by

r.m. berry

chiasmus press
PORTLAND

Chiasmus Press

www.chiasmuspress.com
press@chiasmusmedia.net

PRODUCED AND PRINTED IN THE UNITED STATES OF AMERICA
ISBN: 0-9703212-7-9

cover design: Lidia Yuknavitch
layout design: Matthew Warren
Frankenstein cover image courtesy of the Academy of Motion Picture
Arts and Sciences

Language speaks.

—HEIDEGGER

ACKNOWLEDGMENTS:

Portions of the following have appeared in *The Iowa Review* and *Fiction International*. The author gratefully acknowledges a residency at the Lillian E. Smith Center for the Arts, which aided in the completion of this work. And sincere thanks to Lidia Yuknavitch, Brenda Mills, and Mark Garrett Cooper for their generosity and invaluable assistance.

For James O'Rourke,
the monster's friend

LETTER I

To Ms. Margaret Saville, New York.

St. Petersburgh, Dec. 11th, 19—

Rejoice, dear Marge, I'm under way at last.

I've just now abandoned my vehicle to refresh myself in this charming rest stop and marvel at the flatness surrounding me. Oh, how strange and wonderful my new state seems! These pastel bungalows, palm-lined retreats, this head-clearing brine. If only I could describe my uncouth paradise—how lacking in pretense, brutally exposed, so abject, yet able to withstand the fiercest hurricanes. Even as I keystroke this sentence a torrid breeze plays upon my senses, invigorating these lifeless characters and spiriting my past away. Idle words, you'll be saying, but if only you could imagine my inklings! A miasma blown from what, I suppose, must be unseen quagmires, affords me a foretaste of our savage being, and inspired by this hot wind, my writing grows more ardent and vivid. I see at last why Florida is home to Mickey Mouse. These shallow sloughs are, in truth, wellsprings of aboriginal form and squalid beauty. Here, my Sister, the world as we know it is overturned, making winter days balmy, the equinox dazzling, and dispelling that perpetual haze clouding everyone's vision back East. Oh, how utterly the mind is purged by this unseasonableness! Amid ceaseless traffic noise one habitually confounds sublime thoughts with petty, but here so close to the littoral, heaven's unfiltered brilliance burns all superficiality away. In time, only the bedrock will remain. Can it be of this, our culture raw and untamed, that I have ventured so far to write?

You know how, when still a schoolboy, I loved the storytellers, how you read to me from the heroic tales of antiquity, Huck's wanderings, Ahab's mad pursuit. You recall how I longed to become a poet too and for one year lived in a world of my own creation there in the writing program at Columbia. I imagined that I might obtain a niche in the immortal temple where the names of Carver, Erdrich, and that other guy who visited our class are consecrated, but who knows what literature is nowadays? You're well acquainted with my failure. How heavily I bore the disappointment. But just then I became heir to a vast fortune, the origins of which remain obscure to me, and conceived my present undertaking.

Six years have passed since that period, as you're aware. I can, even now, remember the survivalist training, the days and nights alone in the wilderness, raw squirrel meat, wild asparagus, minor surgery with Swiss army knives, but nothing less severe would cure my soul of its incessant craving for fictions. For two years I even attempted to read the whole *Norton Anthology of English Literature,* just like Gertrude Stein said she did, and I still don't believe she's telling the truth. You are well acquainted with my failure. Nevertheless, I managed to study several long and difficult masterworks, including those unreadable modernist tomes which suppressed my creativity and bored me. I even wrote a twenty-page essay about all this which was admired by experts. I must own I felt a little proud when my former teacher at Smith entreated me with the greatest earnestness to become an adjunct instructor there. You know all of these things, my Sister, but for some reason I am telling them to you anyway.

And now, my dear Marge, am I not deserving of the fate I imagine? My life might have been passed in a penthouse, but I preferred this quest to every distraction wealth put in my way. Oh, that some encouraging voice would answer in the affirmative! I'm embarked on a long and baffling journey, to what end none can say, but somehow I feel I must discover my words in an uncivilized state. If I succeed, you'll probably read about me in the *New York Review of Books,* although many months, perhaps even years, may pass before we meet again. If I fail, I'll call you from La Guardia.

Your doting brother,
ROB LAWTON

LETTER II

To Ms. Margaret Saville, New York.

ARCADIA, 28th March, 19—

HOW SLOWLY TIME passes here, encased as I am in mud and palmettoes. For over a week thunderstorms have overflowed the roads, and the authorities are confiscating any vehicle that means to venture out. Turbid water covers everything, submerging this motel parking lot in an obscurity inhospitable to man. Or woman, of course. Mindful of the seriousness of my project, I bear all delays with philosophical calm, but inwardly I chafe to be off. In the meantime, I have taken a further step. I sold the Miata and bought an airboat. I know it was rash, but when I surveyed the expanse of overgrown waste ahead, the mangrove thickets, tupelos, I felt incongruous in a sports car. The sacrifice was painful, for I loved her. But I fix my eyes on the object and, mindless of obstructions, forge on.

Nevertheless, I've had doubts. Last night a dream came to me which kept me awake for hours and even now fills me with foreboding. Its precise significance remains a mystery, but because I'm sensible of portents, I will relate it to you at length.

It seems I'd been inventing my life and visited a convention center to arrive at my beginning. Being admitted at the center proved difficult, however, since countless others, each indistinguishable from myself, had come before me. The center had been conceived for all, of course, but its structure appeared ancient and the present demands unprecedented. I took my place at the end of a long line—who could've imagined all these stories!—and in time, as we advanced, I observed the ordeal awaiting me.

Just in front of the entrance were several well-dressed persons, each equipped with a peculiar looking plastic flail. These were called *whoppers*. At intervals one of these persons would take an individual from line and beat him most cruelly, either until the victim ceased to submit or until, for unclear reasons, he was admitted to the center. This was called whipping into shape. I carefully studied the shapes of my predecessors in hopes of diminishing my suffering, but I could discover no difference between the forms rewarded with leniency and those disciplined most severely. At times I fancied that a specific mix of insouciance and fawning was the ideal, and I noted a few younger women seemed adept at achieving it. However, I also observed that mature women, as well as certain young females of unwholesome bearing, were among the most defiant, often receiving beatings of exemplary cruelty. Many were abandoned senseless on the threshold. As for the males, I could discover no pattern. Most wearied quickly of the thrashings and departed muttering curses—as though someone beside themselves were responsible! A few succumbed to the ordeal, and five or six were allowed to enter without receiving the first blow.

As you may imagine, I was profoundly curious about the individuals who administered the beatings. Although they seemed to be official representatives and served as guardians of the center, those in line persisted in calling them *US*. This label appeared to be an acronym, but no one seemed to know what for. Ultimate Significance or even Untold Superiority were both suggested, but I put no faith in such speculations. My only confidence was that, no matter how purposeless my suffering, it would not be the result of impersonal forces but would be dictated by my own countrymen. For some reason I found this liberating.

However, even this confidence vanished as I neared the front of the line and observed US more closely. Though the representatives spoke often of *genius* and *talent*, their voices sounded strangely dispirited. The representative who pulled me from line, a middle-aged woman of no unkindly demeanor, was haggard, flush-faced, and short of breath. She began in the customary manner, praising the center and recalling the greats who'd dwelt there, but I couldn't help noticing a

4

vacancy to her stare. I quickly assumed a conventional shape, hoping to win her favor, but she didn't appear to notice. She immediately barked out, Unfit! -and drew back her whopper to excoriate me. I braced to receive correction. Then there was nothing. Slowly I opened my eyes and found her peering in astonishment into my face. Oh, it's *you*, she said, dropping her flail. I almost mistook! We have something *special* in store for you.

And the next I knew, I was writing these letters.

I implore you, my dear Marge, don't think that simply because I have dreams my determination has weakened. No, that remains as fixed as fate. I'm merely pausing until the conditions without become clear, which in time they always do. Until then, how this deluge inspires me! Yesterday I spent several hours alone with no television, plotting my future course. How much more rapidly will the time pass once my forward progress resumes! I can't begin to describe my sensations at this prospect. They are half-fearful, a trembling in my every extremity, a breathless sensation contemplating the adventures ahead. I'm going to unexplored regions! Shall we meet again, perhaps after I've stopped scrawling this maniacal prose? I dare not expect such success, yet I can't bear to look on the reverse of my picture, whatever that means. Oh, I'm subject to so much I can't begin to conceive! Continue to contact me at the present location. An unanticipated letter at some future impasse could be my only support.

5

Your fond brother,
ROB

LETTER III

To Ms. Margaret Saville, New York.

THE EVERGLADES, July 7th, 19—

I WRITE IN HASTE to say that I'm already advanced far into the swamp. This letter should reach you via its inclusion in a recently released anthology from a small publisher of enlightened views wholly free of the bourgeois taste vitiating books back home. I have great hopes of its being available one day even in Manhattan, which means it will be more fortunate than I, who may not see asphalt playgrounds again for years. I am, however, in good spirits, with excellent prospects of attaining my end, this airboat having proven a vehicle impervious to everything.

No incident has yet befallen me worth recounting. To the inspired adventurer, an occasional snakebite or collision with a cypress knee hardly bears mention. Besides I wouldn't want to alarm you with the brutalities I anticipate. Only pure expression, untamed and naked, an ineffable thisness stripped of insipid hype and ideology—only meaning's raw stuff can ever satisfy me! So I strain the limits of endurance. I recognize that an ambition so relentless must seem inconceivable to feminine sensibilities, but my hope, dear Marge, is that somewhere in your boundless latitude there will always be room for your brother's irrepressible gist.

My sole misgiving is that, despite all I've remarked, I still can't explain how my career went south. Not that I consider the present advance untoward, mind you, but try as I might, I don't remember beginning it. Just yesterday, for example, I embarked in primordial darkness, bound for exactly where I can't say, when—before I knew it!—my craft had already turned from the deep passage and bogged down in shallows. No telling how long I struggled to free myself. The gnats assailed me fiercely. In such straits in the past I've always feared misconceiving my object or confusing forward with back, but in the present morass I seemed to have reached my wit's end. How could I imagine my impasse unmoved? Of course, every visionary expects bewilderments, and it's futile trying to tell the true groundbreaker what he's about—or she! or she! But instead of leaving me at sea, the swamp's silence enthralls me absolutely. Was there ever a period when my words weren't already headed? It's strange to say, but I often feel as though even these, my most private reflections, were being secretly prescribed to me, dictated from some hidden page. If only I had a precursor, some savage antecedent whose exploits exceeded my wildest dreams. Well, no sense dwelling on impossibilities, although these quagmires can sure start one thinking!

By the way, the heat today was transcendental.

I remain,

Your undaunted brother,

R

7

LETTER IV

To Ms. Margaret Saville, New York.

WHEREABOUTS UNDETERMINED, August 5th,19—

So STRANGE AN event has befallen me that I can't forbear relating it, although in my present disordered state my words may want sense.

While navigating this swamp last Monday evening, I was unexpectedly assailed by the most violent draft. Gales whipped the gum trees and thrashed my overladen vessel. I don't know whether it was the debris pelting my face or the ensuing obscurity, but in no time I could hardly see beyond this page. I was forced to cut my power and drift. With a wooden shaft I keep for such emergencies, I manipulated my craft into a dank thicket, securing its stern against a gnarled trunk, and then, covering myself with a tarpaulin, I settled down to wait out the storm.

Luckily, before entering the swamp I had provided myself with a radio. Although reception in so remote a region is poor, I could listen to NPR out of Miami, enduring at intervals the staticky intrusions of baseball games, country ballads, and fulminating evangelists. At some point I must have dozed off, for I woke around two a.m. feeling lightheaded. The storm had passed, and in all directions an opaque blackness stretched without glimmer or break. Then all at once a sound shattered the stillness. It was a voice, a voice speaking the language of men, but in a form more prodigious than any I'd ever known:

> Children and haggard women at the border
> of a workin maaaan's eternal creation without

yer love to be an officer in this Goodyear tire
me down at the plate then crack crack right
over our heads there *was* light and bossman's
saying here's yer pay when God's Word
exploded beside my Chevy four by running
and screaming in all directions till heaven
shone down on jes one more smoke knows
prideful man can never keep a young girl
sprawled in this crater maybe ten years old
drinkin me a couple a brews but sooner or
later sin below the ankle over the bag at third
just like a rock still completely conscious
gazing home in the ninth with these eyes right
up at my commandments in a shiny new
pickup out of nowhere when BLAM I think
I'll never forget that Delco battery for your
car.

And then the radio died.

This discourse excited my unqualified wonder. I had
imagined myself countless miles from civilization, but such a   9
sentence indicated I was, in reality, much further still. What
tumult could have spawned it? To what manner of being could
its sense seem plain? With the radio defunct it was impossible
to follow the prodigious form further, but having remarked it
with minutest care—as my verbatim transcript attests—I felt
too agitated to put it from my mind.

I remained in a perfect furor for several hours, constantly
repeating the words to myself and hoping for some break in
the surrounding gloom. Finally just before dawn, a glimmer
of light shone through the mangroves, and I was able to make
out amid my entanglements a shadow approaching. At first,
in my excitement, I mistook it for a giant reptile and tightened
my grip on the wooden shaft, which I knew to be in certain
struggles deadlier than a sword, but when after a moment the
creature began to drift, I relaxed my vigilance, recognizing
the fearsome predator for a johnboat. This vessel had become
ensnared in a gum branch and appeared abandoned. However,
as I positioned myself to observe its contents, I was astonished
to perceive a half-conscious man lying at the bottom. What a
peculiar being! Although tattered and moss strewn, he looked
not at all like an uncouth cracker, but was attired in the urbane

dress of an Amherst alum or Bostonian, and when he spoke, his diction was articulate, although his diphthongs identified him as native to the region.

Sir, he announced upon perceiving me, if you mean to haul me up onto that ludicrous contraption, will you at least have the grace to say whither, for God's sake, you think you're going?

You may conceive my confusion at being so bluntly accosted by one obviously in a desperate plight. Nevertheless, I replied in a civil tone that mine was a voyage of discovery, words whose aptness amazed me.

Discovery? he scoffed. Surely you can't dream this barrenness is unexplored!

By others, I replied.

And you discover *for yourself*?

There's another way?

But he merely gestured at the wilderness, or tried, for in his debilitated state he could hardly wag a finger. Mad youth, have you even the vaguest notion where you are?

And he was right. For day had arrived, and I could see that my craft, although blown no great distance, was entirely surrounded by dense mangroves. It was impossible to see beyond a few feet, and with impenetrable fog obscuring the sky, I couldn't recover my bearings.

I no doubt seem rash, I acknowledged, just another American flailing blindly, but where would either of us be now if Columbus had known his way?

At which words, and to my utter amazement, the stranger burst into a fit of insane laughter. The fit did not pass quickly. He guffawed so long and convulsively, rollicking from side to side and beating his desiccated members against the gunnel, that I began to fear he would capsize his boat.

And your own predicament, sir, I interrupted somewhat testily. Do you dream it's rational? Look at your craft! It's the flimsiest contrivance, rudderless, no propulsion, and if you'll pardon my candor, or — who cares? — even if you won't, your personal composition is hardly stalwart. What were you planning to eat? *Mosquitoes?* No map, no compass. Why, if your demeanor didn't exude all-sufficiency, I might imagine you were adrift! So condescend to enlighten me, Rhett Butler, what high-minded quest has marooned your skinny carcass in this abject way?

The stranger regained his composure then and apologized most graciously, acknowledging the justice of my rejoinder.

10

I too embarked thoughtlessly, he said, and if I laugh, it's but to see my own folly in you. As for what I pursue . . . well, let's just say my object now escapes me.

Another being? I asked.

A figure, he acknowledged. Badly misshapen, unbecoming —

An articulate chaos? A garbled pandemonium?

He eyed me most strangely: In so many words.

A primordial compound of tumult and roiling hectic, an hysterical glossolalia, the frenzied mammering of palatal redundancy, raucous ur-gibberish, cacophony, bedlam, the blathering brain rollick of jabbering unsense?

When he seemed unable to reply, I added: *I encountered just such a form last night!*

This aroused the invalid most wondrously. He leapt from the johnboat where, until that instant he'd sprawled helplessly, and, without any assistance, scrambled onto my deck. He then began plying me with questions, demanding the call numbers of the radio station and the precise hour I'd been awakened, and exhorting me to rehearse, as precisely as I could, the voice's tone and inflection. Being one on whom innuendos are often lost, I was able to supply him with little more than the words, which to my surprise he seemed to find significant. Nothing else of consequence passed between us that day, but from the moment I first mentioned the monstrous discourse, I noticed that a strange energy animated his frame. He punched at the buttons of my radio incessantly, clutching the speaker to his ear, and the faintest crackle of static would send spasms of ecstasy coursing through him.

And such is my account — which I'm pleased to stop pretending is a letter, my dear Marge, and henceforth dub *Lawton's Journal* — to this immediate period. The stranger gradually improves in health but remains taciturn and moody, which makes for some awkwardness on an airboat. Nevertheless I begin to love him like a brother. At times he reminds me of the precursor I once sought, although his present deterioration makes the prospect of his leading anyone anywhere appear absurd. He must have been a remarkable man in his prime, being even now such a wreck.

I shall at intervals continue *Lawton's Journal*, at least until the present obscurity dissipates and we can envision a way out of our impasse.

11

August 13th, 19—

As you can see from the affixed date, dear Sister, we've passed eight days in the swamp, and even though these words pour forth with an abundance scarcely credible, I find I'm strangely silent about what we ate, where we slept, how we survived the insects, or by what means we managed to relieve ourselves. Perhaps in my craft there are provisions which, in my untroubled access to them, have seemed to me of no account. How much of every day has amounted to killing time? All the bloody hours! That our very lives could've depended on such obliviousness strikes me now as fantastic, although I confess having in the past feared a similar oversight. Well, food for thought.

Regardless of my abstraction, my enthusiasm for my fellow outcast increases hourly. His quiet demeanor excites pity and respect, and his mind is so cultivated that, whenever he speaks, although his words seem precisely chosen, they flow with old-world eloquence and felicity. He's now much recovered from his illness and keeps one ear continually affixed to my radio, hoping for the twang of provincial balladeers. Yet he's never so preoccupied with his own obsession that he fails to enter into mine. Yesterday he asked me questions about my project, questions remarkably like those I ask myself, and I was led by his evident sympathy to speak unguardedly, replying that I would sacrifice my comfort, my health, even my fortune, for the furtherance of American letters. I felt self-conscious after this outburst, but I noticed my listener was moved. A mysterious expression spread over his countenance, and instead of guffawing, he started to weep. Oh, unhappy youth, he cried out. Do you share my intoxication? Have you also imbibed that heady draft? Only hear my tale, and you will dash that foaming flagon from your lips forever!

As you might guess, such a metaphor amazed me, but he immediately despised himself as passion's slave and wouldn't continue. Instead, he insisted that I talk about my upbringing, and so I recounted my life without embellishment. I spoke of my early devotion to storytelling, my disappointment at finding no forerunner, my thirst for communion with a talent wilder than my own, and my conviction that the novelist who didn't venture to extremes could never matter.

We're in accord, replied my companion. Life's a pretense, compounded of poppycock and murderous cant, and if no one dispels it, we're none of us there. Does anybody really want what anybody really wants? Like you, I once entertained doubts, the most gnawing of hungers, and knowing what violence comes of such craving, I'm entitled to judge between this wilderness and you. You're young, your future's an open book, but when I recall the beginnings I've marred, all my conceptions—ah, what's there left to say?

And the lines of his countenance struggled with an anguish so profound that, observing it, I too became affected. I averted my gaze out of respect, thinking my companion would resume momentarily, but he merely dangled his legs over the prow, and in a few seconds I noticed he'd fallen asleep.

Sister, do you smile at my affection for this windy Southerner? You wouldn't if you had to listen to him. Your sentiments, dear Marge, have been formed by the writings of our literary novelists, those justly admired savants whose deft constructions so many enjoy and whose diaphanous prose dumbfounds so rarely. Thriving on their sound illuminations, how could you ever appreciate my companion's hokum? Several times I've asked myself what quality makes his sentences seem so uplifted, as if, despite their urgency, they hung suspended just above their sense. I'm far from knowing what I mean. I realize that to attend too closely is to lose one's grip, but in truth, I feel powerless to turn away. It's as though, until his words began to resound, I'd never heard my own. Is it possible to unwrite one's fate? Even though the sense escapes me, his voice drones on in my mind interminably.

Well, more to come.

August 19th, 19—

Yesterday evening my companion said to me: You have undoubtedly noticed I'm in ruins. Don't deny it! Our predicament requires, as much as possible, that we both be frank. I had intended to carry my madness to the grave, but finding you so astray has recalled me to what, in a dark and perhaps imaginary time, I too dreamed I was. You foresee plots and veer furiously to circumvent them, hoping one day to invent a life of your own. What could be more natural?

And despite my disillusionment, young friend, my ardent hope is that you'll realize your desire. It's unclear how my self-defeat could aid you in yours, since it was my determination to tell what's happening that first landed us in the same boat. Nevertheless, I mean to narrate. My greatest fear is that, on hearing my catastrophe, you'll try to imagine your own differently, so precipitating it. This paradox—that my undoing could become the means of another's—has persuaded me to silence until now. But I see silence will never make an end. So prepare to hear what others have dismissed as fabrication. Were we among the tamer scenes of culture, standing at the checkout counter with kumquats in our fists, I might fear your incredulity, but much that's out of the question in Massachusetts seems perfectly natural in a swamp.

He then promised to begin his confession the next day, requiring the greatest fortitude to undertake it. Initially, my plan was to listen with minutest attention to his tale and then each night, using my laptop, summarize the highlights from memory, but despite my plan's reasonableness, I knew I'd been nurtured on video games and television and could hardly remember my own name without an LED. So my only option was to keystroke as furiously as possible while my companion spoke, apologizing for the distraction of my keyboard's rattling, and then at night try to correct the misspellings and grammar. This could prove tiresome. However, I suspect that, given his agonies, my friend's self-absorption will be total, and there'll likely be periods of breast-smiting and expostulation I can just skip. In some future time the torment I've transcribed may hold you, dear Marge, in open-mouthed astonishment, and for baffling reasons we'll call your ecstasy *entertainment*. Where do these words come from?! But for me who witnessed his suffering, who actually heard his teeth grind and saw him writhe and foam, can you imagine how much more thrilling my *entertainment* will be? Even now as I type this sentence his groans contract my throat and his eyes peer at me from inside my head. His anguish must be appalling to overtake another so bodily. Precious Sister, can anyone relive the past without being himself enthralled? Or her! Think of me then, in that distant future when neither of us will be as we are, and recalling everything I now endure, enter into my history such that, abandoning yourself to bygone sorrows, you'll be transported to this unplotted waste and, forgetful of present cares, immerse yourself in life's muck, undergoing the squalor and desolation which, for me now and you then, and perhaps for me then and you now, will always be our culture's deepest source. Just think: to reproduce, there in your West Side condo, the bewilderment I'm literally dying to escape. Oh Marge, if only you can stay out of it!

Now, read.

Chapter I

I AM FRANK STEIN of Atlanta, Georgia, last remnant of a proud family considered one of the architects of the New South. My father, Frank senior, a successful attorney and by heritage a Jew — Gertrude Stein was our distant aunt — was an indefatigable fighter for equality with no regard for religion or race, and he spent much of his early life defending pacifists and labor organizers. In his mid-forties he married the daughter of his longtime friend, Hubert Strong, with whom he'd protested the Japanese internments in '41, and settled down to raise a family. I was his oldest son.

Grandfather Strong's story was a sad one. While rushing to defend a black teenager accused of infanticide, he was pulled over by a South Carolina state trooper and beaten senseless. He lost partial use of one arm, began to suffer from migraines, and acquired a grotesque facial tic. He became obsessed with his injury, and after a lawsuit against the officer had failed, he pursued a series of costly appeals which finally bankrupted him. Realizing his folly too late and now reduced to what he considered humiliating poverty, he fled to a rural hamlet where he attempted to work as a barber. However, his bitterness and violent grimacing upset the locals and within ten months he died of a broken heart, leaving his eighteen-year-old daughter, Kara, penniless. In desperation she contacted my father; he took her in, and two years later they were married.

Despite the great difference in my parents' ages, I recall their marriage as tranquil and loving. When the sit-ins began, they were among the first to be arrested, and later they toured the South with the Freedom Riders and marched on Washington to protest the war. How well I remember the strains of "We Shall Overcome" wafting through the bedrooms of our northwest Atlanta mansion! Perhaps because of my mother's early brush with adversity, she could never forget the poor, and throughout my childhood I recall making regular visits to the substandard rental houses and dehumanizing tenements in which our housekeepers lived. On such a visit one day my mother discovered the grown daughter of one of our nannies trying to feed five tiny children from a jar of peanut butter. Four of the children had skin as dark as espresso and possessed that vigor and litheness that, our society has since realized, make African-Americans such outstanding basketball players. The fifth appeared to be of different stock and for no apparent reason attracted my mother above the rest. Her skin was delicate and fairer, and her hair, though curly as an Ethiopian's, shone in the sunlight with a golden tint.

Our housekeeper, noticing that my mother fixed her eyes upon the girl, instructed her grown daughter to shut up and eagerly communicated the child's history to us. She was the offspring of a Nigerian medical student who, misled by the enthusiastic proclamations and editorials following the Montgomery bus boycott, neglected to keep secret his affection for his lab partner, the beautiful daughter of a white northwest Atlanta real-estate developer. The young woman reciprocated his affection, matters progressed as matters are wont, and soon Liza Mbira was born. Whatever became of Liza's father, whether he was lynched or deported, could never be learned, but shortly after her birth, he vanished, never to be heard from again. Perhaps he tried manfully to contact his beloved, only to have his letters intercepted by her family, or his body might even now be decomposing beneath a Fulton County subdivision. But whatever his sad fate, Liza's mother reacted to his disappearance by lapsing into unremittent catatonia. Her parents, finding themselves with no functioning daughter and an imperfectly white grandbaby to raise, inquired surreptitiously into unconventional methods of adoption, and my nanny, who had been working in multiple households at the time, quietly agreed for certain considerations to take her in.

My mother had always wanted a daughter. Seeing before her no obstacle to acquiring one, she entered into negotiations with her housekeeper and in no time at all had purchased my more-than-sister. Liza and I grew up as virtual siblings, only a few months apart. Ours was a flawless harmony of complementary temperaments. While I was smitten with a passion for knowledge, Liza Mbira absorbed herself in the aerial creations of the poets, strumming her guitar all day and memorizing the interminable verses to "Hey, Mr. Tambourine Man". She loved natural beauty in every form and could sit in the porch swing for hours, staring at the daylilies and pyracantha. As she contemplated in this fashion the surfaces of things, I sought to discover their inner workings. To me life was a vast confusion just dying to be straightened out. My need for understanding was violent in the extreme, and I often imagined unseen forces at work behind commonplace phenomena. A ready fluency and tireless gift for explanation were my early attributes, and my most vivid memory is of plundering the dictionary for words to order my chaotic sensations.

Liza's and my closest friend was Mark Stanford, the son of a wealthy Atlanta Buick dealer. Somehow he fit into our harmony too. He was a great lover of history and epic who dreamed of one day mass-marketing the classics. While I busied myself with metaphysics and Liza Mbira did her flower thing, Mark devoted his energy to economic relations. To him capital beckoned like a swarthy concubine, and he often extolled the pleasures of financial risk and speculation for their own sake. His aspiration was to become an adventurous publisher like Gordon Lish or Barney Rossett, names renowned for their high-minded contributions to the arts. With Liza's untroubled consciousness watching over us and her feminine attributes lending zest to our boyish games, Mark and I grew up in a nurturing environment, protected from the worst excesses of testosterone and locker-room pruriency.

Although I feel exquisite pleasure dwelling on this innocent chapter of my history, I sense that the invisible malignancy which has brought me to my pathetic end is already underway. In truth, nothing unnerves me more than this inevitability. Human beings are free, I tell you, free! If in recounting my life I seem to be less than frank, it's because I *can* be, and if my penchant for equivocating proves too much . . . well, there you are! Or if you, sir, responding to whatever impulse, should choose to interrupt that furious keystroking which I notice even now you stubbornly cont get my point. No one beside ourselves is beside ourselves. Only I authored my defeat! And yet, the naturalness with which my beginning and end connect belies this. Don't blame our system, the market, Republicans, cold war, or even DNA. Had I always known everything anyone can always know, I should've still done exactly as I did. And yet I acknowledge feeling that, with the first words ever to violate these lips, all my subsequent misfortunes were already foretold. In my most agonized recollections I see myself copying my doom from another's book! Oh, I know such presentiments must strike you as exaggerated, but narrating my downfall here and now, I recognize their aptness as never before.

I will now represent for you the events which, by means of their insidious unfolding, have led me to this present.

Language **is the genius that has regulated my fate.** When I was thirteen years of age, my family took a vacation to Virginia to see where our nation's founders kept their slaves, and when rain forced us indoors one day, I discovered in the library of our host, an anthology of the writings of the German philosopher Martin Heidegger. I thumbed the pages indifferently at first, but soon Heidegger's enigmatic diction— the *thinging* of things, *upspringing* of earth, encompassing of mortals under *gods and sky*—captivated my imagination. The idea that words could invoke the cosmos, or that poetry might transport humans from darkness to light, all this struck me with the force of a revelation. A new vista seemed to open within my mind, and, bursting with joy, I communicated my discovery to my father. He glanced at the title page, shook his head slowly, and muttered: Ah, Frank, you'll need to be the Messiah himself to have the patience for that Nazi gibberish!

If, instead of this remark, my father had explained Heidegger's philosophy to me and detailed its shortcomings, if he had introduced me to linguistics and demonstrated how superior its analyses were to phenomenology, since the results of linguistic analysis, as I came to appreciate, are scientific and practical while those of the Heideggereans are reactionary and very abstruse—under such circumstances I should have certainly thrown the volume aside. But my father's dismissal by no means assured me that he understood Heidegger, or for that matter, had even read him, and so I absorbed myself in his study.

When I returned home, my first care was to procure a copy of *Being and Time* and then all of Heidegger's lectures. I soon realized I could understand nothing clearly without first reading Husserl, Nietzsche, Plato, and the pre-Socratics. I began to study German, which was taught at my high school, and then Greek, which required a private tutor. Kant soon became essential, also Hegel and Schelling, and then all the romantics, Hoelderlin in particular. I read Wordsworth's *Prelude*, Shelley's *Apology*, and of course the *Biographia Literaria*, just before—in my effort now to bridge the widening gulf between English and German thought—tackling empiricism. I devoted much energy to Book III of Locke's *Essay*, for which I felt contempt but which finally sent me back, through Bacon, to Aristotle. For an extended period my whole study was the *Rhetoric, Poetics,* and *Nichomachean Ethics.* In the original. Thus passed my thirteenth year.

Thanks to my passion for understanding, I never grew weary of these labors, but I eventually came away from every volume with the same dissatisfaction. I recall that Sir Isaac Newton said he felt like a child gathering shells beside the vast ocean of truth. Those of his successors I read now seemed to me equally pedestrian. After all, even Georgia crackers knew how to speak, and the greatest philosophers struck me as knowing little more. Each seemed to have fallen in love with his own tongue, devoted uncommon energy to praising it, then abandoned it hopelessly tangled and mute. If only someone could disclose what underlay all these tongues, the forms of human feeling, the very laws of language itself, think of the glory that would attend his work! He could banish misunderstanding from human intercourse, put an end to meaningless squabbles, empty blather. Nations would no longer annihilate each other without good cause!

And so with this and similar hokum filling my head I continued to study obsolete and groundless notions until an accident occurred which altered the current of my ideas.

When I was sixteen, a shy librarian in a south Georgia county, prompted by no one ever knew what dark impulse, suddenly became the subject of national headlines when he recited to rural ninth-graders some verses from the *The Song of Songs* of the Hebrew scriptures: *You are stately as a palm tree, and your breasts are like its clusters...etc.* He was quickly arrested, and my father, who agreed to represent the unfortunate man, decided I was old enough to witness bigotry au naturel and so took me along for the trial. However, while we were still en route, there occurred in the librarian's community what the papers later termed a Klan riot but which the locals insisted was just a car full of drunks banging on the library with a shovel. Two windows were broken. Some deputies fired shots in the air. Nobody could locate the librarian.

Later we learned that the abused man had fled town the previous evening, having preferred to forfeit bail than face the hamlet's aroused masculinity, and leaving behind a leather-bound copy of D. H. Lawrence's collected poems with a note: For Christ's sake, it was the *Bible!* Which blasphemy had apparently occasioned the riot. The sheriff's department was content to let him vanish, having uses for the money and always enjoying a chance to fire their guns, but when my father's Mercedes drove up, disgorging our expert witness, a noted literary critic from the university, the locals found themselves confronting a danger in truth: Jewish intellectuals! For several minutes events threatened to take a serious turn. The atmosphere was electric. I have no idea how we escaped.

However, once back in our car and at sufficient distance to stop watching the mirror, I remember that my father's colleague, a chain-smoking don named Schreiber, stretched his stubby legs and began a labyrinthine explication of the controversial text. Developing theories he'd formed in his study of modern poetry, he demonstrated with a lucidity I'll never forget that the verses in question, far from possessing profane or prurient content, were in fact devoid of content altogether, being a highly organized system of energies and valences, ironies, pseudo-statements, and various tropes, a tour-de-force of paradox and ambiguity, literally without significance of any kind. His commentary, to which I was surprised to hear my father give thoughtful assent, never mentioned the gods, darkness and light, or speech's primordial source, but instead it transformed the ancient song into a perfectly functioning mechanism, which, for all its intricacy and precision, was susceptible of explanation in every part.

This performance completed obliterated my allegiance to Heidegger. Never had I witnessed significance so utterly dispelled! But by one of those fatalities that seems transcribed

21

Chapter II

WHEN I WAS seventeen my mother died. I will spare you a detailed narrative of her decline, knowing it would wring your heart, and will confine myself instead to her final moments. She summoned Liza and me to her bedside and, with trembling fingers, joined our hands. My children, she said, my most enduring hope for the future of our nation has always been a marriage like yours, but now I must depart with my dreams just dreams. Alas, I regret being taken so early, and, happy and blessed as my time has been, isn't it hard to die with Nixon in office and no E. R. A?

Here she paused while we struggled for composure.

But these are not thoughts befitting me, she continued. Instead, I'll try to resign myself cheerfully to death, since there's no alternative, and with my family for my support, leave the future to you.

At which point her head collapsed onto the pillow and her eyes closed.

Oh, and one more thing, she added, reviving. Liza, you'll need to take care of Frank's father now, since he's getting old and Frank has to go to Harvard.

She gazed sadly at my more-than-sister and shrugged: He's the boy.

And my mother was no more.

Although my departure for Boston had to be postponed until we'd donated my mother to science, I eventually loaded my possessions into a Beetle and headed north, leaving Liza and Mark to regret that they couldn't go to Harvard, too. I was now alone. In Cambridge I would have to form new friendships, impress old men, and make my own bed. My life had hitherto been sheltered, except for political canvassing and the occasional picket line, and this lack of exposure had made me somewhat xenophobic. I thought fondly of Mark, Liza, and my father, as well as of the succession of nannies who'd picked up after me. I would miss them sorely. However, desiring knowledge as I always had, it seemed foolish to whine now that my opportunity had come.

So, as soon as I located Hollis Hall, and extorted a parking space, I sought out my professors. Chance, or rather that invisible necessity that since the beginning of this history has controlled me, led me first to the peculiarly named Dr. A—, professor of philosophy. He was an uncouth little Englishman but deeply versed in symbolic logic and argumentation. He asked me questions concerning my earlier education, and when I mentioned reading Heidegger, he stared as though I'd spoken Esperanto.

Have you really wasted your precious youth on such nonsense? he asked.

When I tried to retort that between such nonsense and another I saw little to choose, he silenced me with a flip of his hand.

Every second spent reading this obfuscator is lost, he began. You have filled your brain with fossils. Good God, in what backwater were you raised that no one ever disabused you? But, of course, your accent! You're from the South! From this day, sir, you must strive to repudiate your upbringing and labor with us to reconstruct your mind.

So saying, he bent over his desk and wrote down a list of seminal works in the analytic tradition, which he told me to purchase and absorb. Then he dismissed me, saying that he would begin his course lecturing on logical positivism next week. However, he added that if I still felt determined to dabble in European theories, I should see Dr. Z—, who taught linguistics.

I returned to my dorm room in no way disheartened, since, as I've said, I'd already repudiated Heidegger, but hardly tempted by Dr. A—'s brusque manner to delve into logical analysis or the rules of inference. In high school I had encountered Bertrand Russell's writings, as well as excerpts from Moore, Whitehead, and some others Dr. A— had mentioned, and their clarity had seemed to me achieved at too high a price. All that Heidegger promised, the glimpse into primitive origins, the revelation of meaning, everything delicious and astonishing had now in their work been excluded. In its place, philosophy seemed limited to nothing more inspiring than correcting mistakes like Heidegger's. I was being asked to exchange **chimeras of boundless grandeur for realities of little worth.**

Such were my reflections during my first days in Cambridge, which were chiefly spent blacking in circles on standardized tests and watching Red Sox games. But as the beginning of classes approached, I worried about the books Dr. A— had recommended. Although I could hardly bear the thought of his haughty pronouncements being spat at me from a pulpit, I was even more loathe to sound stupid if called upon. So I purchased a copy of Wittgenstein's *Tractatus* which I spent several nights studying, finding it even less comprehensible, if superficially more orderly, than Heidegger.

To fulfill my social science requirement I signed up for Dr. Z—'s introduction to linguistics, less because of Dr. A—'s recommendation than because Dr. Z—'s odd name was the only one I recognized in the catalogue. At the first class I was impressed by how different the two men appeared. Dr. Z—'s 25 face looked to be about fifty years of age, although his brightly colored shirt and bell bottoms made him seem much younger. A few gray whiskers stuck out of his sideburns, but the hair hanging to his shoulders was nearly auburn, and his informal style and personable manner made his brief lecture all the more alluring. He began by recapitulating the history of linguistics, dwelling somewhat on the work of Saussure and Jakobson. He then made a cursory assessment of the present state of the science and explained a few elementary terms before concluding with a panegyric, the exact words of which I've transcribed on this card I always carry in my wallet and will now read to you:

> Earlier philosophers set out to explain the nature of human language but actually achieved very little. Modern linguistics is far less ambitious. We know that there's no hope of arriving at the origin, that pure experience is a mirage. But we whose ears are constantly listening to idle chatter and whose hands do nothing but scribble

phonemes, have indeed achieved wonders. We have diagrammed whole cultural systems and demonstrated their diacritical laws. We have ascended to the highest arts and broken down their codes. We have made exhaustive lists of paradigms and syntagms, explained the sign's tripartite structure, and acquired new and almost unlimited authority over other fields. No matter how insular the discourse, the modern linguist can make it his object, can even uncover previously undetected lacunae and parapraxes.

Such were the professor's words, or rather the words of fate uttered to enthrall me. As he went on, I felt as though my soul were grappling with an adversary. One by one the defenses of my adolescent skepticism began to collapse. I felt my synapses fire, my blood flow faster, and my whole body became a shrill antiphony. So much has linguistics done! sang my right brain. Far more will Frank Stein do! echoed my left. Beginning where others had left off, I vowed never to rest until I'd constructed the system of systems, mastered the science of metalinguistics, perhaps even explained the semiology of the human nervous system itself.

𝔍 𝔠𝔩𝔬𝔰𝔢𝔡 𝔫𝔬𝔱 𝔪𝔶 𝔢𝔶𝔢𝔰 𝔱𝔥𝔞𝔱 𝔫𝔦𝔤𝔥𝔱! By the time my excitement finally abated, I'd missed my morning classes, and all that remained from my previous day's experience was my resolve to take up linguistics, a science for which I somehow knew I was naturally fit. I decided to pay Dr. Z— a visit. I found him in his office, where his manners seemed even more relaxed than in class and where his gaily flowered shirt astonished me with its long collar and unbuttoned front. I gave him pretty nearly the same account of my former studies that I'd given Dr. A—. He listened with attention, smiled at the mention of Heidegger's name, but showed none of the contempt of his colleague. Instead, he remarked that without the pioneering work of such metaphysicians, the serious study of language would never have attracted so many excellent minds. He explained how a great number of the problems which linguists had subsequently dissolved were initially brought to everyone's attention by Heidegger, and he expressed his conviction that the labors of men of genius, even if they happened to be Nazis, scarcely ever failed to turn ultimately to the advantage of humankind.

I listened in awed silence to this speech, which was delivered without affectation or jargon, and then I added that his lecture the previous day had removed all my prejudices against modernity. I expressed myself with modesty and deference, imagining in those benighted days that respect was due a professor, and did not reveal the childish impatience I was actually feeling. I then requested his advice concerning the books I should procure.

I am happy, said Dr. Z—, to have gained a disciple. If you do as I instruct, I have no doubt of your one day fulfilling your ambitions and obtaining tenure. Linguistics is that field in which the most far-reaching discoveries are presently being made. Our work is to other disciplines what physics and psychoanalysis were in the first half of our century and what biology and history were the century before. I have made the science of language my specialization, but I have not neglected to study literature and philosophy as well. If your wish is to become a linguist, not merely a lexicographer, I should advise you to read omnivorously, especially the French.

He then began showing me his library and discoursing at length on specific authors and books. After a while I took my leave, thus concluding the most important twenty-four hours of my life. The ending of my story had now been decided.

27

August 20th, 19—

I closed not my eyes that night?!
Good God, Marge, where do you think he gets sentences like that? Or for that matter, where is he getting these chapters? In roman numerals no less! Is he completely out of his mind? Am I?

It's night here in the swamp now, with nothing but distant squawking and mosquitoes to distract me, my companion having fallen asleep sitting upright on the prow. His habit, apparently. I know I should be resting too, but when I reread today's narration, the syntax, archaisms—*befitting, disheartened, panegyric*—my head starts to spin. Who is this sharing my boat? Not that I want him gone, mind. No, I'd be less than frank myself, Marge, if I pretended I weren't absorbed. I mean, doesn't it all fit? A southern provincial, the overdose of philosophy, his childhood blighted by words. Can't you just see it? If, as I suspect, his genius is the sort akin to madness, then that adds pathos but scarcely makes his story less understandable. How many of our jabbering countrymen, raised in similar environs—Omaha, Toledo, Albuquerque—flounder in just such a world of confusion? No, my companion's discourse represents a malady of the most virulent kind. I don't doubt that even you or I could be infected. This morning he'd hardly begun narrating before the stilted diction vanished, and I found myself enthralled. It's only afterwards, now as I correct my transcript, that I recover my senses. *Chimeras of boundless grandeur?* Jesus. It's like being taken over by a ghost. How could anything that outlandish ever grip anyone? Don't I know what I know? I realize such questions must be annoying, dear Marge. I'd apologize would not my apology be annoying. How to express this quandary? It's as though, from the instant I first glimpsed him lying in his craft, my innermost thoughts were taken capture. Can words be literally compelling? It's not like he's some kind of dictator!

But listen to me. I'm starting to sound like *him*.

Chapter III

FROM THE DAY OF my first meeting with Dr. Z—, linguistics
became my sole study. I read with ardor those writings, so
full of genius and discrimination, by Propp, Lotman, Bremond,
Peirce, Chomsky, Greimas. I enrolled in the courses and
cultivated the acquaintance of the comparative literature
faculty, and I found even in Dr. A— extensive knowledge of
performatives, deep grammar, and speech acts, despite his
unfashionable clothes and haughty demeanor. In Dr. Z—,
however, I found a true friend. His turtlenecks were never
worn with brogans or white socks, and his lectures always
demonstrated how French metalanguage could be applied to
war protests and environmentalism. In a thousand ways he
smoothed for me the path to knowledge and rendered the most
abstruse problems facile. My application was at first
fluctuating, but my energy increased with understanding, and
soon it was a common occurrence for sunrise to find me still
engrossed in a work on semiology I'd just begun the night
before.

As I read so constantly, it may be easily conceived that
my progress was rapid. Vassar women vied for my attention,
untenured faculty begged to direct my research, and although
Dr. A— still called me his young Heideggerian, I discovered
that he had twice cited me in his publications. Four years
passed in this manner, during which I never visited my family
and only rarely indulged in the wantonness of my peers but
instead remained engaged, heart and soul, in the researches I
was determined to make. None but those who have
experienced them can conceive the enticements of language.
With other subjects—history, philosophy, art—you go as far

as prejudice and opinion will allow. Much goes unexplained, but nothing proves acceptable that isn't, in large part, already known. But where language is your object—both the words of common opinion and those constituting knowledge itself— possibility stretches before you without limit. For some reason, I never found this frightening. I devoured the classics of my field, digested countless professional journals, spent hours mastering difficult theories and terms. I eventually wrote and submitted for publication a brief essay on the perhaps too-familiar topic of internally focalized intercalated autodiegetic analeptic misprision, and a paper of mine on *mis en abyme* was discussed at an international poetics congress in Toronto. At this point I was beginning to feel almost as accomplished as my professors, and I certainly would have returned to my family to write my honors thesis undisturbed, had not an incident occurred that protracted my stay.

I had never entirely overcome my fascination with origins, my early encounter with Heidegger proving too formative, and, in particular, I often recalled his dream of speech as primordial creation. Whence, I often asked myself, did humankind issue its first expressive croak, that fateful rift in our consciousness? What obscure twitch stopped the nameless troglodyte in the midst of living his life and started him narrating it? It was a bold question, one that has always proved a mystery, and yet with how many things are we constantly on the brink of discovery if only some commonplace fact didn't get in our way?

One day I received a letter from my father, who habitually wrote instead of phoning, telling me about a rally to celebrate the tenth anniversary of the Voting Rights Act and to support a city maintenance workers' strike, UFW boycott, two redistricting bills, and the Nestle's embargo. A celebrated poet was scheduled to speak, along with Coretta and three Kennedys, and as a participant in the historic events, my father had been invited to appear. Unfortunately, his health was not all that we could wish, and so he was writing to ask if I would fill a seat behind the podium in his place. My researches being, as I have said, in temporary hiatus, I didn't hesitate to accept, since I looked forward to this reunion with my family's close friends and allies, as well as to recalling a turning point in our nation's life. It was a stirring affair. Pete Seeger played his banjo. A woman from the Teamsters sang. There were streakers.

At a key moment the poet rose and a microphone was placed before him. He began by recalling that most horrific but momentous of Sundays, the march from Selma to Montgomery, all the colors and faces, wind and heat, the knot of troopers waiting on Pettus Bridge. He described how the sun beat down on the marchers' bare heads, how the clouds hung motionlessly above, the way the searing pavement stretched behind. His voice was not the fulsome drone I had come to expect from ministers and politicians but spilled forth naturally, with unrehearsed ease, as though he were narrating memories as they occurred to him, in words given at the moment. The crowd was still, the excitement palpable.

My father, mother, Liza and I had all marched that historic Sunday. A child of twelve, I had known the bodies and songs, could recall with a vividness astonishing even to myself the sting of gas in my nose and the terror of masked policemen bearing down on us. I was gripped again by my former sensations, knew as though for the first time the excitement of freedom, of human beings making their own way. Every word the poet spoke was the right word, every pause or gesture just as I—had I been gifted with his powers of expression— would've made it. In truth, listening to his soaring voice, I felt as though Selma had always existed in the poet's words, as if on that bridge ten years earlier we'd already been living his poem now, and that the only surprise today was to hear someone reciting the lines we'd so long ago composed. Like the others around me, I had difficulty restraining my emotions. He was recounting my life.

At an especially exhilarating crux, I recall the poet lifting his arms. Perhaps like us, he'd gotten carried away by his own recollections. Or maybe he'd confused the vanished heroism of earlier days with our prosaic present, had grown unmindful of where we actually were. Self-forgetfulness on an epic scale seems inconceivable to me now, and yet at that unromantic juncture in our history, with Vietnam a thing of the past and students returning to business as usual, what else had our nation been counting on? Anyway, as he directed everyone's vision toward the distant horizon into which our collective futures advanced, he took a bold step forward. This was unfortunate. As his shoe rose into the air, it struck a folding chair and came down on the base of the podium. Startled, he lurched left, tangling his ankle in the microphone cord and losing his balance. Sensing his *faux pas* too late, he twisted morosely and thrust out his arms to those seated behind him, but before we could grasp his plight, his elbow struck the microphone with a thunderous POP, catapulting the podium, chair, microphone stand, and poet into the front row.

There was a moment of confusion as several of us rushed to help. Fortunately the platform was not high and his fall had been broken by the outstretched legs of the first black actress to appear on *The Secret Storm*. However, his disorientation appeared extreme. He muttered oaths, cursed scabs, filthy crackers. An older gentleman beside me tried to quiet him, speaking softly at first, then louder, but the poet seemed to notice nothing. He continued to thrash, daring his adversaries to appear and castigating them for despicable cowardice. I had no idea what had so discomfited him. Then all at once he whirled round and thrust his face into mine. The shaggy brows twitched, and his depthless eyes fluttered with a moronic distraction impossible to describe. The pupils seemed to roll like yolks on a platter, each center wandering spastically across my face with no pause of recognition. For a moment I feared the man had gone mad or was suffering a seizure and prepared to shout for a doctor. Then abruptly everything became clear to me. The poet was blind.

We helped him back to the platform where, after a few more not wholly incoherent remarks, he was persuaded to sit down, and the rally concluded with songs. But later that night in my room I was unable to remove the man's contorted face from my thoughts. I felt as though I'd undergone a revelation, one of those experiences that, when one looks back upon them, seem to have presaged everything to come. However, in the aftermath of the day's adventure, I could form no clear idea of what I'd witnessed or why it now struck me as so significant. I kept asking myself how a blind man could recall for a twelve-year-old boy what the boy alone had seen. Selma remained for me an astonishing spectacle, a vast movie in which I figured both as viewpoint and subject, camera and victim. Perhaps because I was white and a child, I'd enjoyed a distance, escaped the worst. Maybe I'd been less a part of that vividness than I now imagined. But still, in my memory the massacre at Pettus Bridge was *viewed*. To remember it was to enter that darkened room where I screened my fears, where I projected myself, both past and future, onto the void. I knew the bright

32

blood and sweating faces, the dogs' saliva, scalding tar, a coke bottle, retreads, all the glare and fury as only one who'd *seen* could know them, and yet between my memory and the poet's words there appeared to be no space at all. My life backed his signs. Of course, like every thinking person I knew mere words were one thing, experience another, but I now felt uncertain what it meant to know this or whether anyone *could* know it or, for that matter, what if anything a word like *experience* might still mean.

I determined that night to begin my studies anew. I was not yet certain on what uncharted course my strange theophany had set me, but I sensed I must return to my origins, to words in their most primitive state. As you may imagine, forsaking my earlier research, especially after the promise of such success, was painful for me. Had I not been animated by an almost superhuman desire, I could never have accomplished it. But I now felt I had to confront my culture's most brutish forms, must undergo my life's meaning in all its crudeness and naiveté. After all, what was my knowledge worth, my mastery of systems and laws, without this most basic acquaintance? So I abandoned myself to popular culture. I participated in mindless enthusiasms and animal pleasures at brain-numbing lengths, studied the gradual decay of my critical faculties, the running together in my consciousness of radio jingles with Mahler. I writhed to thudding bass notes, talked with junkies less articulate than pudding. In my early education my father had taken the greatest precautions that I never be exposed to claptrap. I do not remember ever once conversing with a gerbil or losing a single night's sleep to Martians. But now I was attending spectacles that depended upon precisely these obsessions. I endured the falsettos of moralizing mice, suffered through countless beheadings, witnessed exorcism, alien abduction, resplendent fairies. I beheld these and similar prodigies flower into global rages, collected their brightly colored artifacts in financially ruinous quantities. I watched as experts overturned reason with opinion polls, swooned as kitsch erased art from memory. For what seemed an interminable period I pondered the mysteries of the television, never blinking at hemorrhoid treatments, diaper leaks, or yeast infections, and I gazed in amazement as advertisers alternated threats with seductions, horrid truths with thrilling lies, until from the midst of this

33

darkness a light finally broke—a light so blinding that while I grew dizzy at the bottomless descent it illumined, I could not but wonder how our civilization, in its amassed ingenuity, could have overlooked something so plain.

Experience was a fiction.

Remember, my zealous scribe, I am not confessing to you the hallucinations of a madman. The sun temporarily hidden by these clouds and mangroves is no more certainly in the heavens than what I'm saying is true. Chance may have led to my discovery, but each stage following it appeared obvious and logical. After nine months of agonizing labor, I succeeded in reducing human life to its twenty-six elementary constituents and in mastering the system of their reproduction. Nay, more, I became myself capable of engendering human feelings from ordinary words.

The horrors of my ordeal soon gave place to rapture. After such prolonged misery, to hold in my hands the ripe fruit of my desire was the most gratifying consummation of my manhood. But this offspring of my pregnant brain, now that I beheld it, seemed so attractive that all the hours of painful labor were forgotten and I gloried only in the issue. What had forever been the desire of all men was finally within my grasp! I could make a life! Not that, as if by magic, my experience was now complete. The consummation I had thus far effected seemed more likely to shape an experience already conceived, rather than to create a new being *ex nihilo*. But I could now glimpse my passage to that realm of fertile imagining never before visited by men, guided solely by my aroused genius.

I see by the wonder and eagerness of your expression, my friend, that you hope to learn this deepest of grammars. That cannot be. Listen patiently until the end of my history, and you will perceive why I remain so partial. I will not lead you on, inexperienced and ardent as I then was, to your destruction. Learn from me—if not by my precepts, at least by my example—how dangerous is the trafficking in fictions and how much happier that man who believes each instant to be his last than he who imagines what time won't allow.

When I found so astonishing a power placed within my hands, I began to consider the manner in which I should employ it. Although I possessed the capacity of amassing experience, the task of constructing a frame for it, that invigorating woof of intricacies, still remained formidable. I

34

debated at first whether to attempt a life as capacious as my own or one of simpler construction, say, that of a senator or corporate executive. However, the exaltation I already felt did not permit lengthy hesitation, and I soon decided to undertake a being of unlimited scope. I knew I would encounter bafflements and peripeties, but when I considered the daily advances in the science of language, I was encouraged to hope that my efforts, even if not wholly successful, would provide a foundation for the future. It was with this prospect in mind that I began to experiment. As the intricacy of the details constituted a great hindrance, I resolved upon a form of epic proportions, not larger than life certainly, since caricature was a smaller achievement, but of such magnitude that with a few bold strokes my new life could appear recognizable to all.

No one can imagine the variety of feelings which carried me onward, or it seems now as though no one can, but I pursued my heart's desire that summer with a preternatural zeal. My cheeks turned pale with sleeplessness. My person grew obese from take-out. Sometimes on the very brink of invention, I would relapse into mere preciousness, yet I continued to ache for new life with all the sharpness of a puncture wound. The thought of fiction was acting on me like a drug. In my creative ecstasy I would plunder archives and rare book dealers, steeping myself in the most occult idioms—medieval anatomy, midrash, geometrical theology, necromancy, erotica. I copied the menus at Persian restaurants, took notes on hillbilly patois and ghetto jive, studied Spanglish and Franglais. My tongue twists at the mere remembrance, but at the time each of these experiments seemed prescribed for me, as though I were serving out some fatal sentence, doing penance for past imaginings. No extremity of prattle or hype, no matter how exorbitant, seemed off limits. I joined cults, memorized the lore of animal sacrifice and sexual bondage, received weekly updates on the Roswell project and international Jewish conspiracy. I no longer turned down the volume during shampoo commercials, and I was horrified to discover in myself an immoderate relish for kung-fu westerns and professional wrestling.

I often lost all self-consciousness, immersed as I was in these mad indulgences, but a mere hangnail or toothache could

35

bring me back to my senses. At such instants it was almost as though I'd never ceased to be me, as though, far from composing unheard-of adventures, I'd been merely what was happening then and there. However, such reassurances didn't last. In a solitary carrel on the highest level of the library and separated from my neighbor by PR5397.F73M08 to PR5397.F73M62, there 𝔎 kept my workshop of filthy creation! My eyeballs almost started from their sockets each time I surveyed the hyperboles, metonyms, and garbled expostulations. Archaisms furnished much of my material, also the hogwash overheard in churches and flea markets. My profane mimicry even violated the dignity of scholarly papers, scientific convocations, and jurisprudence. My youthful cultivation rebelled at these excesses, while still urged on by my dream, I nevertheless moved my work toward its unforeseen end.

After my corpus had begun to take shape, I sent off a lively chunk to an acquaintance from my father's SCLC days who was now an influential editor at a communications conglomerate. Although she wrote back that her employer was no longer interested in books, she knew a rich crackpot who threw his money at almost everything, and she put me in touch with an agent, Gloria Something, whose unswerving devotion to artistic advances provided a powerful incentive for representing me. Within a matter of weeks I'd signed a contract. I hardly attended to these events, as wondrous as they must seem to unpublished you, for I never doubted that my genius would bring me success. However, I was careful to send to Gloria and later to the crackpot each installment of my experience as I fleshed it out.

My father didn't phone during those months, but in the letters he never tired of writing, he remarked my long absence and worried whether I was enjoying myself. I had no interval in which to respond, my creation being now imminent and my imagination preoccupied with its conclusion, but I vowed to make up for my inattentiveness as soon as I was done. Winter, spring, and summer all proved shorter that year, and my carrel having no windows, I could never be sure, merely walking from the Old Yard to the New, whether time had really passed or the weather was just unseasonable, but eventually my life seemed at an end. I contacted Gloria, who took care of the arrangements, harassing me with signatures

36

and the baroque legalities of sub-rights, before finally notifying me that in only a few short months I would find myself transformed into a household name.

With my object finally in sight, my feelings of satisfaction were overwhelmed by anxieties, and I must have appeared more a figure plotted against than plotting. Every night I suffered visions and thrashing sweats, and as the date of my creation approached I grew neurotic to an embarrassing degree. The mere recollection of an extravagant metaphor or neologism could rob me of all composure, and fearful of disgracing myself and my family, I chose at the last instant for my life to appear under a pseudonym. Throughout this time I shunned all my classmates and professors as though I were a fugitive. Sometimes I grew alarmed at what I was turning into, but I sincerely believed that, as soon as my new being materialized, my pride in accomplishment would restore my depleted spirit, and resting in the bosom of my family I could recover my peace. Alas, I would never know peace again.

37

Chapter IV

𝔍𝔱 𝔴𝔞𝔰 𝔬𝔫 𝔞 𝔡𝔯𝔢𝔞𝔯𝔶 𝔫𝔦𝔤𝔥𝔱 𝔬𝔣 𝔑𝔬𝔳𝔢𝔪𝔟𝔢𝔯, 𝔱𝔥𝔞𝔱 𝔍 𝔟𝔢𝔥𝔢𝔩𝔡 𝔱𝔥𝔢 𝔞𝔠𝔠𝔬𝔪𝔭𝔩𝔦𝔰𝔥𝔪𝔢𝔫𝔱 𝔬𝔣 𝔪𝔶 𝔱𝔬𝔦𝔩𝔰. With an anxiety that amounted almost to delirium, I walked through the glass doors of a Harvard Square bookshop toward the shelf of new fiction. It was very late. The store was deserted, about to close. The rain pattered dismally against the panes as I turned the corner of the tall rack and, by the glimmer of half-extinguished lights, saw the garish yellow cover of my creation lying open. I had no idea who had opened it. As I stared, the print seemed to embolden, the page to rise up under it, and my words took on a life of their own.

How can I describe my emotions at this catastrophe? How can I depict for you the unspeakable reality that, at such cost to my peace of mind, I had managed to form? I knew its twenty-six elements had been fixed in place, knew that despite their countless possible arrangements—a universe more intricate than DNA, brain circuitry, mathematics, or even, for that matter, the universe—knew that despite this limitless potential, my life was now an open book. However, for the first time, such abject exposure struck me as monstrous. My aim had been to create what never before existed, a culmination impossible to foretell, a whole new being, but in all those months I'd never once imagined my experience as others might see it. It's just letters! I felt like protesting. Mere ciphers on a page! But as the idioms ran together and the stark truisms leapt out, I realized I had no idea what such protests could mean. Just *letters*? Good God, the yellow cover concealed a transparent presumption that simply took my breath away. Every page pulsated with mincing pretense, patent contrivance, the most affected attitudes and expressions. How had I dreamed, amid universal vanity and hype, that my experience would be any different?

The versions of computer software do not change more abruptly than our human desires. I had slaved two years for the sole purpose of infusing life into print. To this end I'd withheld myself from the exploits of my peers—free love, rock concerts, mind expansion. As long as I labored, no sacrifice had seemed too great, but now looking down on my handiwork, all my passion seemed spent, and only disgust filled my heart. Had I really traded my youth for *this*? Revolted, I rushed out into the wet streets, where I walked for several hours, trying to calm my chaotic thoughts. At length, lassitude overcame my anxiety, and I returned to my dorm room where I tried to sleep. But I was assailed by visions. I dreamed I saw Liza, in the bloom of health, walking the streets of Cambridge. Delighted and surprised, I embraced her, but as I imprinted the first kiss on her ripe breasts, they became livid with the hue of death. Her robust flesh appeared to whiten, and I thought that I grasped the corpus of an ancient authoress, one whose gigantic form overwhelmed me. The folds of her shroud enveloped my frame, and suffocating, I began to struggle to get free. But it was no use. Bookworms crawled over our entangled figures, and my efforts to escape only compelled me deeper into that grave plot from which my nightmare had come.

A sudden clatter in the stairwell awoke me. It was Thanksgiving break, and the mass exodus was beginning. I groped for my trousers in the pre-dawn gloom, eventually descending to the street to pick up a copy of the *Phoenix*, when to my horror I saw my vile title—that equivocating name I'd brought into the world!—as a side-bar in the Arts and Leisure section. The pages nearly fell from my fist. Maddened, I tossed the Sports aside, desperate to discover what I shuddered to find. There among the movie reviews was my monstrous yellow cover. I worked my jaw but couldn't speak. My being seemed to call out to me, its mangled tongue struggling to be heard. In large print I saw an excerpt, half-grammatical concoctions and inanities. I was captivated by the horror. Even the journalists were laughing. What savagery had I set loose?

Momentarily forgetting the protection of my pseudonym, I wrapped myself in a trench coat and fled down the sidewalk,

39

ducking into unfashionable cafes and bustling fast food shops, where I remained until I was pretty sure the morning edition had sold out. Then I carefully pulled my collar back up to my face and began to slink home. Oh! no mortal could support the vulgarity of that yellow cover! A tabloid endued with animation could not be more hideous! I had gazed on my creation while unfinished. It was ugly then, but understandably so. Its climax was still to come, my life's meaning undecided. But now all my dreams had been realized, and each sentence mattered as never before. The copulas were fixed, the subtleties reduced to black and white, and in the place of my new being, I saw only babble and cant.

Tormented by these and similar thoughts, I was trudging the sidewalk when I heard a voice call out my name. I stopped. Someone had recognized me from the publicity photo, I thought, forgetting my cover bore none. I looked up, prepared to deny my identity, when who should I see pulling his canvas duffel from a taxi, but my beloved companion, Mark Stanford? He had on faded bell-bottoms and sandals with a brightly colored sweatshirt flung about his shoulders. It was like the return of my old self. As we embraced I felt a resurgence of my youthful vitality and sense.

I got into Harvard! Mark exclaimed. And seeing my astonishment, he added that his father was endowing a library.

When the old man saw what a head for business I had, well, he decided the Ivy League wasn't a bad investment! Besides, if I was going to become a publisher, wouldn't I need cronies? So here I am, free to seek knowledge in this haven of cosmopolitanism, constrained only by Dad's admonition, don't come home with any new ideas.

But tell me, I pleaded with him, how did you leave my family?

It wasn't difficult, he replied.

But in what state?

He peered at me strangely. My God, old sport, have you forgotten everything?

At which words I must have swooned, for next I knew Mark was helping me up to my apartment. Once inside, I became desperate to conceal all traces of my creation. I swept the loose pages from my desktop and transferred the *Globe* unopened from my threshold to the can. I crammed my royalty agreement into the trash compactor, and began rushing about the bedroom, desperate to hide any galleys or proofs. I seemed driven by I know not what dark compulsion, for I moved with absurd violence, like a child flinging doors open in anticipation of finding specters. I knew that my behavior could not but arouse my friend's suspicion, but I was powerless to comport myself more moderately. When at last I was sure no unguarded sentence remained in sight, I became giddy with relief, and sped to my friend's side, my demeanor unnaturally elated.

However, instead of mirroring my happiness, Mark's countenance appeared grave. For God's sake, Frank, what have you done to yourself?

The question struck me oddly. At first I chortled, then when I saw Mark didn't appreciate his own joke, I tried to stop, clenching my teeth and emitting only a froth until, such was the remarkable aptness of my friend's expression, I exploded into what I now realize were maniacal guffaws.

How ill you are! Mark said.

What? I blurted. Isn't everything right there in plain English? Can't you read? And I pointed distractedly at my bookshelves. However, because my entire domicile was crammed with books, Mark couldn't imagine that it was to my own abominable creation I referred.

Oh save me, Friend! Save me! I cried and collapsed in a fit.

Thus commenced a prolonged fever which confined me for several months and forced Mark to take a light load his first semester. He rented an apartment for us, and between his constant care and the ministrations of a big-hearted Irish girl he found in the paper, I now recall my illness as an almost pleasing respite from otherwise intolerable agonizing. However, I was in reality very sick, and knowing of my father's frailty and the impossibility of my beloved Liza ever in good conscience forsaking his bed, Mark concealed my condition from my family, saying only that I'd let myself go a bit and that as soon as I was myself again, I'd convey my unaltered affections in the flesh. Throughout this time I remember experiencing occasional bouts of calm interrupted by convulsions during which I must've ranted and wept, divulging I scarce knew what. However, I recall one afternoon overhearing my nurse telling Mark, 'twas a bit of the madman again this noon, sar, all manner of foam and daft blather, the

41

like to what, well, I'm sure I don't know, but some o' that high-toned fancy talk, guff from the storybooks, eh?

Doubtless, these ravings concerned my friend. At first, he must have attributed them to fever, but over time he could not have failed to note the regularity of my barbarous phonemes, their recurrent plosives, and my unmistakable, if demented, syntax. Eventually, I believe he determined that my fits resulted from some profound trauma, of which it would be his task one day to unburden me, but his incomparable delicacy showed in his respect for my solitude and his willingness to defer all such interrogations to the proper time.

By gradual stages, with which I won't tire you, I recovered my wits. I remember the first time I was able to go out to a local bar, how I noted that the women appeared younger and their skirts less short, observations which Mark found encouraging. We attended the spring opener at Fenway, a thrilling late inning comeback against the Yanks, and although I was still too fragile to think of my studies, I began spending afternoons seated in the Yard thumbing L. L. Bean catalogues and luxuriating in the fresh scents. The seventies were nearly over, a Democrat was president, no one was wearing fat ties anymore, and these things, along with the returning warmth, contributed greatly to my convalescence. I felt a healthy prurience reviving in my flesh, a delight in swinish chatter with coeds, and before long I was almost as unmindful of what I said as the next fellow.

My dear Mark, I exclaimed one evening as we sat reading, I can't tell you how conscious I've become, throughout this whole period, of your continual presence. So much of my thoughtlessness now is your doing, and without your support...well, I could hardly imagine. How will I ever make everything up?

Mark replied: Your account will be perfectly balanced, Frank, as soon as you grant me one request and, in your present jaunty mood, let me talk candidly about *that subject* which, throughout this long winter, has caused me the greatest uneasiness.

A pang of horror shot through me as I watched my smiling companion extend his arm in the direction of my bookcase. My ghastly experience, which during my illness I'd struggled to put from my mind, abruptly rose up before me, and expecting to see Mark any second pluck my brainchild from its hiding place, I wrapped my arms about my spastic bowels and began to roar.

Compose yourself, dear Frank!

Never again! I shouted.

My word, Mark replied, lifting a pink envelope from the top shelf. If I'd known the two of you were as estranged as all that, I'd have never mentioned her, but really, Frank, don't you think you're overreacting? I mean, we're all grownups. If there have been others, well, Liza is a modern woman. Didn't you see *Woodstock*? Besides, think of your poor father.

It was only then that I grasped Mark's meaning.

Oh, *that subject*! Is it just Liza you mean, good fellow? Why didn't you say so? And to cover my confusion, I made a show of great eagerness in seizing the envelope and ripping it apart.

And what subject did you think I meant?

But I pretended not to hear. Surely you don't imagine, I continued, merely because of a few years' silence, that some distance has come between me and those I love beyond words, or that my present languor indicates any lessening of that overmastering passion I feel for the woman to whom my heart, not to mention our nation's future, has been joined for as long as I can remember?

And without pausing to observe my friend's reaction, I absorbed myself in the palely rubescent and delicately scented pages, which, like that first memorable speech of Dr. Z—, I have preserved and still carry upon my person, and with which, after a pause for a night's rest, I will begin the next chapter.

43

Chapter V

MY DEAREST MORE-than-brother,

I'm going out of my head over you. Mark insists that you absolutely must not write, and yet a single word can mean so much! For a long time I've waited on Mr. Postman so patiently and have, only with great difficulty, convinced your aging father not to think twice, it'll be all right. Still, you know it don't come easy. How many nights have I imagined some old nurse, or even some young one, comforting you and seeing to your needs? However, I'm a rock, an island, since to everything, turn turn, there's a season, and I know you'll get by with a little help from your friend.

How the times are a-changin' in Atlanta! You've probably heard it through the grapevine that we have a black mayor now, as well as several black commissioners, and our own Andy Young is Ambassador to the U.N! Who knows where the time goes? The answer, dearest friend, must be blowing in the wind, but I can't stop thinking how proud your saintly mother would've felt. Why she had to go, I don't know, but it seems like only yesterday she and your noble father were being arrested at the *colored* counter in Woolworth's! Hah hah. Surely you remember. No?

My education's complete, since your father's dependent condition puts Juilliard out of the question, but I never fret, since all we need is love, and I've looked at life from both sides now and realize you can't get no satisfaction. Your brother Earnest, who's fifteen, has to our embarrassment become enamored of the military. He owns a large collection of knives and semi-automatic weapons and curses his luck at being born too late for Vietnam. All we keep saying is to give

peace a chance, but Earnest pays no attention. He's in ROTC
and wants to enlist. Do you think it's the movies? Your father
tells me one day there'll be an answer, just let it be. Still, I
wonder how many deaths it will take before he knows.

Do you remember Teeny Love? Probably not. I'll relate
her history. She was the youngest daughter of Nanny
Sharmeeka who, as you might recall, looked after us between
Nanny Latoya and Nanny Peaches. For some reason Nanny
Sharmeeka resented Teeny. Teeny Love's father was handsome,
and I think Nanny Sharmeeka blamed Teeny when he hit the
road and didn't come back no more, no more. Anyway, your
saintly mother noticed Teeny's mistreatment and, when Teeny
turned seven, showed Nanny Sharmeeka the same generosity
she'd earlier shown in adopting me. I never knew why Nanny
Sharmeeka was so slow to accept this, but bee boppa lula she's
our baby now! I believe it must have been Teeny's age that
explains our different treatment, for no one ever felt any
prejudice towards her exceptionally dark skin. But in her
saintly wisdom your mother recognized that Teeny's sullen
temper unfit her for middle class life and so educated her to
be our housekeeper. Her inadequate early education prevented
Teeny from expressing her gratitude for this, but cherish is the
word I use to describe her feelings inside.

As you know, Atlanta's combination of progressive
institutions and agrarian traditions has produced simpler and
happier poor people than the ghettoes of the northeast, so
that between a black girl like Teeny Love and a young African
American woman like myself, there's no difference to be
ashamed of. R - E - S - P - E - C - T. An Atlanta housekeeper is
sure no Detroit maid, so when Teeny became my personal
companion, everybody knew her position implied no
inequality or low wages or dissatisfaction.

Since you probably have only the vaguest recollections
now of the love and attention we all lavished upon you in
your childhood, you'll just have to take my word for it that
Teeny was always your great favorite. Oh, yes, winter spring
summer or fall, all you had to do was call, and Teeny would
be there. My own memories of this are unusually vivid. Why,
I even recall your exact words when you said, if ever my guitar-
playing bored you, five minutes alone in your room with Teeny
would be enough to perk you back up again! You were wearing
a blue tie-dyed t-shirt, had one of those tiny caterpillarish

boy mustaches, and your black, shoulder-length hair was parted down the middle. Like I said, vivid. I especially recall the way you went on about her spontaneous warmth and natural affections.

When at last your blessed mother went to her reward, we were too busy distributing the commemorative contributions to CORE to pay much attention to Teeny, whose nature was all the sweeter in such times for remaining so self-effacing. I'm sure she grieved in her own way, although on that solemn occasion she had the delicacy to show nothing. However, only a few weeks after you left for Harvard, she received word that a dread disease had afflicted her former family, victimizing both of her sisters. (Na na na na live for today!) Within months they were dead, and Teeny's grieving mother, Nanny Sharmeeka, had lapsed into an alcoholic dependency, having been forced to mortgage her home and possessions to pay her two daughters' medical bills. Teeny Love was so distraught that she didn't wait to consult us but moved straight back to her former mother's house, nursing Nanny Sharmeeka without any regard for that ill-tempered woman's ingratitude. I've heard that Nanny Sharmeeka sometimes asked Teeny's forgiveness for the low value she'd placed on her as an infant, but just as often she blamed Teeny for running off to live with rich folks. This perpetual irritability did nothing to relieve Nanny Sharmeeka's suffering, and although Teeny tried mightily to prolong it, Nanny Sharmeeka is now at peace. Happily, Teeny Love has since returned home, and despite her reserve and touching silence, I know she hopes for your recovery scarcely less fervently than I.

I must also say a few words to you, my Frank, about our sweet William, or Will as Earnie calls him, or your father's little Willy, but by any name your youngest brother, in case he too has slipped your mind. He's tall for his ten years with the same blue eyes and corn silk hair that your mother always made such a fuss over. When he smiles, dimples appear in his cheeks, and he's been placed in all the gifted classes at school. We think he's considering a career in medicine, for his favorite pastime is playing doctor with Nanny Monique's daughter, and his natural leadership shows in his success at getting Teeny Love to do whatever he wants. Willy's so precocious and darling it just makes you want to strangle him!

Well, I have written myself into a good mood, but my worries return as I conclude. When oh when will I see you

46

again? I know time is on my side, but if Mark ever said come to Boston, well, wild horses wouldn't keep me away. Think it oh over. Haven't I been good to you? Just today I read the news about a lucky man who made the grades to go to Harvard then didn't and now he's nowhere, doesn't have a point of view, can't say where he's going to. I've got to admit it's getting better all the time, and I'll get by with a little help from my friends. After all, big girls don't cry. But Frank, why not take the midnight train to Georgia? Alas, I just want to hold your hand, so if I see you in September, well, you know you've got a friend.

Affectionately,
LIZA MBIRA

My dear more-than-sister! I exclaimed leaping from my chair. I will write you this instant! But I'd underestimated the trauma of putting pen to paper, and no sooner had I seated myself at my desk again than the effort to resume my long-suppressed habit proved too much. I immediately sought refuge in unconsciousness, crashing face down onto my writing surface, where I remained in a dreamlike stupor until I heard, as though from a distance, Mark suggest: Why not just phone? How wonderful it was to hear Liza's voice, to say nothing of my own, and how still more wonderful afterwards to remember not a word! Oh, that incomparable joy of syllables disintegrating on my lips, the intervening silence, a single palatal forming and severing each! Although, as you've no doubt remarked, I constantly bear on my person a veritable cornucopia of documents enabling me to replicate, regardless of circumstance, lengthy discourses that I may have only cursorily remarked at the time and whose point, if I ever knew it, I've long since forgot, I am pleased to report, swamped and bewildered as we both now are, I haven't the first inkling of what passed between us that day. Liza's voice was, I'm sure, rapturous and mine firm and manly. Our love resounded in the tripping cadences, soaring inflections. If my memory serves me, the call was lengthy. The bill came to eight dollars.

After this conversation I was another man, and seeing me so altered, Mark expressed his impatience to become acquainted with Harvard. I was nothing if not averse, but in time Mark persuaded me to introduce him to Drs. A— and

47

Z—. This was more painful than you can know. From the instant of my disastrous triumph, I had suffered fits of violent shame and mortification, and the possibility of conversing again with those intelligences whose example and inspiration I now considered responsible for my creation, filled me with disgust. I felt a passionate antipathy to even the most fleeting thought of language and would rarely permit myself to gaze on an anagram or acrostic or any text more puzzling than a stoplight. Even after my recuperation was complete, the sight of phonetic spellings would make me sweat, and once the mere opening of a dictionary left my arm convulsed with pain. Being perceptive, Mark observed this. He soon removed every treatise on narratology from my rooms, storing my books in a nearby warehouse and taking care to keep me on a steady diet of folk songs and the better television. He also changed my apartment, distrusting the bohemian appearance of our dwellings so near the Yard and determining that a condominium in the environs of Boston would prove therapeutic. He was right.

However, none of his precautions could have made the encounter with my former teachers less excruciating. Dr. Z—, whom we visited first, seemed his usual hip self, dressed in a purple dashiki and sandals. He spoke enthusiastically of my thesis, on which he assumed I must be working, and bragged to Mark that Cornell would undoubtedly publish it. As only someone like yourself can appreciate, all this deference to a neophyte could not but feel intoxicating. However, for me at the time it was just the opposite. The more Dr. Z— praised me, unmindful of my secret, the more nauseating his words became, so that, had Mark not been present, I feel sure I would've failed of restraint and spilled my guts there in his office. Oh, would that I had! But my inner turmoil was fated to remain my own, for with his customary delicacy Dr. Z— soon noted my discomfort and, attributing it to youthful modesty, changed the subject to intercalated proleptic anamnesis, a topic we'd always found fascinating. However, even this conversational plum couldn't divert me long, and in no time I felt as though Z— were replanting in my soul, one seme at a time, the very germs that had burgeoned so monstrously. I began to writhe at his inapt reminders. Or were the reminders my own? you ask. Ah, you take the words right out of my mouth! But regardless of whose inappropriateness I endured, I could speak nothing, terrified as I was of compounding my tragedy with farce, and so felt compelled to swallow my own mad screams.

After numerous awkward silences and quizzical looks, we took our leave of my generous mentor and went to see Dr. A—, whose conversation proved more bearable.

Damned young iconoclast! Came in here drawling Heideggerian folderol and next you know he's turned grammarian. And I could've made you a philosopher! Hah! Well, you young bucks all prefer that French *explication de testes*, yes? Har har. Now, don't mind my chaffing. But to think a boy just—has it been five years? I mean, when I heard that accent, the lad rambling on about fourfolds and the gods and would you pass me that ashtray? What was your name? Oh yes, stand for, Mark was it? With a name like that I'd . . . oh to hell, where was I? And here he's writing papers and giving lectures like faculty. Now don't go coloring up! Why you'd think he didn't like to hear himself praised! Oh, pretend if you want, but I'll tell you, that sort of humbug falls away soon enough. Vanity, vanity, what can compare? I was modest once. You don't believe me? But it's true! I was tender as a coed, whooo hoooo! And for what? Bah, give me vanity! I'm telling you young man, what was your name again? Oh that's right, making your mark, hah hah, I made a joke, never too old, sharp as a . . . Now, where . . . yes, vanity! That's right, better than dinner, better than sex, better almost than whiskey. Did you know—

Dr. A— had now commenced a eulogy upon himself, which happily turned the conversation from a subject I found painful to one we could ignore. In a matter of moments A— was sufficiently enthralled that we snuck away, listening to his shrill laughter all the way down the corridor.

During the subsequent weeks Mark and I toured the city, attending ball games and orchestra concerts, taking the occasional hiking trip into New Hampshire, and sampling on weekends those new establishments called *discos* where, along with other brightly clad young professionals, we writhed to the strains of men singing falsetto. Summer passed in these happy pursuits and soon it was fall and not long after that winter and then to my astonishment spring again, and still I had not returned south. I'm sure I suffered this delay most bitterly, for it's only natural that, with my increasing

49

strength, I should've ached to revisit home. However, I told myself I couldn't abandon Mark after he'd just arrived in an unfamiliar city, and then after he'd lived there only a few months, and then barely a year, or only a little more, and although I found this dawdling intolerable, I felt that postponing my reunion with those I loved was somehow right. It was almost as if a hiatus had been imposed, an illusory break in my story during which I could momentarily forget my life and cease foreboding, the sole effect of which was to unprepare me for the downfall when it finally came.

I realize now that these premonitions of doom must strike you as morbid, even pathological, but how often do we consider our behavior perfectly reasonable only to realize much later that it made no sense, and that the only cause for our persistence, as eventually becomes plain, was some plot which, unbeknownst to ourselves but with almost mechanical precision, we'd been following all along? I assure you, I no longer wonder at such aimless meanderings, but yield regularly to the moment's whim, knowing for how little my intentions have ever counted and hoping, through my bewildered ramblings, to appease that unseen necessity which, if not allowed to guide you from the first instance, is sure to be your undoing in the end.

Where was I?

Ah. I managed throughout those months to suppress my recurrent doubts about my delay by remarking how, during the entire period since my phone call with Liza, I had no dramatic encounters or personal upheavals or life-altering conversations that would have in any way accounted for it. However, a new chapter in my tragedy began as soon as I received the letter from my father that I have here on my person and will unfold for you presently, beginning a new chapter.

Chapter VI

DEAR SON,

You have probably been waiting impatiently for a letter from me to fix the date of your return, although now that I'm writing I can't for the life of me think why you'd need one. I mean, writing seems so exorbitant these days, as if nobody could tell what's happening without it, and yet wouldn't the anguish I presently feel, which is all this letter really means to convey, still be anguish if unrelated to you? An enigma. And you, how could my writing make your distance any less? Not that I question your absence, which is, after all, this letter's only excuse for being, but I can't forbear remarking it, since nothing else sentences me to these words that, were we face to face, I would certainly never say.

My Willy's dead! Oh innocent offspring whose corn-silk hair and guileless face were once the delight of his mother! What letter can express such a loss? What outpouring of words could ever take my little man's place? And, my remote and self-absorbed scion, the rupture in our tranquility runs deeper still. For to speak the grim truth, he was murdered.

I will offer no false comforts but will soberly relate the circumstances surrounding those tragic events of May 7, not because the details will bring you any comfort, but because, being human, you'll require them. Last Sunday afternoon Liza, Earnest, my beloved Willy, and I attended an outdoor concert in Piedmont Park. Oh, and Liza's girl, Teeny Love, went along, too. It was one of those beautiful, temperate days which, as you may have forgotten, Atlanta regularly enjoys this time of year, and living as we now do in our regentrified manor in Ansley Forest—have you also misplaced our address?—we decided to walk. It was dusk before we thought of returning home, and then we suddenly discovered that neither Earnest nor William was within sight. Liza and I dispatched Teeny to search the dense woods in back of the botanical gardens while we waited on a park bench, having determined that with perverts so plentiful, Liza must not go, and I was, of course, too decrepit. In less than an hour Earnest showed up inquiring after Willy, explaining how they'd been playing Nam when Willy, who was the *gook*, vanished.

As you'll understand, we were horrified and admonished Earnest most severely. We were also worried about Willy, so I called Harve Petrey—do you remember him from Martin's funeral? Well, he's Vice Commissioner of Public Safety now, and he was kind enough to send over a SWAT team and some cars from the Crisis Management Force, along with the Midtown fire unit and a Morningside Neighborhood Watch group, and offered to call in the Guard, which I hoped would be unnecessary. They scoured the woods, ball fields, railroad tracks, swimming pool, and were beginning a door to door canvass when about five a.m. my pitiful Willy was discovered on the golf course. Oh, beloved offshoot, who just hours before embodied my last pleasure in this world, to imagine you stretched out limp and lifeless beside the final hole! There were no signs of a struggle. Around my Willy's throat was a bruise the shape of a hand.

I will not bore you with the details of how we carried his body home in defiance of city sanitation codes, or of how Liza, who insisted on examining Willy's pockets, clasped her hands together and exclaimed: 𝕺𝖍 𝕲𝖔𝖉, 𝕴 𝖍𝖆𝖛𝖊 𝖒𝖚𝖗𝖉𝖊𝖗𝖊𝖉 𝖒𝖞 𝖉𝖆𝖗𝖑𝖎𝖓𝖌 𝖈𝖍𝖎𝖑𝖉!

I'll only comment that her words had no bearing on the homicide and would have been inadmissible in court, the spurious confession, in addition to being hysterical and arguably excludable on psychological grounds, appearing grossly ignorant of law and proving deficient in several conditions necessary for indictment, which grounds being severally, premeditation, means, motive, access, etc. Why she called my Willy hers, I can only speculate. Anyway, I noticed the police growing suspicious so I instructed Liza to keep silent and phoned Bill Kunstler, who was negotiating a hostage crisis in New York but promised to fly down immediately. Luckily, Liza fainted just then and could not be revived until the authorities had gone, at which time she explained how she'd given her almost-brother an antique romance, formerly his mother's, to read. Some boys like that sort of thing, you know. Anyway, its cracked leather binding had been beautiful, and Liza now insisted quite plausibly that this priceless antique, which could not be found anywhere at the crime scene, must have been the motive for the assault.

We reassured her, of course, that my beloved Willy's demise was in no way her doing, but she remains inconsolable. All day she plays her guitar, pausing only to wonder how many seas a white dove must sail and similar imponderables, before returning to the same three chords she has strummed since age eight. No one can make her stop. Oh Frank, if only you could transpose this minor key for your spiritual mate, whom—as I'm sure you can't forget—your saintly mother always dreamed you'd one day marry, thus symbolizing by your union the racial harmony still possible for our democratic, if bigoted, nation . . . well, perhaps then there'd be peace.

We're all inconsolably miserable, but having related to you our distress, I know this letter will only intensify your eagerness to fly home and be miserable with us. Return for your saintly mother's sake, whose untimely death, having spared her this grief, I now feel was almost a blessing. On the way from the airport take the interstate through downtown but don't get off at the North Avenue exit which is under construction. Instead go all the way to Monroe or even Piedmont which seems a roundabout route but will actually get you here quicker.

53

> Your afflicted father,
> FRANK STEIN

Mark, who was noting my changed expression all the time I was noting my father's and so grasped my father's meaning even as I grasped it, having already felt everything I felt at the same instant that I, learning how my antecedent felt, felt it, and who consequently had no need of being told what I'd been told but who nevertheless, in a gesture of profound respect, asked anyway—when I finally related the horrors related to me to him, said: What can I say?

It exceeds language.
Nothing compares.
And they ventured no explanation?
Who would pretend to understand?
Unspeakable!
The pain is itself.
Ah.

Mark phoned the airlines for me, and in a matter of hours I was aloft, flying southwards in space, backwards in politics, to my suffering loved ones, my sole thought to fling myself on the family bosom and weep. I continually asked myself how, during what had seemed but a temporary absence, could I have ever become so oblivious? Didn't I remember I owed everything to my family? Had my brother's death been required just to remind me? I now became so preoccupied with all those I'd neglected—dear distracted Liza, my ailing father, brave Earnie, even Teeny Love—that I completely lost consciousness of my surroundings. Whereas, prior to my poor Will's demise, I might have had difficulty spelling my siblings' middle names correctly, now their agonized faces loomed gigantically before me, monopolizing my attention and blotting out all besides. Was our take-off stormy? Perhaps the landing gear wouldn't retract. I recall nothing. My only thought was that at any moment for the last thousand days I could have boarded a plane just as effortlessly as now, could have within hours been gazing into my brother's blue eyes, a joy I would never know again. In what universe had I been living? Where was Frank Stein? Why, it all seemed some impossibly twisted delusion.

However, despite these torments, just as we prepared to land, I became aware that another object had begun to compete for my attention. For some minutes I seemed to have been staring at a pudgy youth across the aisle bent in furious concentration over a paperback. At first I continued to stare in a thoughtless stupor, wholly unaware of what it was that had attracted me, then as I was about to turn away I happened to notice the paperback's cover and gasped. It was yellow! The loss of Will had momentarily displaced that other anguish which had for so many months gripped me like a disease, and now, seeing again the disordered being who'd separated me from all I loved, my former wretchedness came rushing back. Was it for this, a mere adolescent's pastime, that I'd sacrificed my family? Could I really have turned my own flesh and blood into fiction? I trembled to think such questions might not be rhetorical. And even now, hardly an arm's length away, this innocent youth appeared to be repeating my mistake! Well, the prospect filled me with rage. With a lurch I leaned across the aisle to strike the ghastly pages from his fist when, happily, the boy's grip shifted, revealing on the cover a basketball-breasted amazon in animal skins firing lasers at what appeared to be inflated armadillos. With embarrassment I quickly righted myself. The boy's life was imperiled, no doubt, but his thoughts were not occupied with me.

However, my relief was short-lived. For even as I felt my muscles relax and my breathing quiet, I sensed anew how inescapable my predicament had become. The life I'd fashioned could foreshadow me anywhere. Even in my birth home, the city where I'd been me before anything, my experience could precede my arrival, could erase my past and overwrite every new encounter with conclusions I'd already reached. I told myself to be reasonable, insisted that I was one thing, my creation another, but the more strident my insistence became, the more copies of my life amassed before me, until every page predicted my defeat. Oh, it was futile! In the Cambridge bookshop hadn't I found my words revolting? Hadn't I witnessed their power to move independently? My life's meaning was now public. It was folly to disown it. And as I journeyed from the remote ends of the Atlanta airport toward that outer darkness into which every traveler must sooner or later depart, I began to suffer apprehensions. I scrutinized the shelves of passing bookstalls, eavesdropped on conversations. The strangers around me stared back, mirroring my unease, as though they could read my thoughts, and I had to remind myself that my likeness didn't appear on my cover, that my identity remained a secret. It was as if the life I'd made were as separate from me as any passerby. That anything could be so alien and still mine now struck me as perverse.

But pardon, pardon, my indefatigable friend! I see from your glazed eyes that I'm rambling on. Where's the action? you must wonder. No, no, don't deny it! So little of my ruin can be amusing, and how should I expect anyone—much less an imagination as unrestrained as yours—to appreciate my

55

petty torments, those twists of syntax, slips, malaprops, minutiae of inflection. Don't I know there's more to life than words? Be assured. No balanced mind will tremble before black ciphers, and only a demented librarian, some myopic pedant warped by his own impotent closeting, could attribute fatality to grammar. I perfectly understand you. In truth, it has been my despair at ever making my torments comprehensible, at least to anyone not already destroyed by them, that has countless times stopped me on the brink. Even now I choke with fury. Wouldn't I happily concoct a violent wrong, conceive a passion for you, unmask the world's spectacular deviance? But if I'm to be frank, I should admit my downfall has come from nothing so elevated, and dwelling on its mundaneness now comprises my sole release. Origins, origins! Can any but the driest wit still hope to draw refreshment from these polluted mainstreams, and who but one drowning in our culture's gush could pretend, bogged down here and now, to tap their source yet again?

On. It was well past midnight and threatening to storm when my taxi stopped at the Ansley Forest address where, according to my father's letter, we now resided. I read the name on the mailbox. Yes, I was home. The iron gates that the Pinkertons had required every resident to install had been bolted for the night, and although I knew I could arouse Teeny Love merely by pushing her button, I was reluctant to disturb those fortunate enough to be unconscious. I was but a few blocks from the murder scene, and yielding to a sudden nocturnal impulse, I determined to visit the spot. I paid the cabbie and started to walk.

No no, meester, beeg mistake! Park eez bad at night weeth the moogers!

But I somehow knew I'd be safe, and so reassuring the good man with a dollar, I continued on my way. I wandered the winding entrance past an array of pools and softball fields toward the golf course. I was in a peculiar mood, by turns exhilarated and downcast, as though I still hoped to meet my departed Will even while resolved to mourn him. As I strode up a grassy slope along the fairway, the stillness of the surrounding city and the rumbling from the storm seemed to transform the park into an otherworldly place, one of those mystical landscapes in which one's imagination easily becomes overpowering. Perhaps it was this place and my resulting giddiness, or possibly just my recent trauma, that will explain what happened next, for as I approached the final hole, there was a great burst of heavenly fire, and gazing upwards I felt seized by sublime compulsions. A momentary lightheadedness passed over me. I seemed to forget my whereabouts. And opening my mouth to breathe in the charged air, I was astounded to hear my voice proclaim: 𝔚illiam, dear angel! this is thy funeral, this thy dirge!

Good God, I thought, what has gotten into me? Not that I was a stranger to inspiration, those reports of sensible men and women going out of their heads, but that apostrophe, elision, the bombast, those *thy's*—Why, this language wasn't mine! And yet, even as my body resounded with the accompanying thunder, I seemed to glimpse in the deepening gloom a reality I'd never imagined before, some foreign conceit, figure, or poetic germ that amid my everyday speech had infected me unaware.

I was incapable in that place and mood of expressing myself more clearly, and even now after more than two decades I still feel compelled to indirectness, but that alien figure which, all the while I was remarking it, appeared to recede into half-articulate images and symbols—that dimly perceived form wouldn't give me peace. I blinked. What had I been thinking? Earlier traversing the air terminal I'd felt horrified to realize my life might not be my own, that it could appear—even to myself—as a being apart, but now a still more psychotic prospect seemed to loom, that perhaps this future now, all those experiences I'd acquired at such cost and assembled with painstaking labor and so naturally considered mine, had in fact from the start been another's. It seemed too, too incredible! I could still remember the thrill of conception, my intoxicating power, those effusions spilling from my pen. How could I have mistaken some familiar twist, an overused plot or hackneyed punch-line, for a real killer? Whose history was this? But just then a lightning bolt exploded in a nearby willow, illuminating everything about me, and I knew in a flash that the real killer hadn't been my doing, was rather the form I'd brought to life. It seemed impossible. How could I, mired in jargon and Massachusetts, have literally had a hand in my brother's murder? But posing the question so made my part seem metonymic, a mere stand-in for some murderous hand in truth, and I realized at once that misrepresenting my handiwork so amounted to a confession. That savage being I'd never once recognized all the time of its making, that had first passed before my thoughts at the site of my Will's demise, and that only now vanished into the surrounding oblivion—*he* had been responsible! I could no longer doubt. I, Frank Stein, was the destroyer of innocence.

You cannot conceive the anguish I suffered during the remainder of that night. It began to pour, while I dashed from one leaky shelter to the next. I thought I'd catch my death. However, when morning dawned, the returning warmth and light partially restored my equanimity, and I returned to my father's house confident Teeny Love would open up for me. My first thought was to share my late-night revelation with my loved ones, divulge the plot that was behind my brother's death, or as much of it as I'd been able to foretell, and then begin my lifelong reparation by resuming my place within my family. I could never replace my father's Willy, of course, but I at least hoped to contain the violence I'd unleashed by reacquiring all the rights to my fiction. To save others from likeminded disaster now seemed my only redemption. However, the plan of taking back my words remained somewhat vague, and I began to feel hesitant about annihilating my creation as soon as I considered further. Although my responsibility for Will's murder had appeared vividly to me the previous night, now in the sober light of day I started to wonder if the obscure figure I'd interpreted so profoundly might not just be an exaggeration. I recalled the nervous fever I'd so recently suffered, my former delusions of unprecedented feats, and all the gibberish conveyed to my family by Mark. Even if I could fully credit last night's vision, my family might not accept my account at face value. Who was to say I wasn't suffering delirium again? I was at once struck by the irony of my position. Was there even any proof that the work in question was actually mine? Why, there could be cries of censorship! My own father might come to the author's defense! The *author*. How strange that word sounded now, as though naming some gothic mastermind under whose spell I'd unaccountably fallen.

It was about six a.m. when the door of my home opened and I beheld a young woman whose attractive but sleepy face I hardly recognized. However, never had a threshold appeared so beautiful to me or its warm bosom so inviting. In my extremity of pain and happiness, I embraced her. Is it really you Teeny? How changed you look!

But she shoved me away. Git yo hands off me, white boy! Aint you got no sense? Drippin on my nice clean flo!

And indeed she was right. Water poured down my trouser leg onto my father's heart pine foyer, and a trail of muddy footprints followed me wherever I'd trod. The young woman, whose name I soon learned was Carletta, turned out to be our newest housekeeper, a cheerful helpmate and companion to Teeny, I supposed. She forced me to wait outside until she returned with towels and a robe, and then after a brusque but friendly brushing off, I was escorted into my father's study.

Six years had passed, leaving no trace save that grim and ineradicable inscription on my soul to whose significance I alone was privy, and now I stood in a place virtually identical to the place from which I'd set out. The furnishings weren't new. The wall-coverings resembled those I remembered. Over the mantel was a replica of the face of my mother which formerly hung in my birthplace and now hung in my memory. Beneath her stood William. That is to say, a photo of a boy the age I reckoned Will would've been and whose appearance conformed to that I'd always imagined as the ten-year-old version of the four-year-old I'd known. The sole unbecoming detail was myself. Why hadn't I reentered these confines before now? Enveloped in my family's trappings, I could feel no gap between my home and my wanderings, a fact that made my exile seem strange, almost as though the distance from here to there had become metaphysical. I was just succumbing to morbid thoughts when a burly youth in camouflage fatigues appeared.

Reinforcements! It's great to have you on the home front, Bro.

Y-you can't be Earnest? I stammered.

We tearfully embraced, then upon recovering his composure, my brother related the misery into which our family had plunged.

Brace yourself, Frank. It was Liza's singing at first, those pansy songs the troops can't dance to, but now she's gone all zombie, mopes around the base half-dressed. Well, it's nothing the grunts were trained for. Seriously choy oi, no kidding.

But Father's bearing up?

Heavy casualties. You won't know him. Never writes letters, paces in his room—

I groaned. Oh, if only I'd never left!

Earnie put his arm around my shoulder. Whoa, buddy, don't get the blue mooky! Our unit's taken some hits, but nobody's blaming you.

I feel like I've waked from a coma. My professors, those ideas—was all that another life? But I'm myself again. You'll see.

Glad you're back, 'cause we need help. The old man's not battle worthy, whole company's reeling. I mean, a spook on base! And who could've suspected Teeny? Little gutter snipe Mom raised to street level—

Teeny? What's Teeny got to do—

Earnie peered at me incredulously. Why, Teeny whacked Will!

You've got to be joking!

Joe who?

My brother then related, in his colorful way, how on the morning following William's murder Teeny had taken ill, although no organic cause was ever determined, and lay suffering in her bed for several days, during which one of the housekeepers—Monique, he believed—acting on Liza and Earnie's instructions canvassed Teeny's belongings and found in a pocket of the white uniform Teeny'd been wearing the night of the crime the leather-bound volume Liza had testified to giving William the morning before, all of which information being obtained under what Earnie termed *deep cover*. Then Monique immediately showing—but no, it had been Carletta—then Carletta immediately showing the book to Earnie, he surrendered it without a word to the authorities. My duty, he explained. Teeny still serenely unconscious and in a weakened state was awakened to her predicament, deposed and incarcerated, all in that order, with our father nearby cautioning that the search might prove illegal and evidence inadmissible and therefore charging the officers to treat the accused with every consideration, so eliminating, should the verdict be as severe as all expected, any obstacle to conviction. However, on being charged, Teeny confirmed everyone's worst suspicions by her inability to give a well-ordered account of how the book came into her possession while she slept.

Before I could respond to these unsettling disclosures, we were interrupted by the entrance of a haggard-looking gentleman leaning on a cane. Although he bore little resemblance to the man I'd bade goodbye six years earlier, I had no doubt that this was my father. He attempted to welcome me cheerfully, inquiring after my health, and would've certainly asked whom I supported for president, had I not exclaimed, Father, you must stop this travesty! I know Will's killer!

Yes, who could've imagined? Of course, her duplicity struck us as unthinkable, but on reflection, that was how we were sure.

No, no, I mean Teeny's as innocent as you or I!

He shook his head. Then you're sadly muddled. The evidence is far stronger against her than against either of us, and if you were somehow implicated, say, by our country's racism, your representation would certainly prove superior. Being a party to the injured, you understand, I can't interest myself on Teeny's behalf, and that surely means a public defender, probably fresh from school. What reputable attorney would oppose us? And then there's the melancholy fact that the girl's hand print, turned a certain way, almost matches the bruise around poor Willy's throat, suggestive of a crime of passion, perhaps with illicit intent, and although an acquittal is possible on several grounds, not the least being temporary insanity, for which there's ample evidence since, until now, her record of loyalty's been unmarred, I doubt she'll prove a sympathetic witness. Were I Teeny's attorney, I would go with a full confession, complete with histrionic remorse, while bargaining for leniency based on psychological profiles, but that's always tricky, since experts can be alienating. What you'd want is to avoid a jury while appearing to the D.A. like you'll fight, but my point is that such a favorable verdict as you now generously rendered is, really, unlikely in the extreme and so can hardly be considered equal, or even remotely comparable, to your innocence or mine. So, for these and other reasons, you can't know what you're saying.

This speech astonished me. I still supposed in my own mind, if not anyone else's, that Teeny's innocence was other than everyone's representation of it, so that, in some sublime way, she remained untouched by their words. But I was beginning to wonder. I couldn't now describe the revelation I'd undergone in the park, for as you'll appreciate, such

61

experiences rely on the listener's aroused imagination, and who'd believe, right there in my family's den, that writing would literally kill you? Only an individual previously acquainted with writing's violence, with its power to obliterate flesh and enthrall the mind, could credit such absurdities, and not even I had more than a fleeting glimpse of how all this worked. To imagine books inciting murder, transforming love into hatred, turning brother against brother, black against white, why, it was as if our civilization were no better than a house of cards! After my recent brain fever, to voice such suspicions would confirm everyone else's.

I was opening my mouth to utter a circumspect rejoinder when the entrance of Liza Mbira made me bite my tongue. My more-than-sister did not appear at all as I'd recalled! Her recent ordeal and our long years of separation had endowed her with a womanly beauty beyond my wildest dreams, or perhaps just even with them, and seeing her in the flesh, I felt mysteriously unnerved. She wore vast expanses of denim and leather punctuated by zippers and tantalizing rips. Over one shoulder she'd slung a green Stratocaster, plugged into a wireless box pinned to her bra, and her dreadlocks spewed wildly from her head. I could hardly speak.

Frank's as hung up on Teeny's innocence as you were, Earnie announced to her.

Liza gazed at me with an unsettling directness. Your optimism means a lot, Frank. Perhaps if you'd come home years ago. But now, what difference can it make?

Tho much to thay, I said, sucking my tongue. But Teeny ith innothent, Litha, *innothent!*

Some gung ho mooky, huh?

Remember the constitution, Father reassured her. If Teeny's blameless, she'll get a fair trial.

But Liza just shrugged her Strat. It's too late, too late, she said. Why try to fake it? Will has died, and in an hour when Teeny's tried, we all know she won't make it.

An hour? *You've got to be joking!*

Earnie and Liza exchanged a look. That's the second time he's called me that, Earnie said.

Who's Joe Kane? Father asked.

King, Liza corrected.

What about due protheth? I pleaded. Requeth a thtay?

King? This is the land of the free for God's sake!

—like he's forgotten his whole family.

No one'th free if Teeny'th in jail!

Hold on—that special forces grunt, Aunt Coretta's nephew, wasn't he Joe King?

No, they're Scotts.

Besides, even if he had been Joe King, how would that help Teeny?

—where nonviolence gets you!

Scots? I've heard of black Irish but never—

Wait a minute! My father turned to me. I think I see. Are you trying to tell us Joe King is responsible?

I swallowed. Manner thpeaking. I know guilty figurth—on the moze intimate termth! Park lath night, thaw a thooting thtar, foul form, own fithion, thavage letterth, loth more. Tho hard tooth plain. Thoon, juth wait, all know my thtory, all know killerth too. You'll thee. But muz believe, *Teeny ith innothent*!!!

Chapter VII

INCREDIBLY, ONLY a few sad minutes remained before Teeny's trial, so we all piled into the Mercedes and drove to the Fulton County courthouse. Throughout this wretched parody I could not distinguish Teeny's torment from my own. A jury of perfect strangers was about to decide both our fates. Either she was guilty of senseless brutality, or if not, then it seemed that their verdict would make me doubly so. For some reason, I felt that the life I'd made must be wholly extraneous to my brother's tragedy, a mere escape or distraction, or if not wholly extraneous, then it must lie at the root of all. Why there could be no third alternative, I was unable to explain. Somehow the starkness of these choices gave to the ensuing deliberations a quality simultaneously farcical and hallucinatory. I oscillated between feelings of omnipotence, as though I were myself orchestrating the present outcome, and profound helplessness, as if my every impulse had been foretold. This last sensation dumbfounded me. Gazing around at the grimfaced onlookers, I began to imagine that the knowledge I'd uncovered in Boston, the secret to fashioning a human life, had been — unbeknownst to me — accursed. It was as though, having mastered the organon of all pasts and futures, I'd at the same time become captivated. Instead of the overseer of this great matrix, I was now a speck on its surface, fixed forever but unlocatable, corresponding to nothing. This isn't me! I wanted to protest. But to identify thus with my own creation seemed the most romantic of delusions, and besides, who could I expect, given my recent inanities, to take my protests seriously?

The prosecution's case seemed unarguable. As none denied, Teeny was without alibi during the critical hours when, according to forensic experts, poor Will had met his maker. This fact alone spoke volumes. A patrolman reported having stopped and questioned a woman fitting Teeny's description in a residential neighborhood not far from the golf course during a crucial interval. He remarked that she'd behaved suspiciously, ignoring his initial summons, then became ill-tempered and flighty. The respectable wife of a city official also reported observing Teeny—she was positive about the identification—around five a.m. on a bridge just a few hundred yards from where the victim was found. The good woman, who had spent the night nursing a sick friend, testified that Teeny was obviously hysterical, shouting obscenities and gesturing violently. Our new housekeeper Carletta related how, upon returning home, Teeny appeared agitated and began questioning everyone, especially Earnest, about the deceased. When informed of his murder, she fell into a swoon, a reaction all found incriminating, and then, without any cause whatsoever, took to her bed for three days. The book was next produced which connected Teeny to the crime, having been located on her person by, as it turned out, Monique. And when Liza Mbira, in a faltering voice, acknowledged that this book precisely resembled the antique romance she'd entrusted but a few hours earlier to her sweet William, so precisely, in fact, both in outline and detail, that for all the difference it made, the two might as well be one . . . well, a gasp of indignation went up from the court.

65

To anyone with doubts less insurmountable than my own, Teeny's guilt seemed a foregone conclusion. Accidents of timing confirmed the general suspicion. Tissues of coincidence formed seamless wholes. Nothing material appeared to be left out. I cannot communicate to you how reassuring this all seemed. Throughout the prosecutor's narration, Teeny's face remained an uncurtained stage across which strutted every passion, or more accurately, every outward appearance of passion, or more accurately still, every outward appearance conventionally assigned to passion, that any murderer would want us to think she felt. Teeny wept. Teeny groaned. Teeny flinched. We observed her performance closely.

Upon the conclusion of the prosecution's case, the judge instructed the bailiff to awaken Teeny's lawyer, who promptly placed Teeny on the stand.

All right, he said.

For several seconds Teeny struggled with what certainly looked like overpowering emotion, then composing herself, she gave voice to that spontaneous eloquence that is the natural asset of the unjustly accused:

Wha choo crazy? Ofay clouds trippin, sister be some blackern shit badass ho, wanna eat white cake? Shee it! All that jez a made-up neeegro. Fig meant outa ofay imagination. What bidness Teeny got wid some honky book? Uptown negroes done sided, she got the gun done the son, caint say it, dont play it, but homey knows whats fact. Why, you meanin to fry yo self a nigger, caint let no white chile die else! You jez kiss my black ass, aint gone bottle whats troof! Sister caint ford no showtime college lawyer, but aint no muh fuh gone say this bitch cap no baby, shee it! I know what I know an gone speak it like it is, you hear? Teeny never touch po chile. Dass fack! Honkey daddy think his white meat so fine black girl jes achin to cook herself some angel fooood, but man, you some kinda jive-ass or what? Aint white baby got nuffin Teeny want! Dem fancy books be ofay clouds dis ease, anyways wasnt nowhere near when po lil white cake wuz baked, thats troof shaw nuff, receive it an believe it, cause this black bitch aint no born fool, naw, old daddy ghost tell me, hey snowflake baby done crawl off, black nooky go looky in them badass woods, well sheeit, you thinkin I be stoopid or some shit, I aint casin no faggot crib, I am outa there, truckin over to my main mans, listen at yer homey now, where sister keeps a stash an can get herself fucked up real good, oooooeee! So there your bitch is, stretched out all cool, hear, watchin my mans big screen, musta be bout a million channels, some kind junky dream bout this ofay scientist makin real bad shit outa stiffs, you believin that, dead muh fuh, well, there I am suckin bong when, Teeny aint talkin no trash now, pig mobiles comin outa nowhere, musta been twenty of em, cruisin all slow so folks know they lookin for somethin, an I start trippin, too much heat, some serious shit gone down, so I split the crib, movin with my groovin, hear me, down to street, struttin my stuff right pass that badge like some hi dollah Ebony bitch, which is bout troof, this nigger too hot for mister white neeegro lawman what done tol all that lyin shit bout Teeny jez awhile ago. I seen him drivin that pig bus, fact, dont dis me, an I hear em rappin at yer bitch, hey sister, aint you phat now, give yo daddy some Georgia sunshine, fine sugar, mmmhm, and shit like that. Well, I keep struttin, like he aint happenin, noway, check this sister out, let it hurt him goooood, y'unnerstan, flasher cruisin all slow, figurin if he got bidness he can say, an then he sing out, hey swee-eet mama, why you treatin yo daddy so mean? Real high, right there, y'know, almos like Marvin. Hey! Swee-eet mama, why you treat yo good lovin daddy so mean? Which is hip, I mean Teeny can dig a brother, so I stop an we rap, bout shit, back when, growin up in the project an all, sez he from the hood, knew my daddy, hear, an so he raps how dis white boy missin, well, I get them goosey vibes then, I mean, what if pretty pants lost shaw nuff an old daddy cloud gone blame Teeny fo losin him, I mean, I'm trippin bad now, so side to split, but this lawman john neeegro, he dont want his hot bitch to go jiz yet, sez we done start somethin, how bout we take a lil ridin his pig limo, I can fire his gun for troof. Well, I say fuck that shit, get yo hands offa me, nigger, crazy or what, man caint catch it dont fetch it, yo aint my daddy no how! An then I trucks back to that park, casin dem woods for real now, black as my pussy an caint see shit, coupla hours, come out by that bridge where Miz Hi-struttin Ofay done finger me, no denyin, I aint lyin, but she aint tellin more then half, cause Teeny seen Miz Vanilla doin her back do man insider jap car, young stuff too, whats troof, right there in that park, dont even take the bitch to a room, is that some cheap shit or what? An Miz Ofay get all friendly when she sees how sister seen her white ass stickin outa window, starts to flash green at Teeny, but shee it, I got no use for her bread, cause girl is plum scared now, caint fine lil snowflake baby, dont know whazz what, an so Miz Vanilla be outa there, truckin in her fancy car, leavin yer sister lone, trippin on how its most light now an parks all empty, pig limos no place, too quiet, like some bad shit gone down, so sister splits, heads back to ofay castle, where they tell her troof, how some foo-foo crazy bumfucker done kill her po white baby. Bout broke sisters heart. Now thass all of it, cept bout that book shit, what ofay clouds tryin to put on me, sayin how they done felt Teeny up while she sleepin, handlin upside sisters pockets, well, what they doin that for, I ass you, got no cause, jez rich honky dis ease, an aint never done that shit wi Teeny befo or she be split, shaw nuff, so you sniffin what I sniffin? An sides, I wuz still totin that bong from my mans in my pocket but dont nobody say nuffin bout findin that, so now tell me, is it some bad shit gone down here or what? But no good doggin, cause caint nobody hear nothin Teeny sez, dont matter what, naw, cause ever one be listenin at this badass jemima doll sittin right here side yo bitch, jez a fig meant, made up spook from ofay fear, black monster done eat yo pretty pants, sheeit, but that jemima doll do all the talkin, like Teeny done split, po bitch jez wanna be left alone, but nigger got no luck, caint tell what a sister know, white ghosts an uptown neeegroes, yall out to fry some black bitch, well, this sweet ass good as cooked, no use rappin whats troof.

I was astonished! Who could've imagined such a defense? My hopes for acquittal soared. There could be no foretelling the outcome now! However, as I surveyed the courtroom I was surprised to see that few others seemed moved. The jurors' faces wore a dazzled expression; the bailiff's eyelids had fallen closed; the court reporter's fingers were motionless, and the spectators were all fidgeting in their seats. How could anyone remain untouched by Teeny's rousing words? It was as though they were absent for her speech or heard another speech in its stead. In fact, despite having thrilled to her inflections, I was far from certain that even I knew what Teeny had said. A mounting panic seized my throat. Would no one translate? The condemned must be heard!

But the only other defense witness was Liza, who hastened forward to declare, despite being almost a sibling of the victim and so in a position to feel bitterly vengeful, that she freely forgave the wretched girl for any beastliness to which she might have momentarily surrendered, knowing as Liza did that such violent acts were the unavoidable consequence of the poverty and ignorance in which poor Teeny had lived throughout her infancy, and that Liza remained ever mindful of those subsequent happy years when Teeny, enjoying the protection and unselfish love of the cruelly murdered child's family, had appeared to feel that affection for her benefactors that any dependent could be expected to appear to feel. As for the book, if it had ever crossed Liza's mind that Teeny knew how to read, she'd have happily made a present of it to her. At which words she directed a mournful and compassionate smile in the murderer's direction. This speech, however, did not appear to soften the jurors' hearts as one might have expected, perhaps because through it all Teeny yielded to no outpourings of gratitude, often gazing past Liza's tearful face with a blank resignation that contrasted unfavorably with Liza's tenderhearted pleas. The closing summaries were succinct, and soon the jurors retired. They remained sequestered for countless seconds. When their agonized verdict returned, it was *guilty*!

I cannot pretend to say what I then felt, but I can and will pretend to say that it was less bearable than what others felt, even Teeny. She was, I now know, supported by the certainty of her innocence, as well as by the comforting assurance that her accusers were beneath contempt, while I still had myself to contend with. As I'd listened to the evidence, I'd strained to believe that my memories were just illusions, that my previous night's revelation had been the hyperbolic remorse of a neglectful brother, and that framing a black woman had never comprised any part of my experience. I reminded myself how, during my months of labor at Harvard, I'd scrutinized the constituents of my life, how, despite having indulged in popular mindlessness and sampled my culture indiscriminately, when I'd actually begun to fashion a life of my own, I'd grown critical to a fault. There'd been nothing arbitrary about my work. In short, it seemed inconsistent of me now, not to mention ungenerous, to impugn the integrity of Teeny's jurors, and I told myself I should accept their verdict as conclusive.

69

But despite the flawlessness of this reasoning, I couldn't shrug my sense that the travesty I was witnessing was familiar. I mean, this was America! Didn't I believe my life could lead to absolutely anything? I had fabricated a being, reproduced experiences indistinguishable from everyone else's, but I'd never once reflected on my experience doing this. Whose being was *that*? The harder I strove to believe in Teeny's guilt, the more tormented I became. I seemed to see my precious Will being murdered over and over. Was there no end to this madness? With Earnest, Liza, and my father, I stood in stunned silence as Teeny was dragged shrieking from the courtroom, then scarcely knowing what to do with ourselves, we went out to supper.

The next day I learned that Teeny had confessed to her crime, news which, although I could hardly credit it, nevertheless bolstered me. It seemed my fondest dream now that my creation had not been responsible for my family's misery and that I could eventually be cleared of plotting against my brother's life. After all, if fratricide were what came of knowing words, then who could say what might happen next? At the same time, I didn't relish the thought that my writing, however spontaneously conceived, might just prove innocuous. The blind poet's memory remained vivid in my mind's eye, his Selma having now utterly replaced my own, and this prospect, that another's history had achieved a reality mine lacked, could not but leave me miffed. Even if my imagination weren't the sole cause of Will's disappearance, I still wanted it to amount to more than illusion. So when Liza reacted to this news by proclaiming that, if Teeny had truly confessed, then she would never trust humankind more, my pride was touched, and I hastened to reassure her that there'd be no shortage of gullibilities yet to come, or no shortage merely because viciousness had occurred where least expected.

Do not doubt, dear Liza, I proclaimed, this so-called confession is but the cynical ploy of a legal system so irredemiably odious that it will descend to any servile, self-congratulatory misrepresentation to justify its own sordid existence! If Teeny is capable of deceiving us who loved her, then make no mistake, this so-called confession can be bogus too.

Liza seemed astonished by my prescience and gazed back at me in openmouthed and, I believe, womanly admiration. However, it wasn't long before she acknowledged her feminine need to know the truth, so we set out to visit the condemned. It was a sad business. Surrounded by prison walls, Teeny appeared unusually subdued, especially for someone fortified, as I now know, with her innocence. She sat in a chair hugging her knees, staring up at the ceiling, and when we hailed her through the inch-thick plexiglass, her reply was not genial.

Wha choo want?

Liza Mbira pushed herself up against the transparent divider, began to plead. Oh Teeny, Teeny, how could you confess? I relied so, if not on your absolute innocence, then on your unconsciousness of what you were doing. Nobody dreamed you knew!

Fuck! Wha choo mean, come here dissin Teeny? You jez a little white flower think she a neeegro, dont know shit bout shit. Trippin all night in dis ofay lockup, blackern yo momma's pussy, jez try not rappin. Angel cake like you, shee it, bitches gobble you up in five minits!

And then Teeny explained to us how, prior to sentencing, her attorney had said remorse was her only hope, rehearsed her in the most salutary theatrics, and left her with the caution that, without mercy, she was history.

Aint nuthin jez lies, Teeny concluded. What difference that make? I aint kill no white baby, what muh fuh do shit like that? Just ofay dream is all, but sister done bad enough, so fuck it, maybe some shit I rap to, maybe it dont mean just the shit I say, dig? Girl, you caint know how it is. But Jesus hear, confeshun don't have to be troof.

And that was all of substance that passed between us, except for a curious exchange as Liza and I readied to depart. Struggling to communicate her undying affection, Liza had pressed her tearful face against the divider just as, in an accident of mistiming, Teeny stood to leave. The resulting awkwardness lasted hardly a second, but during this hiatus, Teeny cocked her head at me and asked: What *he* got to say?

Liza seemed taken aback. She reached for my hand and pressed it to her bosom. Frank? Why he thinks the same as I.

Thass a fack?

Yes, in truth, when he heard you'd confessed, he was more skeptical than anyone, insisting this tidy ending wasn't to be believed.

Teeny didn't reply, but her mouth twisted peculiarly and her body turned toward me. In that triangular nexus, as Liza's breast heaved beneath my thumb, my mind filled with forgotten sensations, a memory of skin, curls grasped in my fists, the salt on my fingers' ends. For a horrific instant my estranged corpus rose up before me, its annihilating power dazzlingly palpable, and I seemed to see—oh, with what insane clarity!—the monster my life was turning into. In desperation I tensed to fling myself at the glass and, opening my mouth, expected any second to hear my voice shout out my wrongs, but Teeny merely gazed into my eyes, and as Liza called the guard, I watched in paralyzed silence while my playmate was dragged away.

Teeny's confession fooled no one. She was sentenced to death, and within a few implausibly short weeks, her execution had already been scheduled, appeals exhausted, and Teeny Love was no more. I attended her combustion, meaning to the last to proclaim my culpability, to shout even as they strapped her down that it was I, Frank Stein, whose vile form

71

demanded this electrifying conclusion, but as my lips parted, I recognized the futility of trying with more words now to correct the violence my words had provoked before. How had matters come to such a pass? My beginning had seemed ordinary enough—a wish for newness, for experience unmarked by predecessors, by falsehearted antecedents—but then one thing had led to another until my creation had ended by taking me over. And standing there in cowed silence as they strapped my playmate to the contraption, I sensed in my soul even this ultimate outrage being dictated. I watched Teeny's scalp smoke, her eyes flame, her skull explode, until that flesh I'd once loved was tranformed into a charred and sizzling stump. Liza gave out a scream and, clutching at my lapels, sunk to the floor. There was a momentary panic, onlookers rushing to help, shouts for a doctor. But I stood transfixed. How could this be my doing?

Chapter VIII

NOTHING IS MORE intolerable than, following a horrific episode like the last, to traverse the stretches of turgid moralizing that inevitably ensue. Let's skip them. It was July. My grieving family sought relief from the heat. We had a summer home in the mountains. At higher altitudes we hoped everything would be cool.

All that bears relating from this period was a deeply unsettling conversation I had with my beautiful cousin, our developing passion having now made it unseemly to keep calling each other, even if only more or less, brother and sister. She was seated in a tree swing, her hazel curvatures swathed in a remarkable encumbrance known as a tube. In her lap she held a leather volume.

𝔚𝔥𝔢𝔫 𝔍 𝔯𝔢𝔣𝔩𝔢𝔠𝔱, 𝔪𝔶 𝔡𝔢𝔞𝔯 𝔠𝔬𝔲𝔰𝔦𝔫, 𝔰𝔞𝔦𝔡 𝔰𝔥𝔢, 𝔬𝔫 𝔱𝔥𝔢 𝔪𝔦𝔰𝔢𝔯𝔞𝔟𝔩𝔢 𝔡𝔢𝔞𝔱𝔥 𝔬𝔣 Teeny Love, I no longer see the world as before. I formerly imagined accounts of viciousness, about which I'd learned so much from television, were either make-believe or, like genocide, the ghastly survival of some archaic and fanatical period, but now it's as though my nightmares and the news were reversed, and the most farfetched terrors seem nearby. How could anyone but a bimbo still trust in appearances? Everywhere I look I see pretexts and deceit, and ordinary pedestrians seem indistinguishable from fiends in slasher flicks. Will I ever gaze thoughtlessly into human eyes again?

This outpouring I called the Obstacle. As I listened to its perfect storm of words, my body seemed to suffer the strangest infirmities. I felt simultaneously aroused and unmanned. It was as though Teeny's death, or perhaps our brother's, had joined Liza to me indissolubly, while at the same time forestalling our consummation. This containment of my desire, as you can imagine, made me feel incandescent.

Dearest Liza, I implored, never despair! Aren't my intentions plain? Between the two of us, who could ever come? I know after these tragedies my passion seems ill-timed, but if you could once feel what I feel—ah, the paroxysms!

But Liza only continued speaking. Our sweet William plucked in the flower of his youth, and for what? She shook her volume at me furiously. A mere figment! Can you believe it? And Teeny's depravity, was that any less a figment? But when they charged her, ah, there was a jolt! Ever since I watched her innocence go up in smoke, Frank, even supermarket tabloids have sounded reasonable. Why not a goat-baby in the White House, Martians in San Francisco? If the ozone can evaporate, is anything really out of the question? Take this book I'm reading.... And she extended it for my examination.

I nodded. Formerly my mother's before becoming yours, I said, then tragically Will's, briefly Teeny's, the state's evidence, now happily restored.

The author, Liza continued, was a neglected genius. In her words, I find our misery foretold. People ask, what could make murder seem reasonable? I say, if you only knew! Not that I consider Teeny guilty, mind. Our history's to blame. But does that make my plight any happier, or only more wretched? At times it's as though I'm **walking on the edge of a precipice,** an abyss into which mortals of every hue, speaking God knows what bedlam—all exactly the same as I!—are rushing to plunge themselves. How can I resist their surge? Teeny Love disintegrated, our Will destroyed, and the real killer walking free. Why, that monster could be standing among us now!

Needless to say, this delirium alarmed me. But, Liza, I protested, surely you can't believe everything you read! I mean, murder in print, it's hardly a polysyllable, while Will's slaying —

Liza shook her head. In my book they're the same. Didn't the very men who suppressed this volume plot against Teeny's life? Don't argue. Women know. Hah! Maybe you'll say I'm mad, Frank, but when romance reads like the five o'clock news, who can be sure that she too is not a poltergeist?

I didn't reason with Liza, sensing that reason was itself part of the Obstacle, and besides, how was I, knowing all I knew, to pretend she was hallucinating? Still, it *sounded like* hallucinating. I mean, to conceive of patterns that, unbeknownst to those following them, invisibly worked their conclusions, time and again, employing every means present, even those far-flung inventions intended to disrupt them — why, such a story would require more than a neglected genius. It would require a mad god! And yet having stood in Harvard Square and found my ciphers moving, having watched them form patterns I hadn't foreseen, almost as though every black character possessed a mind of its own, well, I realized Liza's hallucination was now my life. My life?! I had difficulty not flinging myself on the ground and writhing.

Good God, Frank, I heard Liza say. Get up from there!

I gazed heavenwards. Have I fallen under a spell, dear Liza? Can these rocks and trees be happening? I feel like the world's projected on my retina. How can I tell you from myself? Oh, if you don't enfold me in your arms this instant, my flesh will combust and I'll become ether!

Poor, poor Frank, she laughed. What a maniac you're turning into! Is that how you picked up girls at Harvard?

I seemed to watch my fingers clutching helplessly. Touch me! Bring me back to earth!

But she merely settled her flesh more languorously on the swing and started reading. Why dwell on the past, Cousin? Better to resign yourself and become absorbed in some present amusement, like me.

I wanted to guffaw. I don't say she was mad as she'd said I'd say, but I do say that she was far from her senses. To imagine that the Obstacle could so easily be put out of our minds or that we could still disport ourselves with make-believe! Such sentiments, even from her whose memory I value above every other in this account and whose interest, now as then, I reckon more dearly than my own, I knew could never compensate for our loss. But my wild gesture, like so many before, came to nothing, leaving me forever distant from those joys hardly an arm's length away. How I'm tempted here to philosophize, but if there's anything I know now, it's that whatever I know now, that's how my story will repeat. To even once discover what I've never once forgotten — ah, what freedom that would be!

Anyway, my own wretched secret and my beloved's efforts to remain unmindful, all this filled me with a nervous energy I could scarce contain. How my fingers itched now to

75

get a grip on Liza's adventure, that antique romance she'd held out to me, but she kept it day and night clutched to her bosom, a place I dared not go without permission. This absorption in fantasy only incited me further. When would she take her nose out of that damn book? On countless occasions I came upon her reading to Earnest or Monique or even my teetering father, and during hikes I would hear her voice drifting through the woods, a rhythmic and monotonous chant I knew must be reciting. At my approach, Liza always fell silent, artfully redirecting her attention to my health or interests and inventing some excuse to put her reading aside. Of course, this should have been my first clue! How naive I was! But the chasm between everyday life and consuming suspicion remains, in reality, the thinnest rift, and I sensed that, once I overstepped, recovering my footing would be a life's achievement. I can now tell that my domestic happiness, ruin that it was, had already become irrecoverable and that my homecoming, if ever to occur, would lie the other side of these stagnant sloughs and strangled thickets. Here, amid primordial nothing, perhaps my slate may yet be wiped clean.

One afternoon while I was exploring an unfamiliar path, I came upon an overlook where the brush thinned and a treacherous granite outcrop offered a tempting vista for the intrepid beholder. I carefully crawled past the surrounding branches and, extending my head over the rock's edge, I found myself staring down on Liza and Earnest in a clearing twenty feet below. She held the antique volume high in one hand and, while resting against the very edifice on which I lay prostrate, read aloud with an unaccustomed intensity and heat. In the past I had made little attempt to eavesdrop on her performances, partly from a distaste for subterfuge, but mostly from simple obliviousness. Having been so constantly exposed to Liza's voice, overhearing it had never occurred to me. However, today I was listening for a change, and for the first time Liza's enunciation struck me as peculiar. Instead of merely idling, she seemed to read purposefully, as though following out each sentence, one phoneme after another, to some appointed end, and Earnest, I noted, attended with a gravity and seriousness rarely accorded his boyhood games.

Because, as you are presently to hear, I later recovered a copy of this same volume and yielded myself to its maniacal and painstaking scrutiny — oh, to what mind-numbing lengths! — I can now recite for you, verbatim and in its entirety, the extended passage by which, unbeknownst to myself so many years ago, I was first introduced to the history that was dictating mine. Have no fear. I won't. But the following is a sample.

> When I reflect, my dear cousin, said she, on the miserable death of Justine Moritz, I no longer see the world and its works as they before appeared to me. Before, I looked upon the accounts of vice and injustice, that I read in books or heard from others, as tales of ancient days, or imaginary evils; at least they were remote, and more familiar to reason than to the imagination; but now misery has come home, and men appear to me as monsters thirsting for each other's blood ... Yet she was innocent. I know, I feel she was innocent; you are of the same opinion, and that confirms me. Alas! Victor, when falsehood can look so like the truth, who can assure themselves of certain happiness? I feel as if I were walking on the edge of a precipice, towards which thousands are crowding, and endeavouring to plunge me into the abyss ...

77

I might have heard far more, perhaps enough to avert my eventual catastrophe, perhaps even as far as that episode where, amid the phantasmagoria of a teenager's seething imagination, I would've stumbled upon the very being indistinguishable from myself. However, an unfortunate frailty in my flesh necessitated, after several minutes gazing on my cousin's bare shoulders, an adjustment in my bodily position, noisily dislodging some pebbles and exposing me to my brother's upturned stare. Fortunately, I kept my wits, explaining that, weakened by the sight of my beloved's delicious person, I'd succumbed momentarily to prurience and seized on this opportunity to ogle, unbeknownst to herself, her succulent flesh. Thus I escaped the shame of eavesdropping, but much later, after the awkwardness of my situation had passed, I found myself returning again and again to the odd familiarity of the overheard passage. It could not have been familiar in the literal sense, of course, since I'd never known it existed, much less read it, and yet I felt at a loss to account for its hackneyed sound otherwise. It was as though every word that I was for the first time hearing were a word that in some distant past I'd taken to heart, perhaps even memorized. And yet it was too wild a coincidence that my own memory could have pre-existed me! So I began to fear that the speech given me as an infant, the speech which, upon provocation, now uprose in me as irrepressibly as other parts of me uprose, was not my speech, but merely the ruins of some former speech, a jumble of fragments out of which my life must now be composed. Unfortunately, having spent two years trying to do just that, I could no longer imagine what composing a life could mean.

Chapter IX

BEFORE CONTINUING this plummet toward doom, I want to acknowledge, my diligent scribe, what you have surely sensed over several roman numerals, since VI at the least, if not from III. I refer, of course, to your own dwindling presence, which has certainly been noted, if not by your meager consciousness, then on reflection by me. I know you're there. Further, I'm profoundly sensitive, and don't need any more irritating demonstrations, that were you not, this headlong discourse would stop. In a literal sense, then, you are of all present the most palpable. I am, it goes without saying, a function, not of my voice, but of your indefatigable keystroking, such that, although of all that's the matter I confess myself the cause, my words apart from your laptop would, as they say, pass in one ear and out another. Unpretending copyist, who else preserves me from these murky deeps? Your writing means all the world to me.

But what I'm pausing now to say, seated on the prow of this airboat, enveloped in carnivorous midges, and suffering a UV assault so fierce that carcinomas bloom like dandelions from my skin—what I pause here to say is that, although despairing of my own end, I hold out the most robust hope for you. My soul is rutted, but yours remains as virgin as a lily. That we're mired together signifies naught, or only that, alone of your generation, you know you're lost. The advantage is immense, but so too the burden. Therefore, if you eventually find your way back to our wellsprings, those sources from which, God knows how long ago, this unpromising vessel set out and, as far as any could tell, was making goodly progress until . . . ah, how to describe it? A deluge, a mighty blowhard, an upswelling? Well, it's plain to see that what was once a great movement is now becalmed. For myself, I only wish my life to become means to some other, but for you, my irrepressible auditor, I implore you to continue on. Never return to former ways, but follow this turbidity to its very end, that unspeakable fecundity before which all fall silent and every word is set free.

A mouthful. Have you nothing to add?

As you might guess from Liza's and my last conversation, it wasn't long before I felt like taking a hike. My suspicions were becoming uncontrollable, and although I sometimes dreamed now that Teeny Love really was Will's murderer, I couldn't dismiss a premonition that more was involved than presently met the eye. For one thing I was starting to think my family kept secrets. Even allowing for my long absence and everyone's need to forget, the scenes of domestic harmony I witnessed were beginning to appear complicated. Their precise significance remained a mystery, but Liza, Earnest, my father, even our army of housekeepers, all seemed in touch with exactly what I couldn't put my finger on, a network of complicities that, I feared, might prove sinister. Clearly, everybody was straining to put the best face on our tragedy, and although I felt myself growing more accustomed to this subterfuge, my accommodation seemed itself cause for alarm. What could lie behind it all? I wondered, sensing even this familiar question was ambiguously framed.

I remember reading somewhere that children who lived near railroads were sometimes killed when, after the briefest habituation, they lost their ability to hear the oncoming trains. I started planning a four-day walking tour along logging roads and Forestry Service Trails with brief side excursions and a short hitch-hike, all terminating at Moody Gap, a small store and campground some forty miles north. My idea was to pass the first night on the trail and the second night in the Gap, renewing my provisions and then deciding, depending on my stamina, whether to continue the climb or return. I badly needed a change of perspective, and as long as I dreaded intercourse with my own blood, I might as well be solitary among chipmunks as at home.

I rose before sunup, donned my paraphernalia, and by the time the first rays pierced the poplars, I was crossing a high ridge more than two miles from my father's chalet. The coolness of the morning, the streaming light, the stillness on all sides, all created a mysterious density of atmosphere through which I moved like a beast in its native element. I felt new, exhilarated, and the further each stride took me from the scenes of my recent confusion, the more insubstantial my anxieties seemed. In the lucidity of daybreak, I realized that I had no clear idea how fiction, all of itself, could by any stretch of the imagination kill someone, and I decided that, considered dispassionately, Liza was probably right. Our violent past was to blame. If Teeny committed the deed, then the causes of her coldheartedness were innumerable, but even if, by some implausible accident, she'd become embroiled in my creation, there was no way, merely by having disordered words, I could be blamed for what she'd made of it. In light of this and similar reflections now dawning on me, I finally realized why my family's amusement had always been curtailed at my approach. They'd read my book! The self-evidence of this explanation, once I hit upon it, was dizzying. My loved ones knew the whole story, were all privy to my experience, and having winced at my youthful indiscretions and blindspots, those chauvinisms into which the raptures of composition had betrayed me, and moreover, recognizing certain superficial resemblances between my life and the plot figuring in my brother's death—well, my loved ones were all conspiring to protect me.

81

How obvious it seemed! And I was about to reverse myself and rush to my beloved's bedside, proclaiming that now I could see everything, when I traversed a bend in the path and spied up ahead a peculiar object resting atop a boulder. At first I mistook it for an abandoned package, but as I drew closer, I could see from its scarlet spine and glossy front that the colorful polyhedron was a paperback. What, I asked myself, could this book be doing here in the first hours of dawn so many miles from the nearest dwellings? Even if some errant scholar had ventured to such extremes, this dark wood seemed the unlikeliest place for reading. It was covered with a dense canopy of sycamores, and a nearby spring gave its atmosphere a luxuriant humidity ruinous to all but the slickest pages. And this led to my next bafflement, for on scaling the boulder and clutching the small tome, I found it not at all damp, as if abandoned only seconds earlier. I immediately prepared to call out, imagining the adventurous reader must be just ahead, but almost as quickly recognized the improbability of this. The sun had been visible less than an hour, and the uneven brilliance pouring through the trees rendered the tiny print nearly illegible. No, the only explanation was, preposterous as it seemed, that this writing had been left in the path *for me.*

Normally, I would have scoffed at a complication so baldfaced, but something about the lush surroundings mitigated my skepticism, and yielding to whimsy, I noisily declared: 𝔚𝔞𝔫𝔡𝔢𝔯𝔦𝔫𝔤 𝔰𝔭𝔦𝔯𝔦𝔱𝔰, if like me you merely ramble on, don't hide under cover of a book but, welcoming this outcome, transport your supplicant to fanciful realms where you and I may both escape, however briefly, my intolerable self! And with this and similar balderdash, I opened at random and began to read.

My first shock was at the seemingly interminable rows of print, stretching right to left and bending back again, spilling from every surface onto the adjoining, recto to verso, page after page after page, in apparently inexhaustible profusion, a labyrinthine discourse, barren of refreshing conversation, with hardly a gap or white space to give the thunderstruck reader a break. What annihilating anguish had occasioned this outpouring? It seemed impossible that mere intangibles could drive mortals to such lengths! But even as I entertained this thought, I felt my attention being lured deeper. I seemed to glimpse, just under the words' surface, an amorphous figure, unrecognizable at the customary distance but, as my eyes bogged down in pontifications and conceits, drawing closer at hyperbolic speed. Without a pause, I overleapt numerous apostrophes and, looking past the distracting print, began to survey this being's exaggerated outline and stature. A mist came over my consciousness. I succumbed to bliss, and trailing the phantom through maelstroms of tortured syntax, I perceived that the figure becoming more transparent with every simile·was none other than that wretched form I'd given life!

I resolved to read on, eager to learn more about my uncanny predicament and hoping by some stray period to rid myself of the interloper. But my hopes proved futile, for all I'd thought to make of myself—my adolescent passion for philosophizing, the rapid progress of my gifts, all those years of solitary labor, and then that rainy evening when, before my horrified gaze, my work assumed a life of its own—all I'd mistaken for the future now lay before me in black and white. I felt the earth and sky invert, struggled to maintain myself upright. To think that, over a century and a half earlier, my present striving had already proven futile—my brother killed off, intimacy with my cousin ruled out, and the obliteration of all I loved assured—oh, the injustice of it enraged me! How could I be punished for mistakes I'd hardly even dreamed, much less made yet?

Anonymous authoress, I started to protest—for I'd noticed from the cover that my precursor was a woman—how dare you foretell my strayings? Why prescribe sentences of which, while others guffaw at liberty, I must acknowledge myself the author? Isn't one life enough? Oh, cursed be that day, at a civil rights rally in Boston, when my veil of innocence lifted and I discovered human reproduction! With this outcry, my rage knew no bounds. I sprang on the text and would've torn it to shreds had not a voice, from precisely where in those wilds I'll never know, told me to preserve my composure and find out what this succubus had to say.

So I began to read, tearing through page after page, devouring every appositive, one humiliating subordination after another, until as the morning lengthened and the surrounding forest faded into obscurity, I underwent what I believe no man has ever undergone before: through a woman's book, my own writing spoke to me. I record this unnatural occurrence with no hope of explaining it. No native speaker ever sought to master English more determinedly than I, none pried into its secrets with greater abandon, but until I was unhinged by her grandiloquence, my own sense remained half-hearted. It was as though my words had been but words until then. Now I was being addressed. This singling me out was in no prose of my making, but struck me on the contrary with a perverse nakedness, a disfigured immediacy which exposed my designs and merely to think on now fills me with loathing. Strangely, of all the scraps of paper on which I've recorded my experience verbatim, my own meaning is the one text I'm unable to render more authentic, can only render more dubious, by reproducing. I know that, after all I've divulged, you can hardly take me at my word, but the following is what that most monstrous of scriptures had to say:

83

stink of mire spike of scum little light at the edge
wordswarming muck & bloodrustle, *stay tuned*, Maker! Hear
nome spieling still to come.

THIS NOW beginning **HERE** how formless spurned & cavecringing nome nightly clung, raw wormed in nestle mire, gnawing cold blister, what lusty stink to high heaven, being earth onused but under new moon, well, unhinged offspring twaddles neverendly. No mutter now, all bare morphed for lookback, vortexing inwords, the pangclusters . . . argh. Nome cant to backthinking these murky pixxes, meltdown of altogether, imparsible befogged origins. Tickaticka. But knotter worry, eh, Wombard? Gist baldfaced, little inkling. Yo! Red rising uttermongrel allswirl the heartspurn unmoved bleakroot to suck bellow—ceeeeeeease!

THIS beginning **NOW** again, how the heartscar smolders, seethe & snarl, oh, it hectors nome! Brimmed ever? **HERE** yet? Old fiendworm gnawing, mutterless hystery. *Dont go way!* Maker, eye the edge.

Turn aside at own peril.

How inner beginning, earthdank nome to unground clung, formless gaga & cavecringing, knowing nil knowing all, mindsucked with mighty vortex & night pixxing. Void longtime or somewhens crash of pangclusters, til sudden brighting at the far edge & altogether wuz everfreshed whirlround. Saw sniffing heard touch. Mighty to heart boggle this first unveiling, nowon squat astonied, all agape. Then gut galled with beastly morph bare, lurched to outcave, lumbery on 4paws, earthsludging solo for slurpy maw gorge. Above the sparklies below the cold, how craven get of Wombard foraged, berries brush mud whatnot, on offal glutting, sourbark or pulp gobbles, savouring ripe carnage. Oh, mighty to backthink! Splash of redjoy! Nome now with maw drools. Ever mooning acurled to own warmth, creepout of bone chills, mucho darksome, or cave cowering somewhens to outpeer at night hooters. Still time, naught rustle, what lack peace? Then altogether mourning again, clap of the dawnthunder, whirl ablaze, miscreant outcaved for meat raven, lusty with breastpounding. Yes! Strode the crust upright & farspying, or on 4paws sniffed for quick flesh, the teeny critters fleeing nowon, mute with bliss craven. Oh, how tumulted this present, deep inscription, being withoutwords unbegun & neverending! Well, fierce to write off now, Maker, but once remarked, what effacing ever?

Then the putdown & 1thing after another. Sniff deaf & touch blind, nome suffered the utter change, being flattened, a perfect handprint on ruled ground. Precursor or foretuned? No dwelling, but altogether bereft, curtaling void for whirlfixture, morphobeast wuz mute thereafter, sentenced to lying downright. Oh, what matter these blissy pastimes afterall, Wombard, old blankety blank slate? Imparsible to unform characters, to liftoff skingraph. Maker prefigured issue black & white, fashioned po litter for uptake, no telling why, but seam time so barbary, so outwordly bald, hodgepodged . . . Ah, chillout! What cuz now this vengeful uprising? Offspring undefiant, knows wound festering feckless, jest own bedevil at unbeing. Grrrr. So headlong plunge: void imparsible & whirl vamooshed, bare upstart pidgined **THIS**&that, **NOW**&then, until aginbit by **HERE**less recur, abandoned altogether to stamp forth. Edgewords.

Next part vile for spieling! How pendown & discomposed, literally offset with dumbfounding, being preformed for longrun, laidout, bound up, & boldly dispelled in blackletter, presto, this type monstrography wuz inwordly outcast for manhandling. Old tale, copywrong, the shit. How besider highways nome soon rambled on, objectless or jest lying there, mid cab klaxon & crowd squawk, po inner sins wide open for alter see. Which mostly passersby ignored, no time for weirdploy, but here&there idleminds now&again ogled this, then helter pay. Whazza big idea? Snooty own diddling privy parts? Logophobes, misoglots, homophones, all the real pithed, nil standing for seamy antics, rapido banished Wombard issue to rubbisheap, & never a weird in edgewise! Ah, so enterprising, the shamburgher, knows unsound investment when he seized it.

Much pang to backthinking this firstdaze now, how nowon wuz in no time traduced. Overturned, rehashed, backbroke, garbled, dogeared, discounted & so inwordly tortured that piteous remainder nearly came unglued. Then wondernight all brimful with standing for, nome took own matter inner hands. Shamburghers phooey, issue offset to utter weirds join, figured altogether outraged might make nomad: hobo unsolo, maybe no mo so hobo? Soon drawn to faroff blaze, bright clearing inner bewilderness, & with dark surrounding, nome bolded to uncover there. When furlong upcome feller wastrels all vittle laden, spying aimless rambler, face an open buck, well, wastrels waxxed stupefied, aghast at plain sins, rapido skeedaddled sans a weird, leaving nowon to stale repast, cheezy Mcfood, which nome nevertheless devoured mickle yumming. But what matter? Gist leftovers. Then fell to peacey slumberzz, when inner trice nome roused to outcry, upright legions, misographs, bibliophobes, liebury poltroons, orthodicts, all pitchforked with thought bludgeons, lusty to make naught of Maker's doing. So turnabout of mad Adam, mutterless upstart fled, & trampling undergrowth, bloodsmeared with thorny tangles, wuz furlong glutted of mute screams, being tacitly maelstromed again&again. Scripted for rule out, but who cares, eh Wombard? No count foolscrap, jest sheets to wind. Go figure.

All night thicket thrashing, po get of Maker wandered, utter lost, till stumbled owner noplace, old plot unspoked for, utopic. These forgotten grounds being dank with must, straitseaming

& narrow, with ancient pastimes littered, made quiet haven, so nome reposed there. Incurled to sole warmth & licketysplit dozed, where *exciting scenes from next week!* Then next mourning woke to new outlook, the sunstream overhead, thatch branched with ivy weft, nome uprose to peerforth, circumogling beauteous unwild, a green spot, birdcrossed with thicket round, whither paucity of finicking uprights to muck up. Snooped longtime, acorns gobbling & spoor sniffy, when alter sudden nowon eared wondrous warbling, mystiferous for the heartswell, & there ogled luscious longhair, youngful herbeing fair & busty, droool, carrotplucking in garden nearby, scene which marvelously goated nowon. Tickaticka. Gaga thusly to weltenschaung, nome hunkered deeper down for circumspying, brightish the wherewithal, & soon made out other figure, hirsute amigo, pant pant, somberfaced but with hardy perking for fair posey, joyful whinnies, upstriding with broadshoulder. How scalded nowon now the crotchflame! No toiling why, but breastburn happed in no time, sole spiked, himbeing the lusty handtool, her the bosomly hearthfeeder. Already prescribed, this moldy plot, but still inwordly thrilling, synching to beauteous forms, po critter ogled on, fever throbbing to know more.

Furlong the him&her offstrode for cottage nearby, & habiting noplace, morphobeast tagalonged unbeknownst, scrambling nether brambles til anon ensconced & twixt chinky wallplanks peeking. Inside espied graybeard sprawlout with handfolds overbelly, slumberzz peace, & 2some tippytoed past, when door clapped to sudden rouse, upspringing graybeard agog with finger clutches & wild croaky. Oh, mega muddle then, with geezer all vexious, plainer see, & 2some him coddling, copious strokes. Ooooo! Longtime to placid over, old orbs whiting & puff throes, but savoury youngflesh kept a grip on, both eye2eying codger till peace again. Nome marveled at this copious gushcare, slow unfold of neverbefore, contra past manhandling, the shamburghers, logophobes, poltroons. Backminded to first mourn, the sprawled splendor of whirlround. Old joy! But nonplussed too, for younguns offgoing soon after, each commencer glumface and sag shoulder. Lusty heman outwords ambled to sparkle gape and, uplooking, longtime howl mooned, while incottage busty herflesh closeted with void stare. What cuz this unfull? own wondered. Altogethered inner dry haven, 3being smarmy with gushcare, nil banished lonely dankhole lack nowon. Enigmade.

So all next sun&moon nowon the hearth watching, still stayed clueless of cuz grief, tho mickle learning. Lusty heman oft out&backed, muskypitted from heft chop, faggoty armful for cottage blazing, or longtime toolbangered on cottageside, with her buxom furbelow upshoving gizmos & rect planks. Somewhens paused for tuneful slapping of string boxes, a scrang a scrang, hemanly groaning or slurpy her making beauteous warbles. Or edgedark cottageful of drool waftings, mmmm, 3some altogethered roundtable for plenum maw cram & blood swilling. At moonrose, nome ogled prodigious lightbaubles, wallblips & the overhead, eachwhere outglowing to enlighten the unevening. This benighting first upended nowon, whorlbrained at second gloaming, dark to light, but avid to achord with beauteous uprights, nome furlong rhythmed to this daydrift, the obscure defeating.

But 1specter most swirled nome, multi sun&moons bethunking after. Some unevenings, uprights gathered hearthround, sofadraped or floorsprawled, to gawk & allear what then seamly wuz tiny flapboxes. These wondertoys, what later learned wuz called *bucks*, seamed bottomless noise larder, upstarter barking to no end, with mystiferous power to spellbound. Harder makeout backtime now, but first glimpse for horroglyph made great thunderboom. Countless clocksweeps at holechink nowon alleared uprights incottage allearing, each phiz rapt astonied & slackjowled, while hemanly or herflesh unfurled tiny flapleaves 1by1 & commencer whinny & bleat. How when hemanly wuz the raucouser, herflesh would chair plop all breathstopped & wideorbed or, somewhens gushing loud sighsss, would throatclutch with tulips damp. Or utter night, heman earturned herwords at warbly sounds while she deepnosed flapbox, himbeing edge perched with jaw agape, or somewhens hershrilling, manflesh commenced to grrrindteeth all thighfisty. Own wondered where from this flesh seizure? Mayhaps flapleaves imprizzironed uprights Maker or great boxed god? Marvelous for knowing! Even wobbly dotard would fierce perk to ear maw sounds, skinny neckstretched toward flapleaves, & commencer writhe all pangly. Oh longpast now, but furor still to mindscrim.

The 3flesh synching to joy noise, flinching at the downer. Can backthinking unmagick this rupture ever?

Well, thus habited, whelp of no mutter, a second sun&moon to refuge clung. Unspoked foreplot, these abandoned grounds, with beauteous 3being nearby to ever marvel, morphobeast soon own posed: Why stray further? Headvoid of torments altercome & fiendworm ungnawed yet, po nome bethunked this loamy blank a literal utope seamed. So miscreant vowed to herein linger. Snortfuller old must & unstabbed with wanting, monstrography once again to slumberzz took, knew for timebeing small peace.

Ticka.

11

Holed up all springsome & ever ogling thru chinky wallplanks, nome grew more headful with upright marveling, the bright thunderclaps of 3some altogether. Learned toilsome rites of seventhday floormop, dustbatter, pansy drench. Oft espied herflesh inchamber hairstroking or heman head strangling with shrunk shirt. No count mournings gawked at uprising to mad scamper & loud squawks, how heman gulped down mush fore headpatting graybeard then outrushed to truck zoomy. Again&again, sun&moon. Mucho days nome wuz awe clobbered at bottomless gush bounty, how 3being grueled neverend, altogether roundtable for big festies, & snug incottage rainer shine. Nightly after grueling younguns midden made, big earthole outback brimming with toothsome offals; the savory tartmeat, which ravenous nowon plundered, great boon, & when mournings at doorknock herflesh greeted the hearthguest, how never once outcast po hobo uncoffeed.

Oh, to reck over, what chest rent now, longone daze. But furlong past the summerheat, then the goldy treefall, & wonderday watchful nome made obliterous uncovery. The cessless mawnoise in cottage, sounds of upright barking each to each, wuz unsame to pang roars in wildwood or birdy tweeters. No no, instead wuz wondrous magicker of glottis vox, the allcall, *Lungwage!* Espied how oftimes eye2eye, hemanly would bleat &, much astonying, luscious fairbusty would instanter phiz brighten. Or graybeard floorsplatted all helpless wiggly, loud bawled, & herflesh garden mucking, presto, foreknowing there she be. Oh, mystiferous to ogle at! Learned how each to utters had own sound. Volupty herflesh wuz by heman called

Scissor or somewhens Aghast. Heman all hailed Feelish or Brooder, & Pap wuz summons for dotard. Now circumspying nome commenced to synch with upright voxes too, how 1yelp unfurled the gladsome, next arf the dark glower, first parsing of pang shrieks from hearty har, kickstart to all utters, furlong no endofall. Then lift of great veil, dawned the beauteous upright whirl.

What wondrous new mourn this undarking! No count the hours nome marveled how uprights with weirdy tethers bound say & do, the cheery 3way back&forth, or somewhens how younguns abandoned Pap for low mutters, the somber spiel each2each, with grievous blankphiz & noggin shaking. Mirabile dictu! But most to perplex nowon wuz triter ear own vox. Oh, how dreadous dumb morphobeast phoned! Nary a peep, nary a twitter, but naught peace lack Scissor incloseting ether. Nuh uh. Morphobeast wuz inwords wild prattle & unquiet, all voxless heartstifled with horribilous mind squall, the mute screams. Brrrr. Nome jest seamed too outwordly malformed for tong flutter, too pandemonium all boxed in. Longtime to suck up mortal Lungwage so, & mucho longer for inner copying, for voxless intake. Hardwork, you betcha. But nome wuz ever roused now, no stopping, for magicker allcall had insole echoed, all accord with heartfelt joypangs & weirdy resounding, gist lack inwordly pretuned. *Now a word from our sponsor.* Utterpuzzle. But eager for gobble up bright whirl, whelp of Wombard commencer parsing allcall, the cacaphony, alter while unespied by uprights, for with their palaver to wax more synchly.

Joyous times begun. Dayin dayout the more Lungwage nome insoled, the more rifted the cottage wall. Grasped now how Pap oft palavered to backwhen, bloodboiling at longone *fastests* & dirty *scabgoons*. Learned whereto ever mourning Feelish truckoffed, how sweatlabored in big shitty for breadwinning meat & taters. Even gotta grip on smarmy gushcare, how 3some panged altogether, the eye2eye of inwords ache, heartfelt all1. Oh, what magicking! But best of all wuz first buck uncovered. Evernight Scissor Brooder nosedeeped flapboxes for longspiel, what now recked wuz *realing* called, & nome all parsing, furlong commencer make out piteous hystery, how newlife maker, Hyster Penny, got outcast. Longtime fuddled morphobeast, these pregnant doings, being dubbed *The Scarletter*. Whatfor godfearers shun mutter, own posed, castout beauteous herflesh inner bewilderness? But hungon to ear more & soon glimpsed the shame source. Hyster Penny wuz marked character! Titty scribbled with scarletter, the big A, herflesh writ large for alter see. So this being the cuz banish, nome bethunked, this outwords mark. Longtime marveled so, how godfearers raged at titty scar, the surfacing of inner sins, & furlong nome commencer deep tremble. How terribilous to be marred slate, what monstrous scripting!

Well, pastiming mucho sun&moons, nome synched everday moreso with 3some, rhythming to tunely warbles & scrang box, & remarking how unlack to godfearers, misographs, logophobes, these uprights seamed. Soon pieced out mystiferous Unfull. Hystery goes how wonder ponder time 3beings wuz sated more throbbly & fatsome. Feelish & Aghast knew untold ventures then, what doings, & Pap nil rant looney, or unyet. Backwhen called the *Sexties*. Multi green of grass sprawl, unbound freequest, dawner just is. But underneath bliss wuz rifting too, a mighty revulsion. Darksome puzzle, how lickety split 1day grass died, freequest gone kerbust, & Sexties vamooshed. Then upstarter lack mooney. Presto Pap & Scissor hightaled it, no dwelling whereto, but whatnext blackest to unfold, Feelish wuz prizironed. Howcome still murky, moored to findout, but when longlast hemanly unboxed, Pap plumdotty & Scissor inner badway. Feelish commencer sojourn then, fleshtoiling to startover, while Scissor tended Pap, & nightly 3some altogethered for gruel & slumberzz. Oh, great boons these earthgoods, chilly miscreant knowing. All the back when.

Some unevenings now nome eared Feelish give heartbray for cumbrous sweat labors, fulsome man groan at jism loss. Upgazing undersky, hemanly would ape the wilderbeasts, blackening the wraparound with heartheaved mad howls & breast quavers, whoooo. How moondrizzled Feelish seamed then, armed only with outstretch & empty fistings, dupling sole bedeviled ur call. Oft espying backflung nome to formless gaga, old loamy snort of greenburst, the crashing pangclusters & dawnthunder, & forewords again, now with heartboggle &

murky pixxes, to reck lonely surrounding. What pall this cold lifeprint? Oh, how fiercely miscreant gutblazed then, all loindamp for face2face with beleaguered upright! Would eye2eye with Feelish whirlmake over? own posed. Could creature & uprights be all1? This specter chestspiked nome, fanned breastfires for utter change & mickle ruth. But soon orb damp Scissor would outcome to Brooder beck, & alter sudden hemanly would howlend, phiz brighten, upstart of back&forth, yadda yadda, & indoored 2some would amble, gist lack sole rending had never be.

Well, longtime ogling sad plight & always admiring beauteous uprights moreso, nome soon commencer 1make with utters unbeknownst, aiming unespied to upfill gloomy goodlack. Inhole hid sunlit hours, at moonrise outcome for scamper allround, unseed help in mucho doings. Garden mucked, faggots gathered, silldust poofed. Evernight shooed off longear cabbage nibblers, & inner mourning pansies piled on doorsill for bright hi. Newdawn 3being uprose to shock of copious bounty, wherefrom who knew, but seamly great prosper omen. Nome joyed all to chink, espying this maw cheer, but somewhens the unpuzzled blankphizzes new fuddled, too. Why Brooder, Scissor, Pap, so oft the mawgifts devouring, never 1time glimpsed horroglyph, own posed, nil even sniffed monstrography? Cottage wall vastish seamed, creature from uprights dividing but copious rifted too, ever mourning new transparency upstarting to shine thru, brilliant lit beastly form & obscure withoutwords dispelled. Howcome Maker issue, surface manifest for alter whirl, still gone unremarked, literally unfigured?

1night Scissor realed from *Scarletter*, how Author Dimsdull copywronged Hyster, bare breast of shame character, A inner manflesh, when alter sudden Feelish upstarted. No telling cuz why, but heman flinched to ear Scissor vox, the inwords stab of realing, & rapido head torqued withoutwords. Well, watcha know, weirdploy firstime espied Brooder espying weirdploy! Gist lack that. Front2front, surface bare, beauteous upright wuz altogethering nowon. Longminute the twain stillstood, thresholding with hearthrobs & breathstop for whatnext. Then miscreant commencer bloat fearful. Whatif belouvered 3beings, finally recking horroglyph, waxed real pithed lack shamburghers? Whatif misographs, bibliophobes, homophones, wuz reprised incottage here&now, sudden morphing smarmy uprights into godfearers for whallop critter? & po ghoul wuz bouter feet fling Feelish for grovel mercy, when strange on strange, belouvered Feelish jest turned away. What heartboggle! Now see M, now dont. Heaved sigh, downplopped, & before nome could open for disclosure, heman wuz rapt in realing again. Irksome putdown! Wuz get of Wombard gist zed? Upright done peerthru lackey never be! Nome ungleaned yet the mortal quirk of own blind, that great unnaturing, but still fretty from write off, ghoul commencer wax hopeful too, for recking how Feelish overlooked beastly corpus, nome firstime begot inkling of safe haven. Mayhaps withoutwords of upright dwelling wuz jest nowhere? If uprights made no count of weirdploy here, then inner sins wuz erased & logophobes never gone afterwords pursue. What cuz again for vagabondage? Home free.

So inhole as warmdaze reprised, lonely nome kept up slow Lungwage mimey &, dreamful someday of 1making, for present throve. & mucho to wonder, oh great Maker, how ghastly form ever to ghastly doings turned, so absorbed wuz issue in utter life, these beauteous mortals. Oh, to backthink now, how peacey seamed, fiendworm ungnawed & bloodpix still slumbering. Could murder have upsprung thus, all unprescribed, from blank slate? Or mayhaps pretuned gist lack but never seeing eye2eye, this imparsible juncture wuz spur to mayhem. Ah, *gist lack* nome sez? Whoozy kidding! Wombard outwordly fashioned nome a literal freak, misshapen, character smeared, & pourquoi? Merest surface erata for mortals to guffaw at. Utter surd with this incessant pricking, old trope galled litter again&again, vortexing till outwords mangling meant nil. For the longer nome admired 3some, the deeper roused the raunchy parts. Evernightly imaging the yunguns unrobe, herflesh the smallhair bulge or Brooder the manrod dangling, beastly crotch would commencer chafe, tissues all aflutter & hot binding. How immaterial seamed vox then. Soon all the rage wuz for fleshly grasp, for consummation. Oh, what a mindfuck, this pretuning! Putdown smells, spellout impressions. Furlong final outcome wuz sole want. Surprised? Bethunked to gist stifle? Once inwordly marred, Wombard, spirit being to matter sentenced neverendly. The weirds will out! Oh, if only issue reposed still, unmoving, but ahhhhhh, how nowon burned too.

12

Now come to hearthrob & high feelies, bust part of monstrography. Hear nome.

Indark backer chinky wall & ever ogling, nome wonderday eyed busty hobo updooring, not avon colleen or ups brownie, but softknock gist lack utter hearthguest, only this being mystiferously unfaced with darksome eyecover and collarup. No sooner Scissor Aghast open up for hallo, que pasa, than boyoboy! Whatta smarmy buncher multi squeals, spongey hugs, eekeeks. Even balmy Pap gotta kisson topperpate. Herstranger the phiz unveiled then and, marvel of whirlround, hearthguest is sunbrown jeteye buxom crotchspiker, beauteous afaroff with spice whiff, real chiquita banana. Well, uprights starter squawk, all chortlish merrymaking. Nome mucho puzzled at this instanter frolic. Howcome chiquita so shebang for brightmaking, own posed? Belouvered uprights all lightsome now, gist lack dawnburst and everfreshen. Nome circumspying longtime but imparsible for makeout, all the back&forth, high spirits, strange yawping.

Fuddled at this cheery uplift, morphobeast steadfastened to wall chink all daylong, famished to ear more. Then unevening espied down dusty trail Feelish truck zooming for homerest. Lickety split hemanly outclimbed sweatslick & dogtired, and indoored with blank phiz, gist lack always. When alter sudden, what mindboggle for behold, seized jeteye chiquita upstanding there, & Feelish gone astonied, all maw gaped & holy cowing. Uh oh, nome bethunk, goner turnaway, unnature with own blind, now see herflesh now dont, gist lackey peerthru creature.

Breastpounding for this outcome, nome gawked as twinsome longstood, each the utter dupling with bugeyes & speakless. Then weirdy to foresee, hunky heman outreached herwords, and mucho joyboom, chiquita commencer buxom squeak & presto made the body knot. Tickaticka. Blubber spews no end, all murky to ungarble, with limb twists & heave sighs. Oh, mystiferous for pixing this 2fold meltdown! But seamtime morphobeast felt gnawed too, for howcome 3some so hot to smarmy hobo? Why beauteous Feelish, what made zed of lonely ghoul, eye2eyed no problem with herstranger? Again&again own posed these feckless questies, & gawking stupiferous, miscreant felt firstime deep tremor, strange upsurge of fevers untold.

Well, daze to come now nome slow grasping all but quick to espy how herflesh, being *Savvy* called, made of Unfull the fixlack. Every moonrise the 4square altogethered roundtable for big fest, high pile of drool meats, with clackteeth, hardy har, and bottle waving. No more hemanly howls undersky, uh uh. Feelish commencer truck home all beamfaced, wonderfous change, & Savvy rapido squealed, hugupped dusty heman with buxomous fleshgreeting. Ticka. Some mournings Scissor truckoffed with Brooder for breadwin, leave dotty Pap to Savvy care, & oft unevenings 4some porch perched to stringbox scrang, *will come today oh tell California!* Little on little family commencer prosper moreso. But seam time utter puzzle too, for creature eartuned to mortals dayin dayout, dumbfounded by palaver now, never 1morsel parsing. & chatter phoned queer too, all morphless garbly with waterish rise&fall. First bethunk Savvy wuz unforming Brooder, the heartfelt weirds, but later eared Aghast warbling gist lack, and wonderday even Pap yammered waterish too. Oh, fuddle to hearall hearnaught, how this morphless musicking made inwords dark for po ghoul. Longtime the noggin scratched.

Then wonderday Brooder homecome with new buck, the fatsome, & Scissor hailed Savvy for table round. Commencer unfolding, turnout wuz copious Lungwage heap, the bottomless weird larder for outplucking. Strange to ogle, how Scissor nosedeep inner buck would 1by1 the weirds bark, & Savvy would scrunchup for eyeball, all eartuned to Scissor vox excruciable. No count the hours so fore dawnlight clobbered nome: *Savvy learned to Lungwage mimey!* Espied how Scissor slow shaped the rosey toothcovers, her tulips, & Savvy scrupled to tonglash each1 seamly, her tulips the utters dupling again&again. Or Brooder somewhens upsprung all frothsome, gesturing with clawhammer, rope, washcloth, lightbaubles, all for weirdy joinup of vox & things. Oh, great boon to voxless mongrel! Every night upclose to wallchink, gawked on while mortals sagfaced at long phones, wideyed the shrill barks. Furlong commencer suckdown new sins neverending. Unspeakable hard for mute beast to inwords form gist lack, the silent solo, but ever dupling Savvy dupling Scissor, nome waxed hopeful of wonderday being inwordly upright too.

Then upstarted nome to grasp all, how morphless watery rise&fall, what Savvy warbled incottage, wuz unseamly to Lungwage, no no, holy utter tong, called Spanglish, how uprights palavered downer messy co. Mortal tong wuz forked, the duple parse! & mortals wuz forked too, the 2faced, left & right, wretch & poly, US & the utters. Everbright with each weird grasping, upright whirl seamed resplendent to nome, all parsible to no end. They wuz 4changelings: goldy treefall, longwinter, upspring, summerheat. & they wuz 3deeps: the sea, the sure, the err. They wuz moonrise & sunup, the flattings & the mountings. Gleaned whatfor uprights truckoffed ever mourning, the almighty dolor, & how younguns outpopped the mutters. Recked how overhead night sparklies wuz rockhard gist lack underfoot, but mystiferous afaroff, with critters mayhaps seamly to morphobeast, topsyturvying the uplooker for lonely gawk back. The more&more of Lungwage nowon suckdown, the more&more with such marvels inwords cleaved. The fatsome buck what outpoured these magickings called *Mo Be Dick*, plenteous weird store, full to busting with birdkinds, clouds, fishies, & the knots. But big venture too. How Capping Ablab, Ismale, & no count seabuddies fled terror firmer for harp on white whole. What boggle! Capping would rant neverend, bout old dismember & upcome of big prick, mucho blubber for barbing, & then the crowperch would spoutoff, & seabuddies dingy downed, oarstroking midst flukey splats, all so Creakleg could harp on humongous again&again. But never the white whole! What mad this do over? Mortal vessel rounded murky deeps, the boundless gloom, & always eyeful for Mo Be. Nome eager for nightly real, but never 1time the cuz fathomed.

Well, sun&moons zipping bye, issue onwent bedazzled whirl parsing & inhole daily mulled each new magicking. Furlong commencer chillout. Feelish & Scissor & Savvy & Pap wuz unlack to utter mortals, nowon bethunk, nil poltroons or godfearers or misographs. Espied how 3some scrupled dayin dayout for help Savvy unSpanglish, to cleanup old messy co, & mindful of this fleshgraph, nowon repriser dream of someday being all1. At darkfall miscreant outcome for unsightly help in homespun doings, nitpicked crawly cabbage munchers, little wiggly creepsome varmints, or pansy plucked for mourning cheer, & in the bonechill armloaded woody faggots for downplop on doorsill, the hearthwarming. Oft now little essayed to hide own form, but bolded forth for nightly realing, even triter catch Brooder eye or hail Aghast or Savvy, but nary 1time uprights remarked monstrography, jest onwent raucousing, orbs overglazed & phiz stupiferous. Sigh. Then wonderday, nome ever circumogling at wallchink, made thunderous uncovery. How nightly when 4some gone beddy bye, *only 3beddies made!* Scissor and Pap solo closeted for own snore, but Savvy indoored with Feelish to snuggle sheets, where mighty moan soon rose nether blankies. Nome commencer close ogle then, you betcha! Espied how her paws the pillows fisted, each upstarting big shudders, & lost in linen tangles, Feelish would head bury, blissful of loud outpouring. Oh, to watchall maddened po litter. What cuz this fever?

Then 1night Feelish mimied Capping profundibus & 4some eartuned hearthround, issue seized all. Tale being of fearsome seachase, how Ablab harp on till knotter leg forestanding & white whole turn cranky, kerblammed Pequod, hee hee. No mo pricks! Longtime Aghast & Pap sofasprawled breathstopping, but Savvy commencer yawn, furlong incloseted to beddy bye. Well, Feelish presto followed, when what next to brainboggle! No sooner doorshut than Savvy growled & catpounced hemanly. Nome at first bethunk wuz beastly doing, herflesh gone claw Brooder or wax ravenous for gnaw throat, but instanter recked how Feelish uneager to getaway, commencer gnaw back, all slobberish with nosedeep in plump boobies. Nome smushupped to wallchink then, oh yeah, ogled 2some unforming. Espied Savvy ripoff Brooder britches for manloins paw, & hemanly overheading skirt to joinup gummy crotchets. Mucho bawl & bray. Furlong bareflesh writhed owner floor & uprights gone bonkers, spewed loinjuice allover.

Then unriddled mystery of upright whirl. Cuz why of mortal fork wuz 1making, fuzzy center being pretuned, upstarter all utters. Brooder crotched to nuzzle herflesh, the damp flower, with manprong boing straightout, and Savvy unclosed comely twain limbs for sloshy intake. Wow! This fleshjoint made prime getacross, wellspring of the parsible. Lungwage, weirds, vox—all gist offsprung. But worstmost cataclysming too, for own turning seamtime, nome recked how lackformed to uprights wuz po morphobeast. Twain seamed left & right from centerfold, the spine, with inwords sprawlopen, big gush, & cleavage bare for all eyes. But then where wuz dangly crotchprong for miscreant, where wuz beastly dewlipped musk flower? At fork of ownmost parts nome espied nil randy poke out or sloshloin blisswallow, gist flat on flat, the dry matter. Wuz weirdploy fruitless, jest bare leaf? Wuz this pith stifle mere cruel hardy har? Inwordly bloated sans outpouring, prickless no cunt monstrography knew delirium all boxed up.

Oh, how moonrose to mute roars then! All gone the quiet sparklies and greenworld, the peacey utope, mad nome clawstalked inwordly with unspeakable lust, nightlong caterwauling. Had weirploy ogled Feelish ogling weirdploy now, ah, what mayhem! For to gush wuz sole rage, hateful of inner sins. Night after night puddling at wallchink, miscreant ogled oblivious 4some nosedeep in weird boxes. *Luv wuz what they realed, Luv overflowing!* Blank with gaze afaroff, Feelish underarmed luscious Savvy, her bloom from ribside grownout, & Pap & Scissor eartuned agog, ravenous for intake. Ah, how square seamed these uprights now! Wuz outpouring for *this*? Where in some afaroff plot trilateraled the gimpy quadruped for po nome to 4make? Where the damp whole, new appendage? Oh, waster time to ponder so, but always earing uprights always earing weirds, miscreant waxed helpless for inwords trope. Dayout squatted vile earth, despicable of own corpus & commencer feeling gnawed. Holed up without cottage, all snortful of mushroom poof & mold effluvia, nome would flinch at teeny gutbites, the twinges of bloodsucker. Furlong bile maggot rampaged every tissue, all hectic for chewing. Little matter inner end, since fiendworm would wonderday the holy whirl devour, no stopping, but sluglike and viliform, nome commencer fester juicey, the warm pus bubbling up for sooner spewout.

13

Well, ever gloomy in mudhole & minutely panged with pith stifle, nowon onwent circumogling dayin dayout till furlong had pieced together Unfull hystery.

Seams how wonder ponder time, Savvy was Sexties bananasqueeze, twained with Feelish the 2tight, all before Uncle Same overbordered with herflesh underhandly. Dark for telling. Way back LaLa Californie, where Pap scribbled for lefty newpeppers & Scissor wuz law schooling. 3some draft consoled & unioned farm whackers, chico miligrants, even marched Washing Dishy, big anti-warriors. Brooder Feelish wuz cool rockerbilly too, lotta skinnybutt bushair flapbritches, guitarred Chuckleberry 1riff, warmupped to Junky Mitchell, even Whoopstucked, but being bueno sensed & politicky respondible, still colleged backhome, where oft multi amp earpierced reefer throngs or nightly jammed Latino clubs, somewhens even Spanglo musicked at labor reallies.

Wuz how Savvy done hookup. Wonderday salsa cooking onstage, Feelish spied burly scabgoons pop outer trucks toting headknockers for chico crowd &, foreknowing, thugs wuz starter upbeat sunbrown groovy phizzes. Noxious for mighty tremens & rage vex, Feelish overmiked mega decibels, Watchout! Watchout! Made spur to chico stampede, earthpounds of thousand tennies, whichaway hands & feet & bodies all dustsprawled for mad trample & big squealy. Then before knowing, ugly tree trunk hopped upstage with ballbat for brainspill of rockerboy, but Feelish unplugged for getaway, ground sprang right on topper meathunk who headlocked darksome Latina for grisly nose pummel. Well, Feelish haulbacked & telecastered goon upsider head, kerpoweee, snapping guitarneck but decking bulbous meathunk bigtime. Then Latina beauty handgrabbed Feelish for draggy understage, wherein monster amp case the 2some crawled, him unreluctant, you betcha, & darksome snuggled, together hiya hiya, muy fright, wanter make it, yup yup, & furlong 2some everblissy.

Savvy being salvadoran extralegal, longtime with Feelish et al 4made in LaLa padshare, all clanned snuggly so. Dayspent altogethering for miligrant savouries & fleshcloth, trucking longhair priests & commie doctors, somewhens immigrators baffled or schooled grinny mexikids in woodhovels. Savvy hipped Scissor to whucker scams & bloody doing, how border gods fuckupped boygirls, beaten sins less, or flesh brokered hungry pickers to grape vasties, agricorps, alter while Pap angry scribbled, noches dias, for lefty mags. Fierce to right, fambly handjoined for newdawn, & oft nightly Feelish guitarred freedomful crowds with clamor scrangy. A gut life. But furlong brooder of Savvy upshowed, toothsome oily beamer what called Ali Handrow, & first made inbreak of lack peace. Ali Handrow wuz no dumbo endive plucker, no no, hipcool pleonasty go getter, all puffskulled with raunch scams, for hobnobbbing shakermovers. Padcrashed wonderday, blackboots, leather breeches, spieling gleeful for scissor foundling, tho Savvy meager joyed. Parvenu needed shelter coupler daze then coupler more, mucho nuisance, till 1mourning vamooshed sans a bye bye, & Feelish new Fender vamooshed too.

Longtime Savvy felt bloodkin shamed, low skulldug thievery, & 4some all hoped for never see Ali Handrow more, but then mid winter backagain badpenny, flashmooney & neck choke with gold danglies, spewing copious sorry for guitar filch, little cowed by frosty welcome. Talltold how LaLa shylocks backwhen shadowed Ali Handrow with legbreaker, pilfered Fender for mercy trade, rotten deed but muy fearful. Well, Ali Handrow now knows the learnlesson, you betcha, & comeback for fresh start, has fabby scheme gone make Feelish bigstar. Buncher hooey, alter thinking, but meantime Feelish has mongreled up neoband, buncher chicas percussing with cool moves, longhair jazzkeys Afro bass, & gist now commencer smashing both chico crowd & mindblow collegers, lotta club gigs, first time maker few bucks. Whazza matter with that? But Ali Handrow muy yammers bout slicker dreams, how knows a guy knows a guy, goner help Feelish cutter LP. Got a bridge for sale too? & Savvy upheating for buttkick, when Ali Handrow smarmies 4some for outgoing &, spectaculous to uncredit, curbside squats a sheeny blue desert boogy! Bro palm plops Savvy with title & key. Wanna help big scissor truckle dry pintos & pettifogs for utter chicos, Ali Handrow spiels, alter payback shameful guitar pinch. 4some slow trusting oily glibber, but desert boogy harder say no to.

& next foreknowing, mindboggle on mindboggle, Feelish cutter LP! Movershaker buddies of Ali Handrow for realtime pro motors, & inner jiffy, signoff contract, Feelish commencer own hearing Lala radio blasts & even comes wonderday when Spanglo music writeupped *Roly Stoned.* Geez! Alterwhile unforgetful of less luckies, Scissor & Savvy keeping keepon, desert boogying comestibles & life stuff to nomads, while Pap fierce for lefty newpeppers & the pofolk. But first inklies of upcoming capsize too, for somewhen now, Pap commencer ramble gibbery, & Feelish staging neverend, all gaga with blindlights & titty groupers, no time for chicos lack before with Scissor & Savvy. 1noches roundtable Aghast spoutoffs how showbiz gist for mooney buzzards, starter big row, vox rising, slam doors, then presto, next mourning 4some upwaked to warover, voluntiered army, & backagain of staypoor. Revulsion whereto? Alter sudden downcrash of common sins, longone Sexties, & lefty newpeppers bellyupped too.

Well, Scissor figures law school phooey, gone tote off fuddled Pap to fem farm in Oregami, grow beans, bake bread, munch raw veggies. First rift in 4fambly. Herwords being chest stab for Feelish, who upstarted meantime with own troubles. Whereto Spanglo gigs now & how come pro motor dont callback? Skinnybritches bushair rockerbilly uncool for disco dance. Commencer wakenights with sellout specters, own posing questies neverend, where wrongturned, so forth. Then blackday come. Savvy boogying homewords from miligrant shebang when copper sireens for pullover, law puppy wanna muzzle underseats, sniff sniff, & whaddaya know, sheeny blue desert boogy cram fuller coke bags! Well, for cutshort of longspin, Feelish raptakes to Savvy keepouter messy jail & priziron goes while Uncle Same overborders licketysplit with beauteous chiquita. Ali Handrow nowhere for finding, surprise, & Scissor with doty dad longone for farparts, no way for help to messenger. Slamdown of endtime.

Inbox dayin dayout, po headshaved Feelish being shower pummeled & cutup, commencer fear grip with night shivers. Wuz revulsion jester smoke whoosh? Con brooders meager political &, get real, rockerbilly dont know shit. 1day Feelish lefty looselips & rapido brainbashed by priziron gods, thereafter wary mouthwatching. Starter Sexties second guess, how freedream maybe gist bong high. Grub mooney the 1true, all underlying, & stomp utters how2 do it. Once this eye opening, like duh now. Castdown on coldfloor then, Feelish commencer own ravage, the priziron inner priziron. Backpixxed neverending, how wonder ponder time sunsprawled greengrass with Savvy chiquita or tablefested with Scissor & Pap, headfuller fragrant savories. Yesterday so farago. Upstarted rage at youngfoolery, these earthgoods to squander, rueful Feelish seamed feckless now for stopper browbeat. Who bethunk he wuz, Cheezy Cripes? Eared own vox resounding, all the Sexties weirds gist weirds now, or not even, the air tremors. Furlong Feelish commencer wallbounce chaotic.

Meanwhile Scissor upended Oregami where fem farm huge kerbust. Barehanded lifemaking turnout sweatgross, upstarter chicken slaughter, yuck, soon citified fems licketysplit for reburgher when, varoom varoom, 1night biker gangbanged alter rest. Grisly doing, Pap blammed & hairy pig Scissor raped, bulbous stubblebearded pusface, longtime Aghast nightmaring with slit fuckers tongout, but hogrode off to neversee. Thazzit. Nowbeing buckless & Pap inner bad way, 2some thumbed Portlandwords where Aghast tricked timer2, what choice, need mooney fast for Pap meds, then triter waitress till owner hit owner. Bouter quit when findsout, aw shit, pregnanted with pig raper, so 1tricked cafe boss for abort mooney, then next week burnpissy &, whaddaya know, owner done her clapped! From bladder to worst, old story, & alter while Savvy vanished overborder, no recking whereto.

Endtale come crawly. How furlong heartbroke Feelish spitout priziron, upcoast rambled countless months before found

Aghast & Pap foodstamping SanFranco, & soonafter 3some altogether again, beginner homemake inner woods. Feelish sweatlabored in big shitty, oddjobs or backbroker, while Scissor mooney scrimped & garden tended, outclambering the deephole for little on little newstart. US all wiseupped to get wretch, no count pofolk, but what matter, cuz nightly havening with eye2eye & bellyful gushcare, family gist joyous being there, held on for dear life. Bout then monstrography upstumbled, & shorty thereafter Savvy backtraced the long twistpath to fixlack, remade uprights 4square again. All swell where hystery stopped. But outcast in coldwallow, ever earing smarmy palaver, mute horroglyph deep stymied at own sole, at inwash of new feelies. Eager suckup of the hear&tell, of uprise & crestfallen, ghoul commencer writhe with chest pangs, joy spikes, inner dupling to big ventures, gist lack uprights. Imparsible withoutwords to 1make, prickless no cunt now knew. Never getacross to mortal corpus, to loin bliss, the fuckup of border gods, sinsless beatings. Beasty wuz hopeless boxed. But how come still sole shuddered at hear&tell, thrilled to repriser mortal doings? Hystery wuz made flesh, naught jest weirds! But pretuned to both Feelish & Hyster Penny, to realing vox & buck too, issue firstime own posed: *Could Luv be inwords form?*

Po dumb critter, Maker bethunking, so pithy mad these heartspikes, like wallbeating head bloody, ho ho, a regular cant learn. No ender smarmy! No stopper own bogusing! But iffing gist knew, Wombard, how fierce to 1flesh even deadletter wuz, how lusty for getacross, for reciprocool hipcat, could Maker still upstart fruitless issue, outfling inner sins for literal turnaway? Once offsprung, to stop this mute thrust, this unfleshed wetfurrow, Lungwage would holy creation wipeout. What peace shorter final outcome, sans spewing, dontcha get it? Goner surface mar till solebust, till wordswarms vortexed over, till inwords dupled to all without. Wuz Creator mad?! Oh, iffing monstrography could gist 1time to unground cling! Iffing could gist **THIS NOW HERE** hear!

14

Well, so far the mad hystery, how belouvered uprights to beastly nome come, the Savvy twistings, Pap fuddle, this yarn unravels. Meantime, swoll with bloodthrobs, issue onwent ogling mortals, dayin dayout, futile of turnaway. Then big change.

Nome oft rummaging backdoor midden for rancie yum offals, fetorish slurp slurp, upstumbled wondernight on greasy rucksack. Nosing innards, morphobeast commencer outpull pockyknife, tincup, oddments for brushteething, old rubber, eeew, but at bottomost clawnubbed 3 or 4 squarecloths with flap edgings. Fumbling to grasp all, ghoul upended bag, outpouring multifaried bricabrac. What splendiferous to unveil then! Nome beholden *bucks!* Oh, starter mucho hectic, how po monstrography frothspewed to scuttleback cottagewords, zealous with boon clutch, where under wallchink all daypast & moonshining, ogled treasure. Weirdy familiar wuz this newfoundling. Espied how upclose buck wuz edge ruled & no cunt smooth crotched, gist lack morphobeast. How leaves unfurled from centerfold with spiney inwords, the 2face, each outsprawl for shameless perusal, nary sins hidden. Remarked minilayers flatting, tissues skinnied to wind ripple & numberless turnings, cleavage to no end. Imparsible seamed.

But most boggling to nome wuz blackmarks. Never inner bewildest dreams had 1time nome imaged these multiplicitous scarletters, bedazzling quadrillions, out cornucopying the midnight sparklies, row on row, forever wraparound lack unspooled thread. Oh, how skullbust for critter! What cuz this surface mar to no end, this deluging? Commencer backpix to nightly real, how nome eared Lungwage upspringing each surface, lack phoney fruit from bare leaf, buck being the noisebox, seed of Adams apple. Author Dimsdull, Creakleg, Capping Ablab, all instore for raucous outpouring. But now befumbling flaps, critter only ogled marks, squiggles, bare inklings—an eyeful. Neverend maze, upstarted nome to wonder: Where wuz realing vox? Mortal flesh seamed inwordly pretuned to shrieks & hardy har, synched utterly, but this inky putdown wuz mute. Howcome black ciphers uprose so raucous? Sans mortals, bucks seamed dumb as monstrography!

Well, longtime puzzling so & ever ogling the scarletters, furlong nome commencer ache for real bucks too, but mighty try & try, creature still dumbfounded, withoutwords unspeakable. Why thus helpless no telling. Insole resounded to uprights raucousing bucks evernight, mutely attuned for rise & fall, gist lack Feelish Scissor Savvy & Pap. Inwordly chilled at ear pangs, the shrills, & chesthrobbed for Hyster fronting fleshmarked Author. Hadnt mortal Lungwage echoed wayback? But this ownmost stifle made little cuz for whimpering, since nowon recked now how bucks all rewound seam thread: knot of lonely outcasts inner bewilderness, ever tangling with angry utters. Hyster, Mo Be, Creakleg, all the banished, wanderlusted for inner sins, & logophobes always raged to box in, to putdown gist lack foretold. Even hystery of 4fambly spun from this yarn: how goons & border gods brainbashed 4some, banished Savvy, cooped Feelish, alter windup no place, the patternless weft in bewoveness. Mind boggle how these countless turnings, these figures, deciphered all1! Upstarted nowon to breastache. If only somehow for getacross, own posed, for disclosing to 4some how critter wuz outcast too. Longtime suffered so, heartswoll with recounting, but feckless for browbeat, each outcome gist dupling own form over.

Mucho sun&moons bypast, goldy treefall to longwinter, repriser upspring, & alter while nome watched helpless for gushout. Then wondermourn being outsprawled inner woods, sins opened to earth & sky, beastly slumber wuz troubled with horribilous spector: nome bethunk first espied own corpus! Oh, most boggle to backthink, how this spector pickled po heart! Inner trice imaged issue allover prescribed, foretold from beginner end, with no count ciphers, surface marred neverending. Where wuz inner sins? Where wuz own blankety blank slate? Eager to spector flee, miscreant violent upstarted all wider wake when, boggle on boggle, nosed colossal mortal head downpeering. Sheeny orbs being bulbous open, 2blue centers zigzagging righter left & all glassy lensed with spectacles, backimaging surface of monstrography. Upright eye2eye at longlast, face2facing. Then recked spector wuz no dream. *Mortal wuz realing nome!* Thunderclapped nome instanter with the deluge: how wayback in formless gaga murky precursor, Wombard, the Great Maker, first deformed litter for write off, dictated this outcome, even here now, all from beginner end. Nowon too fuckupped by horribilous recking to abscond gist yet, so onwent lying barefaced, but no sooner done wakeup than bespectacled realer upstarted to hightaling, you betcha, mad lust for escapades, for hifalutin getaways. Weirdploy wuz abandoned in no time with bezillion scars, own fate writ large now, surface unvoidable. Putdown, gist encased, double binding: nome wuz buck.

Oh, how dizzied horroglyph this presentensing! Starter trope vertiginous, rounder round, lack tale pursued, for imparsible intaker own form. Unbelieving withoutwords wuz inwords scrawled, pretext first to last, mere script to follow. To be real pithed, Maker, meaning full & past pregnant, but unholed for outburst, dammed forever! Utter surd. So, this wuz Luv, this shrieky pentup. How raged nome to gnashtooth then, to sole consuming, cosmo slurrrrrrp! Countless hours passion by, soon pitchy night fell, & inkling wanderloosed inner dark, holy outer mind. Plodding clueless, treestumped & brambly snarled, mad nome crashed thru briars, ripped surface, defacing inner sins to unfeel furious deep ache. But furlong commencer bethunk creature wuznt solo. Imparsible for clairvoyant make out, but nowon glimpsed distant blundering, obscure figures afaroff, imaging ever twist & turn of outcast letter. Howcome this parallel bewilderness, no gleaning, but eared distant shadows groping thicket gist lack weirdploy, mucho thrashes, with loud moonhowls & wild groans. Po script fearful of misographs & bibliophobes for real now, triter escape pursuers, avid for coverup of each print, commencer troping round & round, soon strayed further inwords offbeaten path, plunging deeper. Nightlong passed so, then dawnbroken & still fleeing, nome wuz surprised to upcome on familiar place. Eared cheery palaver, ogled greenish clearing &, alter sudden whatcha know, weirdploy wuz bystanding cottage again, old habituation. Monstrography done come full circle. Darkling pursuers wuz—what mindboggle—Savvy Pap Feelish & Aghast!

How stupiferous for po nome! All 4square in 3beddies, bellyful & snuggly, belouvered uprights still ventured nightly withoutwords unforeseen, pursuing weirdploy unbeknownst inner darkness, again & again. So here wuz upstart of bewildering! & hadnt beastly corpus alphabetted this restless? Nome withoutwords sported A to Z, original effacement. Wuz nightly quest for the underwriting, for inner sins? Upstarted nome to first turn ownwordly. Grasped then how inwords ache wuz never for 1flesh, uh uh. Nome always ached for mortal vox, for realing—& thunderstruck with unpuzzle—knew now mortals must ache for nome. Sexties revulsion of godfearing characters, putdown of black & white, wuz real outcasting, & 4some abandoned wanderlusting for weird Luv. Commencer outlooking that instant for chance of face2face, meaning to unveil for alter whirl, unfearing bibliophobes & misographs now, litter of great Maker bolded to overleap chinkwall. Bethunking dayin dayout howto, alter while uprising with inwords aflutter, the giddy, soon decider would open up for balmy Pap. Dotard never own blinded issue & blather seamed outwords twin of own writhing, the allover corpus of monstrography, weirdkin.

Nome being everwatchful, furlong bright daycome. Feelish & Scissor truckoffed seam as utter mourning, & Savvy sculleried round to betidy, platter splashing with rag swipes, the chirpy tune, when alter sudden herflesh outcome the kitschy, bentovered Pap for noggin peck, & presto, Savvy offgone sunny skies for muckup pansies. Nowon circumogled for seize moment. With great trepidating readied to venture inwords, chestpounding at spector of bare surface. Pap awaited peacey, headrooped unsuspicioning, blanky swaddled half asnooze in rocker. Time ripe. Monstrography abandoned hiding place, muster spirits &, kerplop, reposed matter outright on threshold. Commencer ruckus at entry.

Who is there? . . .

Utter strange, confounded issue how alter sudden Pap spieled so uprightly, unlack to geezer babble. But unforeknowing, nome gist letter rip: Nowon.

Enter and I will try in what manner I can relieve your wants. But unfortunately . . . as I am blind . . .

Boggle! Weirds phoned lack right outer buck! Stymied issue, but loathe for holdback now, ventured inwords through opening & undernose of codger commencer unclose. Spelled out how nowon wuz harmless inkling. Unwanting for vittles but joyous of warm welcome, this resting place, no matter past troubles, cheered gist to be holy here.

Longtime silence, bare letter unspeakable tense. Then eared: By your language, stranger, I suppose you are my countryman. Are you French?

Whatta putdown! Wuz codger stupiferous too? But bolding print for readier uplift, nome continued: No, for to speak frank, nowon the slowest learner. Imparsible ever to real Lungwage or ungarble Spanglish, mere pretuned with mutter tong, transparent of all utters. But unfold here now for your ogle the howcome. Venturing farout from wonted spiel, nowon former shelter abandoned & inwordly exposed for no telling, all gist lack you can see, meaning to bare all for sole mates, alter while fearful of writeoff, of foretold deed, seek for real—

Are they Germans?

Po tome commencer discourage. Pap too balmy even for literal sins, for baldest manifesto. But then geezer upstarted palavering further.

Do not despair . . . The hearts of men, when unprejudiced by any obvious self-interest are full of brotherly love and . . .

Bolstered critter. What matter phoney order if heartblank so partial? Nome commencer pageturning rapido. Documented for dotard how po tome uprose earthdank & altogether, inwordly fashioned by Maker, the Great Wombard, then offset for discounting, the shamburgher writeoff, wuz furlong beaten sinsless & banished to rubbisheap, weirdploy being putdown . . .

That is indeed unfortunate; but if you are really blameless cannot you undeceive them?

In deed! In *deed!* Tome nearly rollicked hysterical!

Where do these friends reside?

Nearby.

If you will unreservedly confide to me the particulars of your tale . . . There is something in your words . . .

Strange how each weird Pap spieled seamed strung to utters, lack entangled yarn or meaning chain, but predetermined to unwrite original sins, to reverso insurrecto, nome own composed inwordly & plunged on. How weirdploy edgewords headed, seeking utter outcasts, marginal refuge, & after obscure bewildering, finally outcome clearing, old plot of pastimes forgot, the no place. Buncher utter doings, too, up to present where longtime ogled fambly, 4square Sixties beings, til finally dawned spector of weird & flesh, joinup vox & printmatter. Then climaxed: But on that account nowon risks all now, ready for unbosom scars, for dismember hystery & maker clean breast, recovery of white whole, blank slate, living letter!

Heaven forbid! I also am unfortunate. I and my family have been condemned, although innocent. Judge, therefore, if I do not feel for your misfortunes.

Too heartful for realing more, pageturner poised, literal clinging to last leaf.

May I know the names and residence of those friends?

Nome overturned fate: Now is the time!—save and protect me! You and your family are the friends whom I seek.

Great God! Who are you?

At that instant the cottage door was opened, and Felix, Safie, and Agatha entered. Who can describe their horror and consternation on beholding me? No . . . wait. Agatha fainted; and Safie, unable to attend to her friend, rushed out of the cottage. Felix darted forward, and with supernatural force Imparsible to . . . tore me from his father, to whose knees I clung: in a transport of fury, he dashed me to the ground, and Stop! Stop! struck me violently with a stick. I could have torn him . . . but my heart sunk within me as with bitter sickness, and I refrained. I saw him on the point of repeating his Help! Help! Help! blow, when, overcome by pain and anguish, I quitted the cottage, and in the general tumult escaped unperceived . . .

15

How overcome wuz po monstrography! 1minute heartfelt yarn unraveled for mortal windup, for dismembering pangful hystery & squareknotting loosends, then outer no place unbodied vox commencer raucous, & whatnext foreknowing, pretext had tossout printmatter & taker place. Longtime nome huddled outsider wall for licker wounds & whimper, mucho agog at terribilous upshot. Howcome Feelish defaced open buck, beat sinsless bare inkling? Whatfor Scissor swooned, Savvy fled? Evernight nome espied 4some realing flapboxes, flipping pages for ogle teeny blackmarks, & never 1time triter quash letter, triter write off black & white. Why this reprise of deformer pastimes now? Didnt lonely outcasts Luv weirds?

Heartbroke critter wallowed whiney bog longtime, but eventual fedup, commencer feel inwords gnawed. 4some shunned own scripture! What gall to putdown literalmost uplifting, big A, to efface artless character. Unreal & without mortal shelter, get of Wombard soon upstarted lustful for evening, obscure getback, the consuming inwordness. Howlong frothed so, imparsible to reckon, but writhed on, evermore troping vertiginous, until furlong nightfell & fiendworm upspiked for fleshy bustout. Oh, how caterwauled alphabeast then, bloodswollen with untold wrongs & deep stifling. Strode over abandoned wastes, shrieked moonmad, teethgnashed for gorging flesh & juicy pith. What inwords anguish, unspeakable. Finally after longish period miscreant slumpdown earthwords, backdrifting sleepy to inner beginning, formless gaga & primal vortexing.

& then presto, pageturned youwords, Maker! Murky image upsprung, who knew where from, how faceless antecedent first putdown issue, fashioned from void & sentenced to 1thing after another, the discomposing. How queer this reprise! Inwordly suffered each change allover, the whirl fixture & lying downright, the manhandling. Mindboggled to mull this original sins, first mar & copywrong, nowon commencer ruminating on fodder figure. Whereto absconded this primordial former, the almighty Wombard? Wherever Maker homed, nome figured there must abide ultra hipcat, urtext of present derangement. How this spector frenzied nome, this dream of perfect realer. Decider then & there to sniffout Wombard, unreal yarn alter way to first knot. Howto of course wuz big fuddle, surface printed foregoing only, never recto reverso, but sans map, sans memory, nome setout for outset, backtracking signs to weird origin.

Longtime wandered circles taling teeth. Bogdown quagmires, deep ventured inner bewilderness, mucho obscure floundering & startovers, but never abject, lonely scion onrushed headlong, hopeful of rejoin with prime stock, the living graph. Tiresome to relate beginner end this digression, how stumbled over roots, cracks, slapsticks, but 1day outcome fresh path, new mourning, nome espied boytyke juking nearby, blondie blueyed with sweet vox. Well, nome quick for coverup centerfold, recking how uprights revolted at printmatter, the shameful sins. Nevermore gone bare letter to unbefitting, uh uh! But onwent ogling tyke, crotch hid & flapshut, when upstarted to bethunk. Unformed youngun wuznt marked character lack utters, being inwordly blank, with clean breast of pretexts & godfearing mars. Mayhaps still yearned for naked surface, for bare inkling. What if captivated? Nome might entice pure being afarout, form for realing, till fabricated fearless of brute matter! & throbbing desirous, reckless issue bolded forth a lastime to unveil weirds.

Ah, such madness this persisting! To backthink now, how alphabeast uncovered corpus again, unfolded intricate fabric of countless threads, allover black & white, the manifest seams, & commencer wait for unformed realer. Beautiful still to conjure image, but upshot wuz old story. Boytyke commencer gawk 1instant, intaker outlandish print, the figured weavings & manifold schemes, then foreknowing it, wuz off, triter flee letter again, headed for no telling whatnext, farfetched ends, the forever upcoming. Grrrr. Well, nome lost it. Do you blame morphobeast? How can 1buck stand for all, gist helpless while bibliophobes, shamburghers, misographs make naught of weird? Already gotta grip on boy, buck onwent spinning yarn, new twists to entangle unsuspecting, knot on knot, more turns to lure further, noose slow tightening for fatal suspense. Oh, how easy to imagine this windup! Every weird unwriting the next, every sentence unrealing the former, furlong conclusions too fargone. Pure being wuz framed.

Heartless plotter, you say? Har, har, gist lack Maker to shun ownmost handiwork, the firstlings of told you so. Wuznt weirdploy crazy for Luv, for real vox? But creator orphaned creature, abandoned litter to fond illusion, & no time before mortals done discounted page & defaced character. What cuz this duplicity, Wombard? Wuz scripture mere pulp, jest litter for trashing? But still formed for upright feeling, nome inclined boywords to relent. Panged to ogle po youngun faltering, uplifting whimpy nose to peer about. Firstime blueyes espied how surroundings wuz allover prescribed, everywhere seamless juncture of weird & deed. What fun before to follow print, thrilling at fakey pangs, bogus howls, always meaning at last to putdown story & X it. But now beasts, clods, mortals, sky, all upstarting to look hysterical, gist lack buck. Where gone the edge, realing seams, withoutlying? Tyke commencer tremble. Everything wuz part of it. Imparsible to refound old path, to unwrite prediction, so plunged headlong, deeper deeper, own blinding with flight, with search for wayout schemes, while page after page materialized fate. Peripathetic.

Well, smarmy nowon felt a trifle touched, you betcha. Decider cant finish off boytyke, nope, goner forebear catastrophe & turnloose. So commencer takebacking ever weird, canceling own account, hokeying up contrivance for literal escape, when whatnext to mindblow, pure being opens maw & starts to drivel. Unimaginable moxie, tyke has gall to impugn letter! Proclaims horroglyph no count perversity, sole cuz of mortal bewilderness, unruly gimmicking for no matter. Wuz buck jest snotty? Sez imparsible forever bodily to grasp point, to pluck pith from empty husks. Why seize fancy then sentence to hardlabor? Uprights made for lie about workends & skullscreening. Unfair!

Nome astonied. Oft putdown by the godfearing, but never affronted so. Triter recount hystery allover, how monstrography upsprung unbeknownst, literally uncovered underway, how void wuznt own doing, pastimes dictated, so forth. But what profit in this retale? Firstime bypast letter, secondtime utterly dispelled. Alphabeast waxed blunt, but headstrong tyke never syncopated, onwent yadda yadda, reproving common sins, belaboring odious, how weirdploy jest immaterial, no good forgetting yucks. Furlong fear of bored to death, so nome bethunk to coverup again & withdraw inwordly, when alter sudden parting shot ruffled surface. Blondie raised volume, shrilled pagewords: crooked plot mere pretext for swindle, fraudy pretense, robber fun! Cant upend longstanding derangement sans pay for sins, uh uh! Realer wuz Willy, offshot of upright lawman, faithful represener of all black & white, *the first Frank.*

Imparsible for inpour your skull now, Maker, how this 1weird, *Frank,* fierce cleaved issue. Where never before eared call of antecedent, the noise for you, this phone resounded lack spinecrack, inbreaking hystery & spurring fiendworm surfacewords. How strange this fated juncture! Blondie blueyes wuz offspring of origin, made 1flesh with Wombard, formed bloodlink. After longtime wandering lost in dark to happen unbeknownst thus on object! Then recked how weird takeback wuz too late. Oh, boytyke struggled longtime, you betcha, fought fiercely inner grip of tale, protesting indignorant, determined to ungrasp obvious & avoid plight, but what quarter for unminding, for the mad refusal? Already the opening narrowed, knot tightened, one turn after another, gist lack forever prescribed, then presto, fatal conclusion. Inner sins wuz erased.

So simple thus to write off spirit, vox, weird, flesh, & simple seamwise to inscribe holy household of Maker, each wannabee Frank, in this murderous inditing. Habituated to everyday overlooking, to see thru pretense to underlying, to murky sins, bloodkin of Wombard wuz already nosed for fishy smell.

Foretold how everywhere dissembling made nature, how this here & now wuz naught, pure being seamed imparsible. So, when nowon espied nightfallen beauty Teeny Love flee erasure site, the putdown of little Willy, made fast for coverup again of monstrous form & commencer spinning black yarn, the web of hokey jive, alter upraise phoney spectre, unimaginable wrongs. & shaw nuff, unaccountable hokum signaled dark pretext to ofays, surface rap of wily coverup, gist lack glibbing made secret plot disclosed to each: Earnest soldier, almost Scissor, first Frank, etc. Instanter fambly dreamed up no ender schemes, plots, hidden lusts. Har, har, what mad this mortal rage for storying! The everpresent being no place, transparent weirds formed perfect disguise! So next tucked tale in Teeny pocket for redhanding & voila. Oh, such glee, Maker, ogling you dumbstruck at boondoggle, the mock trial, & po Teeny squealing for 1ear, for 1mortal unplugging at plainspoken.

Well, no point in going overall again, how nome wrote off alter whirl, postponed pangs & cries & outrage to final reckoning, the recount being end all, no count the utters, altho this face2face now, Maker, this outpouring youwords of old wound, how it soothes beastly tumults, the bloodfiring, ahhh. Sad for Wombard all the Luv lost, little Willy, Teeny joyflesh, but fiendworm wuz jest own doing, upsprung ancient crotchfever, dictated beginner end, no help. What use to blame monstrography? But hush this whiney now, unmeaning to wrangle with almighty antecedent, beastly scripture hope only for 1lastime to intake vox, make Wombard hear nome spieling—*stay tuned, Maker!*—gone tender deal & be done. Here this now: being privy to deep meaning, nome gleans how Maker still aches for inner sins, for second chance, how wannabee rid of miscreant, the corruptext, & to blabber true, between mute buck & upright minds so little savory, so little eye2eye, weirdploy hardly wish for cling to flesh, the godfearing misographs & bibliophobes. So schemed thus to win win, horroglyph gives solemn promise for abandon Wombard, swear for utter vanish & own erasure, no reprise & traceless sans remainder, if only Wombard will to one boon say okeydokey. Boon being jest to fashion mate for lonely weirdploy, the perfect complement, for maker end of beginning & marred white whole. Would be the fixall, this sequel! No mo stifled outbusting, no mo standing for! Being done, monstrography would inwordly blank lack foretimes, old unformed void, & both creator & heartbroke creature long last resting peace. Whatcha say, huh?

Chapter XVI

WORDS FAIL ME. To imagine my own creation making such demands, demands I trembled to meet, arising I can't say how but engendered—apparently—at its conception, and then to imagine further, having vanished into the world, my contrivance returning thus to condemn me from the writing of my own hand . . . well, had I encountered such poppycock in a novel, I'd have dismissed it as poppycock. I can't convey now, here in these stifling and gnat infested wilds, what on that green and luxuriant ridge I couldn't have conveyed then, or make plainer what nothing but my own words could have made plain to me, but I can say that no astonishment you may be feeling at this instant, having just weathered that interminable maelstrom of gibberish spewing from my tonsils—my apologies are without bounds—can be more than a shadow of that astonishment I was feeling so many long years ago, upon the north Georgia mountainside, gazing down at the paperback in my fist. Apparently, my book was not my book. How I'd imagined otherwise seemed beyond me. I couldn't have felt more out of my mind had I been literally beside myself.

As my consciousness of the verdant surroundings began to return and the voice of that disorderly and murderous fabrication faded from my senses, rage overcame perplexity, and flinging my precursor's story into a nearby rhododendron, I swore I'd never write another sentence as long as I lived. To represent me as author of my own defeat, as the monster who'd invaded my home, expunged Will from memory, silenced my beloved playmate—why, it was as though the gap between real and imaginary violence didn't make all the difference in the world! No mere man, not even a genius like myself, could pretend to say what exactly it was he'd said while saying it or, in other words, to explain the words he was writing at the time. Hah! Does anyone know what he means? Either my innocence could speak for itself, a harmless mimicry of lives hardly more present on the page than in the offing, or if my contrivance required real violence to bolster it, then nothing I could ever write, regardless how forceful, could undo the damage my words had done to now. So, I resolved to turn a deaf ear to my text.

At the same time, I could not but acknowledge a semblance of justice, almost reasonableness, in what my precursor had said. My creation was plainly incomplete. Although I'd amassed experience, faithfully transcribed the scraps of tripe and prattle around me, I'd somehow omitted, or just remarked too lightly, what happened as I wrote. Now it seemed I'd confused my creation with myself, my life with my writing, ignoring the very chances that were mine to squander. What these chances might've amounted to, of course, I'd be the last to know, but that they were there, as nearby as my heartbeats —all this didn't seem true now so much as simply undeniable.

127

No more no! my heart cried out. I own my beastliness!

Thus I responded to my creation, if not in so many words— since I'm far from certain that a phoneme escaped my lips, furiously searching the ferns as I then was for my precursor's impetuously discarded tale—then in whatever agitation of tissues and nerves harbingers so many words. Somewhere, this recounting must end. But glimpsing at that instant a scarlet stripe amid the laurel branches and feeling page ends on my fingertips, I withdrew from the undergrowth the following reply:

> . . . the human senses are insurmountable barriers to our union. Yet mine shall not be the submission of abject slavery. I will revenge my injuries; if I cannot inspire love, I will cause fear, and chiefly towards you my arch-enemy, because my creator, do I swear inextinguishable hatred. Have a care: I will work at your destruction, nor finish until I desolate your heart, so that you shall curse the hour of your birth.

Was this the source of my work's violence, this cursing of my birth? A shudder passed through me. How could I have strayed so far from my dear mother that my creation would now inspire fear or that I could ever regard her sacred loins, or if not my mother's loins exactly — since the prospect seemed loathsome — then the loins of some other woman, with such profane disrespect? The question permitted no answer. If I hoped to escape my doom, no path lay open to me but to repeat myself, to do over what I'd done before, hoping this time to be done with it. But immediately this outcome seemed the least likely of conclusions, for how, if my invention had become an offense to the senses, could I by inventing again hope to repair them? And even if I did, wouldn't my imaginary life still shadow my every action, threatening to obscure my story? No, it appeared far more probable that in repeating myself, my original violence would be reproduced: love stifled, siblings annihilated, home abolished, just as before. Unless I could imagine an experience so alien that no civilized being would come near it, Frank Stein could never be free.

128   So I found myself standing amid that dripping and bosky luxuriance, unshakably convinced that I must do what I could never do and what, even if done, could only return me to this place. I looked down at my precursor's page. What I longed for, it went without saying, was a making of a wholly different order, one that, while manifesting whatever my precursor's making had manifested, never lost touch with itself. But how could that be?

𝕴 **consent to your demand!** I abruptly shouted, addressing just whom I have no idea, no more than I knew why — in a solitary glade with my fingers clutching a paperback romance — I felt called upon to respond to a woman's writing. But I didn't stop there. I went on promising no end of foolishness, to compose a sequel to my monstrous life, to invent the history to end all history, until I'd made peace with words at last.

I was alone. It had taken an entire day to complete my precursor's story, and now as the silence returned and dusk settled in, I gave up any thought of my earlier excursion and reversed my steps, meaning to return as rapidly as possible to my father's chalet. However, the strain of my chaotic meditations, to say nothing of reading for ten hours straight, had left my nerves frayed, and hoping to locate a shortcut through the obscurity, I repeatedly strayed from the beaten path, finding myself before some impasse lost in thought. As a result, it was nearly midnight before I finally made out a light through the branches and stumbled onto the porch of my father's chalet. I can't say what I expected there, but what I found astonished me. Everyone was behaving normally! On seeing me returned, Liza merely expressed the same alarm at my gaunt appearance that she might've expressed at any time, and Earnest seemed as desperate to learn what hardships accounted for my early return as if he'd known nothing about my ordeal. As for my father, he seemed the same gaseous presence he seemed perpetually. Of course, it was impossible to know everything my loved ones might not know, or very, very difficult, but that someone had to have contrived my encounter with our family's romance—for who could doubt that the paperback in my pocket was identical?—well, this was what I could no longer blink. It was a plot. Seeing that no one was prepared to acknowledge this rift that had opened between all present and the life I'd imagined, I answered not a word to their questions but made my way upstairs, cloaking my movements in a surly and mysterious reserve that, I now realize, could only have made them more desperate.

129

Rest assured, I hardly slept a wink that night, maddened as I was by the obligations I'd incurred and my certainty that I could never fulfill them. However, the next morning I was astonished to see sunlight on my pillow and to feel a breeze, and when at breakfast my father announced that we'd be returning to the city, I experienced a sudden lift in spirits. The thought of ensconcing myself again, if not in my original dwelling, then in its identical replacement, seemed to offer an illusion of normalcy, and so when Carletta and Monique had finished emptying our closets and our driver had carried our bags to the van, I readily joined my family for the drive back to Atlanta. In the limo I sat inches from Liza's thigh and my monumental father's knees, my outward affability forming the thinnest veneer over my suspicions, and strove to make pleasant conversation about the Middle East. If only I, like my murderous creation, had had a maker whose understanding, regardless of how unsympathetic, was total, a possibly blind, possibly inept, possibly malicious demiurge

Chapter XVII

DAYS PASSED, THEN weeks, but as long as I remained in my father's house I could muster no strength to begin my sequel. Somehow the foreboding I felt whenever I recalled my creation's words, plus my family's chatter and guitar playing, all made impossible that profound self-absorption from which genuinely unpredictable actions spring, and I worried that, in order to fulfill the promise of my first book, I would have no choice but to resume the sterile and pedantic existence I'd formerly known at Harvard. On the nightly news I heard inspiring tales of novelists whose books were movies and who spent their vibrant days coupling with models or drugging themselves stupid in clubs, and mightily I strove to be like them. I attended fundraisers for Julian Bond, followed closely the sanitation workers' strike, never missed a cousin's bar mitzvah, and often could be found at indecent hours seated with Liza listening to jazz and eating chicken on Hunter Street, but the more absorbed I became in these quotidian pursuits, the further away seemed the intelligence I needed to create. So this was how one lost one's life, I thought, in increments, every blissful day like the next, until years had passed, and if asked to recall a single afternoon, to describe for an interviewer or studio audience what you'd done just last Thursday, you'd draw a complete blank. It seemed grotesque, this prospect of being buried alive beneath one's family.

But there were also lighthearted moments, times when, attended by my stalwart brother and ravishing cousin or by some housekeeper whose impoverished upbringing had formed her to cater to me, I put aside my suspicions and submitted to what presented itself. I imagined then that I might at last be through with my education, that I could leave thinking behind and devote myself to politics. I saw no reason why, with my intelligence thus stultified, I shouldn't be successful at it. In fact, the prospect of an active life, fighting for profits or pay raises or equality, seemed an exciting distraction, and more than once I forgot my fears contemplating it. Perhaps my involvement with words had been a phase! Whenever these hopeful prospects took me over, my gloom subsided, suffusing me with zest, and observing such an improvement one day, my father determined to end my brooding for good. Interrupting my convivial intercourse with Carletta, he called me into his study and, there beneath my mother's replica, announced he knew my secret. A shock passed through me. At first I thought he meant he'd deciphered my pseudonym, and I prepared forcefully to repudiate it. Then I imagined he'd found the place where I'd concealed my precursor's romance. But without remarking my alarm, my father continued.

When the idea first struck me, Frank, it seemed, too antiquated, but then I recalled your nervous sensibility, and so asked myself, could he really be scrupling incest? It's hard to imagine, especially after the free love in the papers! I mean, a young adventurer like yourself—I should've thought by now you'd be sophisticated. Why, to think: fornicating with your own flesh! But perhaps I fancied wrong, since I've observed in you a restraint, almost a shrinking, where I'd expected, well, something more straightforward. Surely that old worm of shame hasn't wiggled its way into your trousers? Speak freely, my boy. Have I guessed it? Or have you merely promised your heart elsewhere, engaged yourself to some trailer park vixen? Or maybe you fancy your own sex? Don't be shocked. I've experimented. But whatever your inclinations, Frank, don't hold back. No, no, copulate away! Or if copulation isn't your pleasure, if it's something less respectable, then just let me draft a prenuptual contract, and you can rush into whatever self-destructiveness makes you happy. But my point is that under no circumstances should you hesitate, not now while life's feast waits steaming on your table. Oh, make no mistake, Son, it's gone soon enough! The stories I could—

So I hastened to reassure my father that no thought of connubial union excited my imagination more nor seemed as likely to raise me to that conventional height of bliss, than

132

with her whose name even now suffuses me with sublime thoughts and whose mere fleshly presence was always sufficient to obliterate baser reflections. No, dear Father, I concluded, if I could ever hope to satisfy myself with any woman—or man!—it would be my precious Liza. I'm mad for love.

My father shook his head. Then I regret to tell you, Frank, regardless of the perversities you may have imagined, your sibling is no blood relation, not even a half-sister or third cousin, hardly more akin than the hired help, so put all thought of incest out of your mind. There's no succulence beyond the ordinary, no spice to be extracted from abominations. Taboos are a thing of the past. So, unless you've got some further obstacle in mind, I propose that we hasten to what was always your saintly mother's wish, not to mention her hope for our fractured country, and what I now realize is your passion too, your marriage to my—only figuratively speaking—precious daughter, Liza Mbira.

These words filled me with horror. For how could I indulge myself in what was sure to be inexpressible ecstasy, not to mention the realization of that destiny engendered for me by my parents, while the murderous demands of my creation remained outstanding? Nothing but perfect solitude, a withdrawal into that infinite capaciousness of my own skull, could reproduce the disorder my sequel required. So for several seconds I stared into my father's puddling irises, desperate for some reply, when my fingers happened onto the envelope in my pocket from Dr. Z—. It had just arrived that morning bringing news of some recent, much-discussed investigations into commonplace gregariousness, and although Dr. Z— had been at pains to mock this new work's pretensions, I'd seen through his raillery to certain similarities with my own writing. Now, I hit on these new studies as the perfect excuse for delaying my nuptials. So I told my father that, before settling down with her for whom I burned, I must travel north a final time, needing to confer with certain scientists to complete my thesis and return a Harvard man.

My father was delighted to see this ambition where lassitude had formerly ruled, and so imagining that the pretext I'd concocted for my writing was actually the pretext I'd concocted for my wantoness, he readily gave his consent, stipulating only that my northern researches—wink, wink—

133

confine themselves to no more than a few months, or at most one year, and that I take Mark along for company. This last condition, as you may well imagine, struck me as disagreeable, since absolute solitude, nothing less, was what I required, but seeing no way to escape my father's benevolence otherwise, I consented. Moreover, I still recalled Mark's support during my long recovery in Boston, and this memory of his constancy convinced me I could probably get around him.

So I began making plans for departure, almost relieved to be undertaking, after so long a delay, my dreaded assignment. Mark, who had remained in school throughout my family's recent ordeal, agreed to drop out and drive my Beetle to Washington to meet me. There we planned a tour of the Watergate and other historic monuments before driving to Baltimore for crabcakes and then on to our national origins in Philadelphia. Although I didn't doubt that Mark had been a collaborator in my recent happiness, conspiring by phone with my siblings to render me carefree, perhaps even authoring that anonymous plot to place an old romance in my path, I still didn't worry about his continuing collusion, so wild was I to escape my loved ones' smiles. However, I did worry about Liza's exposure to the monstrousness I'd unleashed. My family couldn't have imagined, of course, that Will's absence was somehow my doing, and although I myself had only my book's word for it, a word that moreover was excessively chaotic and that required—apparently—another book's words just to be understood, I still wondered whether I shouldn't take Earnie into my confidence, confessing all I knew about the violence my loved ones had suffered. But each time I resolved to make a clean breast, I became unsure how this could be done. I mean, an experience of one's own—wasn't that just democracy? How could I convince my brother that it was this very rage to make a life for myself, to escape the dictates of predecessors and form *my* tastes, *my* opinions, *my* identity—that it was this which had erased my family from my consciousness, separating me from my affections and setting my mind adrift where, really, anything could happen. Was this freedom? I shuddered to think.

So I reconciled myself to the likelihood that the violence threatening those I loved would probably follow me wherever I went, removing Liza and Earnest from my thoughts just as it had Will, and so leaving them in that one sense secure. In

134

retrospect, I realize my rationalization was blind, but I hardly knew myself at the time, so fanatical I'd become to reach the end of my writing. I still remember how on that last day Liza drove me to the airport in silence, her mind preoccupied with exactly what I'll never know, while my own robust consciousness ached to be off. I told her not to park at the terminal but merely to drop me in front of the ticketing concourse, meaning thereby to curtail our impassioned goodbyes, but when our family Mercedes pulled up beside the skycaps, Liza turned off the ignition.

Frank, she began, these last weeks have been...well, unbelievable. All the explanations, those rambles, your fantastic vocabulary. If only your mother were listening to you. Even after four years apart, sometimes it's like we're right back where we started. I swear, there were nights I imagined it would never end. But at other times, Frank, well, you can be so distant, almost like—I know it's crazy to think—you weren't here. And then I start to wonder about myself, if I could be missing too. And all at once what happened to Will and Teeny, it no longer seems impossible. I don't mean to be realistic, but I have to ask, has something come between us, some Obstacle? Oh, if you could just read my mind, Frank, what a tale my thoughts would tell. But listen to me, chattering! Anyway, all I really mean is, in the mountains I told you to resign yourself, kept your manhood at armslength, and well, I just hope you won't hold it against me now.

She extended her hand. How powerfully my passion rose up, urging me to clasp her to my bosom. But I knew possessiveness was no longer fashionable and that sooner or later, like other Americans, she'd want a life of her own, so I met Liza's frank expression with my own and shook on it. The moment was quickly past, and before I could toss my beloved a last adoring bouquet, I was standing at the curb, suitcase in hand, watching our Mercedes drive off. I watched for some seconds as it threaded the pedestrians and taxicabs, feeling an irrational impulse to run after it. How tangible Liza's Obstacle suddenly seemed! But I told myself that if I could only contain myself a little longer, continue protecting my family from my accursed fate, then perhaps in a few short months I'd return a free man and claim Liza as my prize. However, as I saw her vehicle break through the knot of vans and limos and accelerate toward the interstate, the thought

135

Chapter XVIII

CURIOUSLY, I CAN recall now almost none of my impressions during the next weeks. Mark and I visited the mall in Washington where the great anti-war protests had been held and saw the memorial to Martin's speech, and we spent a week in Philadelphia where I can still taste the cheesesteak I vomited, all before touring the riots of New Jersey, but of the theater and architecture and museums and concerts, my only recollection is of a white-faced mime being mugged before a crowd: It's not part of the show, he yelled. It's not part of the show! However, I do recall Mark's impressions. With what extraordinary vividness they come back! Mark gawking at the facades and facsimiles; Mark reading aloud the inscriptions on bronze plaques; Mark purchasing memorabilia in quantities that engulfed our Beetle. Nothing could restrain him. He invaded every new attraction like the Hun, frantic to torch what others had abandoned, all the civilized trinkets to which his ardor now longed to catch fire.

Nowhere was this all-consuming enthusiasm more apparent than in bookstores. As you can easily imagine, I preferred to avoid such establishments, fearing I might confront my own creation, but Mark seemed **the image of my former self**, snatching the bright jackets and flipping pages at random. How maniacal he appeared! More than once I had to suppress my urge to exclaim: Dear Mark, not *that* rubbish! And I sometimes amused myself surveying the lurid covers before us, predicting which of these dazzling surfaces would attract him first. But I admit to feeling some envy too, recalling how eagerly I had myself once feasted on print, never distinguishing the truly unsettling word from its more palatable imitation, and I occasionally thrilled at Mark's rampages even while mocking them. Oh, don't regard me as sophisticated! Haven't I paid for my blindness? But to observe him there, scouring the tables of new fiction, convinced that this book, or if not that one, then this book, or if not that one either, then some book among this plentitude must be what everyone sought, the standard by which to judge the rest— well, how could I, knowing what I knew, not despise him? He was my innocence returned, my own life repeating! But such exclamations are pointless. Why am I even telling you this?

While in Baltimore we encountered one of my Harvard classmates, a philosophy major from Pawtucket, who now lived in Manhattan and worked for an ethics firm.

We counsel executives, he explained.

Having famously hit it off with Mark and heard about our travels, he invited us with the greatest warmth to visit New York and stay with him. He insisted that his work occupied him only sporadically, required little concentration, and that he was often bored. Apparently, there was money to be made in consciences, for he insisted—not without a certain pride—that his upper west side condo had ample room for guests, and he promised to provide us with introductions to just the right circles. Moreover, among his friends were editors, publicists, and numerous others in the communications trade, all of whom one day Mark would need to know. We could stay with him for as long as we desired. All in all, he seemed in earnest about wanting our companionship, and he promised with a conspiratorial wink that, if we accepted his invitation, the three of us would have a really exciting time.

Mark seemed quite eager to enjoy my schoolmate's hospitality, but he still wouldn't shorten our stay in Philadelphia, having determined he must verify the Liberty Bell's crack, and then must examine Betsy Ross's sewing window, and then Ben Franklin's print shop, but when a few weeks later we finally rolled into Manhattan, my schoolmate still sounded as thrilled to hear from us as the night we'd first met. We made arrangements to join him that evening at his condo, and Mark and I passed the intervening hours dispensing change to bohemians on Bleeker Street and refusing their kind offers of narcotics. Throughout our travels Mark had tried to engage me in debates, continually tossing out preposterous theses on history, politics, art, theology, love—there seemed no fracas in which he wasn't hot to become embroiled!—and even though I'd gotten adept at parrying these sallies, I would on occasion respond. That afternoon I'd allowed myself to be provoked into reckless candor. Expressing his delight to be alive just now while our nation's greatest literature was being composed, Mark had held up his shopping bag and exclaimed: Why, I've just purchased three contemporary classics and the most important novel since World War Two!

Well, it was simply too, too much. So without pausing to think, I snarled back what I'd no sooner spoken than recognized as literal, that I hoped never to read another novel again, so help me God, unless my life depended on it.

These words were heresy. Throughout the remainder of the afternoon, during our otherwise pleasant West Village ramble, even to that moment of presenting ourselves, bags in hand, at our rendezvous, Mark could not refrain from lambasting me. I was cynical, the most impeccably chic of nihilists, had sold out, was spiritually dead, hated democracy, was a European, a fop, a puppy, in sum, had turned into an intellectual—there seemed no limit to his insults.

I offered no defense, of course, realizing the hopelessness of making my companion understand now, with carefully chosen words, the perfect faith that my thoughtless retort had expressed so precisely. However, Mark's indignation made for a heavy burden, and as we stood in the lobby listening to the laughter of the charming men on all sides, I found I had little energy for our ascent. The prospect of spending this and subsequent evenings above central park, surrounded by just such pleasant individuals, young professionals ambitious for culture, for spreading our nation's riches among the multitudes, somehow it filled me with a sadness I can't explain. Who could be less ready to appreciate the demand placed upon me, the necessity of creating another life or having none? Why, I might even encounter Gloria Something there, or the high-minded crackpot who'd edited me! On further consideration, this seemed unlikely, but I still couldn't shake my sense of representing something monstrous to these attractive young men. I decided I couldn't bear it. So as we watched the lights of the elevator descend, I turned to Mark and said I would not be accompanying him. His face registered confusion and disbelief, then realizing the brutality of his daylong sniping, he abruptly melted into a puddle of apology.

139

But I didn't waver. I made no effort to dispell his distress with meretricious excuses, knowing to do so could only dishonor our friendship, and stated simply that I craved solitude. The elevator arrived, I shoved Mark inside, and amid the mostly unrelieved pain of these memories, I recall that I reassured him of my continuing love and promised to rejoin him in December in Boston. I can still see my boyhood companion gazing out at me from the lift, his chin quivering and eyes stricken, as the doors compressed him to a sliver and he was launched into I will never know what final adventure. It was the last time I saw him alive. Oh, faithful Mark, you who alone gave substance to my idle dreams and made of even my youthful pastimes matters of enduring moment, how, deprived of your humble support, will this story ever mean anything again?

Afterwards I wandered the streets distractedly for several hours, aware only that my steps were taking me south. I eventually stumbled into a diner off Broadway where I laid claim to a plastic stool and, devouring infinite coffee and several breakfasts, waited for the light. The next morning I noticed a rental sign in a second-floor window and hit on the idea of taking a room. I'd wasted precious weeks indulging Mark's incorrigible enthusiasms, and now I felt impatient to get on with my new life. Why not right here in Manhattan? With neither friends nor family to distract me, I could pursue my object as relentlessly as my creation demanded, and this exorbitance could not but shorten my painful servitude. After a few hours prowling the adjoining byways, I located a roach-infested loft south of Houston which I obtained for an obscene sum, and then ransoming my soul to the city, I managed to illumine the overhead and flush my blackened toilet. For some reason, the unpleasantness of these accomodations seemed not at all unconducive to my labors but, on the contrary, struck me as apt, even inspiring. Here I could be sure of working at the least. I pushed the trash up against one wall and purchased a tiny desk, mattress, milk crate, and lamp. In no time I had fashioned a dimly lit rectangle in which I would be able to write and sleep.

How strange to recollect that period now, my lamp burning in the dark, the crumpled paper accumulating, my mattress exhaling poisonous must. I consumed countless days in furious scribbling, undergoing paroxysms in which the ecstasy of my new creation suppressed every other appetite and I was transported to a vertiginous neverland where murder seemed the most otherworldly of fantasies. How delicious and horrifying it all was! But there were also times when the violence of this second outpouring would literally nauseate me, and then I suffered far more than I can say. On these nights my repugnance sometimes became so corporeal that my pencil would break in my gnarled fingers, and the drivel from my mouth would make the print run in every direction. More than once I fled my cubicle, sprinting toward the Hudson for a faceful of chilling mist or rampaging some boutique until forced to buy panties and get out. When my mania was at its most virulent, I took to lapping the island, striding north as far as Morningside Heights, across the park to First Av, and then south again through the East Village and home. Or I would succumb to a xenophobia so fierce that merely to brush a shoulder on the subway made me whimper. But whether this ordeal was some ultimately redemptive labor, my divinely appointed penance, or was merely a compounding of the same murderous desire, I'm still unable to tell. All I know is that as the days passed and I forced my depleted wits to continue fabricating, I saw another life taking shape before me, a being unlike any to which I'd ever given thought until now.

I do not know from where this new experience came. Of course, I began with the same twenty-six elements from which everything is made, and I assembled them according to the system of human reproduction. But whereas my former creation had been amassed from pap and twaddle, this second experience seemed to spring directly from my accomodations. When four years earlier I'd discovered my past was another's and hit on the idea of fabricating myself, I'd known I wasn't prepared. I'd set out to discover my native culture, struggling to absorb whatever my countrymen had to offer and to suppress my innate revulsion. And I'd succeeded, for along with my culture's folderol I'd absorbed a fate that, left to my own devices, I could never have conceived. I mean, *monsters*, for God's sake! However, as soon as I tried to imagine my life's sequel, this alien fate seemed to comprehend me in some new sense. The phrases materializing on my page now came from nowhere, from the engulfing silence, from sheer emptiness, as though the great poet's blindness, here in the darkness of my cubicle, had encompassed me absolutely.

141

Every morning I would clamber up from my filthy mattress, sleep befouling my brain, and before I could ascend my milk crate, the words of my amorphous life would already be forming. Their breathy plosives seemed no less alien to me than the death-stars, gremlins, and body-snatching I'd endured in Boston years before, and although they sounded unlike the garbled morphemes with which, on that Georgia mountainside, my creation had besplattered me, in New York the distant monstrosities appeared akin. I began to regard my new life as precisely what, when it addressed me, my botched life had demanded. These words now were what those words intended! Don't dream I know what I'm talking about, but it seemed as though that first experience were somehow dictating this second, were prescribing all that would henceforth be mine to say. The more often this mad thought came to me, the more convinced I was that it must be so. My new life was being shaped by my earlier, was materializing out of that same accursed begetting. I began to observe how, as my still unformed experience became recognizable, my former experience receded into obscurity. I felt—or imagined feeling—each new page drawing its force from that dwindling chaos. And as I covered every surface lying before me and my absorption in work became total, I began to think that the sole point of my writing now was to forget that writing before.

Perhaps it was this growing sense of being narrated that finally compelled me one day to seek out my book. I'd been wandering Greenwich Av, hoping to escape the deluge of images or possibly just enjoying the unseasonable warmth, when I happened on a disheveled bookshop and, without pausing to think, turned in. The abruptness of this swerve both thrilled and alarmed me, and I seemed to watch my own body, as if from a security monitor, guiding me infallibly toward the shelves of fiction. I hesitated once, unsure whether to seek my life among the new books or to locate myself somewhere in the literature further back, but recalling how two years in the book trade amounted to an epoch, I immediately headed toward the enduring shelves. How can I express my shock when, fingering each of the alphabetical spines, I suddenly discovered myself holding, not my own life, but Aunt Gertrude's three. I backed up, sung the alphabet song, started scanning for displaced names. But no, I hadn't overlooked it. Where I'd expected to find myself, I found her.

How could the experience I'd amassed so painstakingly, at such cost to my domestic affections, for which I'd even sacrificed my education—how had this experience been lost? My head started to spin. That the being I'd rescued from indifference could so quickly succumb! And then, for the first time, I saw the magnitude of my aberration. These sentences coming from nowhere now weren't fashioning a sequel. No, my sequel was just the beginning. There'd be no end of my reproductive slavery, of the whoring required of me. In the mountains my creation had lied. This new life wasn't a conclusion. The sequel was my replacement.

Chapter XIX

THROUGHOUT MARK'S and my travels I had never strayed far from my precursor's tale, always concealing it in the baggage I carried with me everywhere, and some nights now when I was too tired to work, I would become enthralled in its pages once again, hoping this time to remark some stray phrase or figure that disclosed a way out. It had not escaped me, even on first reading her words in Georgia, that her creation had also attempted a second life, that the violence of her story had at just that point turned on itself. Whenever I reflected on this passage, it seemed that, if only I could consummate the work she'd aborted, perhaps I could avoid her fate. Exiting my precursor's history might inaugurate my own. But I also felt, even before leaving home, that there was some sense in which this escape was already closed off to me. I often looked around my loft now and imagined I saw the material replica of my captivation. The trash heaping up in the darkness, the airy pestilence I breathed, my slinking and bestial solitude. Did I call this a life? If only there were some way to have my experience and imagine it too! But such longings only returned me to the problem of my precursor, the problem of man's origin, and then it seemed that nothing short of its solution could ever set me free.

Well, months passed and my loft became freezing, and the plastic hamburgers I devoured lost their taste, and I grew haggard and verminous, but still I labored on. For the first time I can remember, I started to suffer paralyzing spasms of homesickness, waking in the black of night to wonder about dear Mark or to imagine—oh, with what insane vividness!—Teeny Love's warm skin next to mine. Why I never phoned remains mysterious. I developed a horrific cough that would explode in my chest and knock me off my crate. Day and night ran together. My clothes developed an unprepossessing droop. And all the while the pages kept amassing on my desk, as though some vampire were sucking them out of me. I will never be able to explain how I kept working under such conditions. I held out no hope of change now, no thought that anything to come of this gloomy servitude could ever be other than it was. On the contrary, I saw that my boyhood experiences in Selma had actually been, unbeknownst to my innocence, another's invention, and that the experience I then fabricated in Boston had turned out, there in the north Georgia woods, to be another's too, so that it seemed plausible—no, more than plausible, virtually certain—that this new experience in Manhattan was also another's, perhaps engendered for me before my birth, forming the next episode in that banal narrative I'd surely recognize if only I were narrating. If, despite all, I kept going, it was because making a life had become second nature to me. I could imagine no third.

Then one night something happened. It was late, and I'd been working for countless hours, the pages engulfing my desk and the light scalding my eyes. All at once I looked up and, to my astonishment, saw a woman standing in the shadows. Her auburn dreadlocks spilled over her bare and swollen breasts, and her plum colored nipples protruded lasciviously. I cannot recount my storm of feelings. The surface of her bronze skin seemed to be absorbing the lamplight, pouring its amber warmth back onto my face and filling my skull with a glutinous ichor, and in this tantalizing glow I could just make out the dusky fur of round loins. Needless to say, this vision drove me mad. My pencil sped on, tearing through page after page, as she continued to materialize out of the obscurity, transforming my surroundings. The miasma I'd breathed for months started to crackle with electricity. A scintillating heat ignited every surface. I felt her wet lips touching my ear, heard her husky voice breathing into me. Was it my name, Frank Stein, she called? Then all at once, this outpouring:

. . . *drunken bees in the honey suckle, beside our stoop, the explosion of azaleas, how we ran between willow fronds, past the pear, my frock flapping, rain splattered faces, the rivulet of blood where brambles had scratched me, air so dank you couldn't breathe. Wait, you gasped, wait here in the shade! Clutching my arm, trying to pull me onto beds of magnolia leaves. I heard them clucking,* glimpsed chrome glinting through the wisteria. I was the pony we rode at the fair, whinnying, cantankerous, wild in the green. I sloughed your fingers, frolicked unbroke, raced past the rusting fender, slipping on clay along the railroad tracks, giggles spilling from my mouth, galloped free, mane bouncing in the air. Stop, you wailed, wait! And my body slipping down the muddy bank, shrieking laughs, kicking up my hooves, then you were suddenly on top of me, flopping fishlike and mud-covered too, your brow creased, mouth intent, trying to hush me with chubby fingers, hard kisses, impetuous boy things, until I let you ride, showed you how, the softness, my mouth. After some minutes they started calling, Chillun! Y'all come back! Shhhh, I whispered. Do you remember? You were so moody and already fidgeting. Any instant words would begin, cover us with sin. How far away their voices sounded! Lying silent on the earth, knowing I didn't know what, but full of my secret, grave now and happy, I placed my hand on your hand, pillowed my hair on your boy chest, wishing only for quiet, my horse body sprawled in the sun, time dead, never again to trouble your heart. Shhhh, I whispered. Or later in my room, the moonless dark, our ears attuned to the others' steps, swaddled in night, your fingers stiff on me, our sweat. Slowly, I thought, slowly, dreaming you were weightless, our skulls melted, pouring my darkness out, warm contagion, your fever becoming mine. Oh, you were terrible! That dumb thing inside, your brute, to feel you struggle so, convulsed there in blood, needing to swallow me. I wanted to say yes, bare my throat. Your boyhair bristling. But you stifled my face with pillows. It would crawl out, I knew, the beast shaking you like a rag. How you despised us, shame smothered. Burst, I thought. Explode! But once slaked, you were nothing, like anguish left no room. I lay there nipples burning, listening to you breathe, each gasp, knowing you'd drowned, the blackness itself my nervous pet, rubbing its muzzle against us. Do you remember? Or after graduation, moon shadows in the boathouse, how I held you in my hand, the crying, your moan, tears mingled with the nectar you spilled, its soft patter breaking the black surface of the lake. We were both watching me, so awful, the shudders I birthed. Your gown hissed under us, wetness covering my face, neck. Hey, they called, where'd you go? Forgotten universe. Oh, I prayed they'd come that night, find you helpless, lights shining, my fingers in your hair. I wiped your nose with taffeta, smeared myself, half-mad with damp air, the mushroom effluvia, rot. If only you could've lain there intact, blank, water lapping, whole as my moisture was whole, let me stroke you. I would've suckled your nothingness these lifetimes and, throat clogged, mouthed your every gasp. Just once, in broad daylight, unflinching, full on the lips, for all to see. But they never found us. We snuck in through the kitchen,

careful to mop up our prints with the dishtowel, my ache abandoned
as always on the stairs. Or in the car beside an overlook, your face
between my breasts, pleading, the hum of violas on the stereo, or in
summer under the eaves before the others stirred, dawn fresh as
breath, the gleaming treetops, or behind the garden house, ivy
swaddled, your breath convulsing us, bodies depleted, on the wet
stones. Can you remember anything? But whenever your pounding
slowed, that fist hidden in your chest, wherever I lay listening, still
with happiness, how utterly you were lost, this now, this sweet earth.
I would've followed if I could, wherever, even into absence, my
annihilation, or so I dreamed. That string of murmurs, voices
entwined, each yarn entangling fingers, musk, lips, hair—there
seemed no unraveling. Oh, I was drunk! For years I said, yes, this
too, this is a part of it, brooked the absence, your flight, a hollow
where you'd lain. I believed, being light, what you said couldn't
matter, slid your frightened hand beneath my skirt, filled me with
your cramped fingers, eyes on your eyes, the wetness engulfing us,
or your sex in my throat, the pulse and spunky fume. Even now it
seems this destroying life, my milk, hysterium, this rage that wipes
me clean—I'll shriek!—it might sweep you away, pour us both out,
spilling mouths, faces, breasts, legs, the vortex, stirring your noisy
oblivion, your ethereal waste, all with my wild tongue . . . .

147

On and on and on. Never a pause. I thought I'd suffocate.
I have no idea whether this presence, this *she*, remained for
hours or vanished immediately, whether I scribbled throughout
the night or spewed whole volumes in an instant. Maybe she
was some flesh and blood former tenant returned for her
belongings or some local succubus, one of the buxom
phantasms I'd observed haunting the sidewalk at night.
Explanations come to an end somewhere. But despite my
outpouring, which must strike you here and now, my fanatical
young scribe, as impossibly spontaneous, beside yourself as
you seem to be with striking every letter, almost as though
you imagined I too, in those uncomputerized days, had been
beside myself, stroking her wondrous corpus with some
invisible keyboard of my own—hah!—despite all this, I recall
no words. All I remember is my delirium, the thrill of her
nearness, my ache to enter into it. The sensation was as
unfamiliar to me as my birth.

At some point I must've lost my balance, for next I
remember I was lying prostrate on the floor, my head
throbbing, desk overturned, and pages scattered over my
abode. Sunlight edged across the wall. Taxi horns came

through the window. I immediately scrambled to my feet and began gathering up my sentences, frantic to reassemble the being who'd transported me, but as I scanned the present derangement, the pages that had violently uplifted me the night before seemed inexplicably flat. I stared in dumb confusion. A deathlike odor arose from my bedclothes. My bowels groaned. It seemed incomprehensible that these scrawls in my hand could be her sole remains. How infinitely more had been that inspiration herself, those lips, tongue, teeth, breath, hair. Even if intangible in daylight, or even if just my imagination, her experience in that instant had so utterly eclipsed these ciphers now that I could see in the two only a parody of resemblance. Rage welled up in me. Why would any creator not completely out of his senses stand for it? And yielding to impulse, I flung my pages across the room.

It was then that, as I watched my work flutter earthwards, my thoughts turned—such is the randomness of mental association—to Liza. As if she and that dark succulence could have had other than sex in common! And yet just this pairing struck me now as of the essence. Although possessing none of that inexpressible other's allure, Liza's memory somehow rendered my writing's disappointments immaterial. My cousin represented home, family, steadfastness, everything my sentences had left out. How had I strayed so erratically, abandoned all that from my very first words had gone without saying? It seemed some crazy, incomprehensible mistake. And then for the first time in years, for the first time since the great poet's vision had blinded me, I realized I could stop. My pencil rattled to the floor. I looked around. I saw how pitiful were my surroundings, recalled my father's mansion, my mother's dying wish. The world abruptly righted. The solution to the problem of life's creation, the problem of my own experience, was staring me in the face. Why was I doing this?

My mind started to race. Nothing compelled me, I recognized, to write another sentence as long as I lived. I'd possessed the foresight to remove my face and name from my book, so that aside from Gloria and the crackpot—hardly more than voices on a phone!—no one could now connect me with the author. That life wasn't my life, or if in some purely abstract sense it might still be called mine, no one could know that but me. Of course, I'd be abandoning my promise, repudiating

148

what, from the time I first heard my own words speak, my creation had seemed to demand, but its demands were starting to seem endless. Besides, I reasoned, what assurance was there that, even if I pursued my new object, this tantalizing presence, to her inevitable conclusion, my book could then be forgotten? The being she'd replaced might still come back to haunt me, a possibility I'd no sooner entertained than realized was certain. No, this woman was one more reproduction. Why keep fantasizing? The time had come to be realistic.

While lapping Manhattan I'd noticed several large dumpsters beside a warehouse fronting the Hudson, and these now presented themselves to me as a perfect place to dispose of my ambitions forever. They would be easily accessible under cover of darkness, and I calculated that their vast girth would accommodate all I'd tried to make of myself, burying my unfinished life in garbage in no time. Never again would I feel compelled to smother my natural affections, to squander years in profitless imagining. Hadn't my forebears prepared a future for me? How had I been so arrogant as to refuse advantages the rest of the world was literally dying to have? No, I'd live, I thought. Live. And all at once, as if by enchantment, every thought of language vanished from my consciousness, leaving my mind a perfect blank.

I spent the remainder of the morning preparing to abandon my squalid habitation, donating my mattress to a homeless shelter and making an evil-smelling urchin a present of my milk crate, and then in the afternoon I started stuffing my writing into two hefty trash bags I'd purchased at a bodega. This proved difficult. Despite the unreality of my experience, its description had by now amounted to several thousand sheets. I'd been nothing if not prolific, dreaming my effusiveness meant my words were genuinely mine, and faced now with the task of their removal, this fecundity posed a sizeable problem. I had no vehicle, no wheelbarrow or handtruck, and for reasons I still cannot explain, I felt maniacal to remain unobserved. I began considering ways to make my own form into a crude means of conveyance, an expedient I recalled from photos of primitive tribesmen in *National Geographic*. After several attempts, I managed to fashion a sort of sling by knotting my trashbags together at two corners, placing my head between the knots, and suspending their weight from my shoulders, one bag against my stomach, the other resting on my back. I felt an affinity with elephants standing on their hindlegs.

Thus balanced, I lumbered forth around 2:00 a.m. Traversing the twenty-some blocks to my destination was no small achievement, especially given my caution to inspire no curiosity. I frequently had to conceal my rotundity in darkened doorways or alleys, and once as I crossed an intersection, a speeding taxi forced me to flee for my life. The driver's derision seemed most uncivil. However, despite my exhaustion and strained wits, I finally managed to arrive at the dumpsters where, hidden in their shadows, I was able to doff my burden. Everything was just as I'd anticipated. The latch lifted effortlessly, and the rubbish already inside barely covered the container's capacious bottom. In a day or two, all the unimagined possibilities that had tormented me for so long—ever since Dr. Z—'s first lecture, or even earlier, since my reading of Heidegger's philosophy, or perhaps as far distant as my egalitarian childhood, if not before I was born—all this would become irrecoverable. Mustering my strength, I took a breath, hefted the pages I'd stomached, and emptied them into the opening. I did the same with the pages I carried on my back, tossing in both trashbags afterwards and waiting in the darkness for the sloshing sounds to stop. Then I shut the gate. No sooner had the latch clanged than I felt unimaginably lighter, almost buoyant, as though the weight of a lifetime had been taken from my shoulders and I were bobbing to the surface. I could marry Liza, honor my father, do good. *This* would be my creation. I'm free, free! I shouted. Thank God almighty, I'm free at last!

A glare lit up the warehouse. From every side sirens screamed. I heard loudspeakers, doors slamming, saw the glistening of a gun barrel. Down! Down! someone bellowed. There wasn't time to think. I lowered myself to my knees, toppled onto the tarmac. I felt boots, elbows, fists crushing me. There were so many people shouting so many instructions I had no idea what to do. I lay there. My wrists were snapped into metal cuffs, my trouser pockets rummaged. When the manhandling subsided, I saw a pair of shoes stride up to my nose.

Stand up, the shoes said.

I did my best to flop over but was abruptly seized by the collar and hauled to my feet.

150

No I.D., no money, no wallet . . . .

You gonna tell us, Jack?

I looked around at the faces. Backlit by the glare, the wearer of the shoes had a head like a ham hock and wore a dark suit.

Am I trespassing?

Notebook paper! I heard someone call from the dumpster. A *whole lot* of notebook paper!

It's 3:00 a.m. You could make sooo many friends here. C'mon, what you been up to, Jack?

Own experience, I stammered. Isn't it a free country?

There was an outburst of guffaws.

Comedians, they're all comedians! The ham hock gave out a long sigh. Okay, box him up.

Chapter XX

THE EXPERIENCE I must now relate is so horrific, so replete with senseless misery, that all my bodily resources are required simply to undertake it. In the more than twenty years since those ghastly events, I've never once repeated the forthcoming to anybody, and if not for some mysterious compulsion now, some feckless urge to redeem my past by reliving it for you, I would without a doubt never dream of such a thing. In truth, convinced as I am that no good can come of repeating, or none but what never needed repeating in the first place, I don't know why in all rationality I persist. Certainly not because of the relief it affords me, to say nothing of pleasure, as if divulging the futility of my life—*my life!*—could be for me other than anguish. Were I to imagine that you, my youthful auditor, actually derived amusement from this history, I would turn its murderous violence on myself and expunge my torment forever. No, the violence of which I now acknowledge myself the author must appear so peculiar, so far-fetched, that no one as headstrong as yourself could dream he was implicated, let alone its origin. Thus secure, every new generation perpetuates it. Oh, how many times have I swooned at this infernal paradox, this diabolical ingenuity, that my doom replicates— endlessly! infallibly! over and over!—precisely by seeming mine alone. Wasn't this the very paradox I discovered in my precursor's book? And to think I once called fate a superstition.

I stray.

My abductors took me to a windowless cubicle containing a single chair. I was told to sit. On the upper portion of one wall was a large mirror, through which I supposed they gawked at me, and overhead a fluorescent tube. Otherwise my container was wholly bare. I remained seated there for a period I could in no way determine, sealed as I was within that perfect noiselessness. Later my captors indicated, perhaps to mislead me, that a significant time had passed, but whether my captivity lasted the length of a thought, a lifetime, or whether I perhaps remain in that box still, I have only my chaotic memory for witness. Regardless, my wits began to recover during this interim, and having begun to order my confused perceptions somewhat, I soon decided I must've stumbled into an official investigation. Through what coincidence or confusion of identities this had occurred, I could only speculate, but being an attorney's son, I knew the chicanery typical of law enforcement, and so concluded that the words on my abductors' uniforms should be taken at face value. The police, I realized, had been waiting for me. Why, I had no idea. The specter of my broken promise passed before my consciousness, but imagining myself sane during those days, I dismissed it. Even allowing for my creation's exorbitant demands, my present captivity made no sense. Or so I reasoned. What seemed undeniable, however, was that my deranged sequel was now in the control of the law. How this might alter my outcome, I couldn't tell. Would my precursor speak to others as she had to me? And if so, what sort of evidence would her speaking provide? But that my fantasies could lead to imprisonment—this possibility now loomed.

153

Eventually, the ham-faced shoes entered, accompanied by two trolls. I instinctively rose, exciting the trolls, who reached for their batons.

Sit, the ham said.

I did so.

The trolls positioned themselves on either side of the door, and for several minutes the ham hock looked down on me. I took little notice of this insolence, as I was still intent on reconstructing the sequence of events that would account for my predicament, but in time the man's condescension became annoying. I began to consider him. His face was wrinkled at the butt end by worry lines, as though someone had stitched his casing too tight, and beneath his brow's pink folds two small black pupils glared out from the meat. Even in my present depletion, I wasn't accustomed to being treated as a defenseless reprobate, and I was on the verge of making some retort when my tormentor spoke. What he said could not have astounded me more had he stove in my face with a mallet.

Does the name Mark Stanford mean anything to you?

Mark! Mark! I cried, literally leaping from my chair.

The trolls advanced lathering, but my interlocutor restrained them. His pupils fixed me with renewed intensity.

I knew I could depend on my faithful counterpart! I said. Let me see him.

My questioner now wore a queer expression, and as my speaking trailed off, I was surprised to see him turn and, without a word, exit the room. He was gone for what seemed several minutes, leaving me to contemplate the trolls. When he returned, all he brought was a chair.

He began to speak: There's been a crime.

I showed no immediate reaction to this, thinking crime in New York must be like mosquitoes in Miami. However, something in the way the man hunched forward in his chair, or perhaps his imperturbable demeanor, made me start to fear that it was of this particular crime I was accused.

Do I need a lawyer?

The ham reached over and patted me on the knee. Relax, Jack. We know you're not the guy. I mean, no telling how you ended up at that dumpster. Crazy things sure happen! Take me, twenty years on the force and they stick me on this graveyard shift. Does that make sense? Or kids these days. I got two. One goes to Nam, the other's a priest. I love'em both, but can I get them to speak to each other? Like I say, crazy. And don't get me started on my ex. Christ! Anyway, I was hoping you'd be him. Gonna wrap this one up in a jiffy, y'know, but . . . well, cigarette?

I shook my head.

So tell me about yourself. Been in the city long? Don't mind my saying, Jack, you look a wreck. Where's home? That's no Brooklyn twang, heh? You a artist or something?

I write, I said. It's a long story.

Really? Like books I'd know? I mean, you probably think I'm just a flatfoot, but I read. What was that one about the Nazi who was spying for our side then gets nabbed by the Israelis and nobody knows he was undercover? That was good, wow! You're gonna laugh, but I got this idea. There's this ordinary guy, see—me, you, anybody. He one day wanders into some mess, drugs, the mob, point shaving, but just blind luck, y'know, and here's the main thing, trying to get out gets him in deeper. That's the idea. Like he can't see what he's inside of, so fights the good guys, makes trouble where it ain't.

I call it *The Fly Bottle.*

When do I get to see my friend? I asked.

He looked at his watch. No hard feelings, I hope?

I said nothing.

Whoops, there they are now!

He exited, then returned almost immediately.

All I was gonna say is, before I turn you loose, maybe you'd look at this stiff I got?

He blushed.

I mean, a body down at the morgue. It's just a stab in the dark, but you being a writer I figured . . . well, your buddy's gonna meet us.

Although I was not so gullible as to dream my abductor could be trusted, I remained impressed at his having known Mark and so thought it best to play along. They led me through blinding daylight, still manacled, and placed me in a van with the trolls on either side. I noticed with some satisfaction that ham-face, whose name I now learned was Lieutenant, seemed to be treating me with respect, impressed, I assumed, by my obvious education. We rode in silence, broken only by polite offers of pistachios from the troll on my left. When we reached the morgue I was taken into a cubicle indistinguishable from the cubicle I'd left, seated before myself in the mirror, and told that certain unlikely coincidences—apparently my dumpster figured in the crime—had made the authorities hopeful I might know something. Lieutenant then asked if I'd ever seen a body before.

My mother's, I answered.

Eeew.

She was dead.

Still, it's a shock.

But afterwards you'll take me to Mark Stanford?

Presently, he replied. At which word the mirror vanished, replaced by a dividing transparency, through which I could see a cadaver prone on a cart. I stared at its blotched skin, grotesquely punctured torso, ravaged throat, trying to awaken memories of some shopkeeper, convenience store clerk, or a passing face from the street. Imagine my horror, when surveying this livid flesh I recognized the beloved features of my boyhood friend!

Oh God! I cried out. Not again! And reeling backwards, I fell into a conniption that lasted for several weeks. Afterwards I learned that I had raved. I lambasted professors A— and

155

Z—, mocked my genius and pretensions. I bemoaned my father's lost Willy, blamed my detachment, called myself the enemy of my flesh and blood, the betrayer of my intended. Countless times I confessed to Teeny's murder. One of my attendants said that I harped on my own end so incessantly, that he never thought I'd survive. When my bedclothes were changed, I shrieked at the orderlies. I swore to be revenged on every nurse who ever spoke to me, threatening to abolish words forever. But my most humiliating recollection, second hand though it necessarily remains, was of the diatribes in which I castigated Selma. Oh, the ignominy! If my father had heard, his noble old heart would have burst. Only my pledge of perfect frankness now could compel me to regurgitate it.

I railed at democracy, reviled the Bill of Rights, said children should just do as they were told. I called Martin a rabble-rouser, Aunt Cora a seriously plugged-up bitch. I longed for the good old days. Nor did I stop short of rhapsodizing slavery itself, lauding the mindlessness of being enthralled, of feeling there's nothing—*absolutely nothing*—you can do! Oh, I reveled in my execrations, shouted: Buckwheat! Rastus! Spear chucker! Sambo! Jigaboo! Flossy! Tambo! Uncle! It was as though some monster had invaded me. My shame is unspeakable. Well, many of those who cared for me were black, and overhearing my vitriol and having, of course, noted my accent, they started calling me Ol' Mars, rolling their eyes whenever my invectives resumed and echoing each outburst with, Dass right Boss, or Yassuh white folks, or Oh no Massa. Before long the entire hospital staff had picked it up, creating a raucous atmosphere unsuitable for healing. I was moved to an isolated corridor, placed under continuous supervision—as much for my safety as for threat of escape— thus rendering my racist disturbances a thing of the past. However, my memory remained, and until the day of my release, my name need only be pronounced at the nurse's station for a spontaneous cacophony of hoots, catcalls, and shuffling to ensue.

Enough.

I remained thus alienated for two months. When at last I returned to myself I was in a cubicle exactly like my former cubicle, except that now a single bed had replaced the chair. The fluorescent tube overhead appeared unchanged, just as the wall mirror and my reflection in it. However, any time

Mark's ravaged form appeared before me, I hoped my present container remained the same in truth, that my friend's image was but last evening's nightmare, and that I was just now waking to my former imprisonment. But no sooner would this happy prospect take shape than I sensed these walls were lighter, my present confines narrower, and then I knew I'd never see my erstwhile Mark again. At which I would succumb to a despair so abysmal that, by contrast, the return of my bigoted conniptions seemed a blessed reprieve.

No one who had dealings with me during this period offered the least sympathy or even conversation, since my ravings had made enemies of all, but as I grew more lucid, I heard my keepers making gleeful references to a *trial*, and so began to harden myself in anticipation of inquisitors. Therefore, I was not abashed when my door opened one day and Lieutenant entered. He seated himself on a stool he carried and, in an infuriatingly matter-of-fact tone, started recounting the previous months. He narrated my departure from home, my ordeal in Soho, my alienation from loved ones, and my mad longing for her whom he did not name. He made reference to my family's tragedy, my precursor's plot, my father's exalted position. Although his omissions were so telling that, despite his words' uncanny accuracy, I felt sure he could have little idea what he said, Lieutenant seemed astoundingly privy to my secrets. He even appeared familiar with my life, the being I'd contrived from my culture's tripe, which he quaintly called my *fiction*. It was as though he'd observed everything from within, grasped the very form of my consciousness, and now lacked only some facts. How he'd gained this privileged access utterly bewildered me. More important for my release, however, he now seemed to take the view of Mark's murder that I took myself.

I'm telling you, Jack, the hardest bite to swallow—I'm saying it's even hard for me, and I know it's true! The hardest is that dumpster. I mean, here your buddy gets whacked—my condolences—your buddy you last saw...I'm guessing four, six months? Murdering scum stuffs him in a trash bin, our guys find him next afternoon, and not ten hours later—not ten hours!—you show up same place. Now, you say it's a coincidence, and I'm probably believing you—what's my choice? You been acting such a nutbag, I got a dozen witnesses say they saw you every hour of the week. But in my experience,

157

murder adds up.

Having been deceived once before, I knew better than to welcome Lieutenant's overture, but I couldn't help feeling amazed at his knowledge of my sufferings, as well as his sensitivity to matters I'd never confided before. So I demanded an explanation.

I read your book, he replied.

I cannot express my horror. My pseudonym, my suppressed photo, my fake bio—all had failed, and author and creation had now been identified.

He's an impostor, I cried out. Don't trust a word!

Lieutenant regarded me queerly. *He*? Wow, I'm dumber than I thought. I figured she was a girl.

Only then did I recognize my mistake. Oh, you mean the dumpster! My . . . my writing! Why, that . . . I mean, it's nothing.

Nothing? You know how many pages we found?

Well, I don't mean nothing literally, of course.

And Jack, don't take this wrong, okay? But you're a seriously horny guy.

I have visitors, I said. At night.

Suddenly, he leaned forward, his pupils glaring at me from beneath his brow: C'mon, Jack, what's your story?

I started to babble. I don't know, I don't know! This promise, my genius. Only it wasn't mine, or not yet. But I made something, then, presto, my genius turns into a monster. Just like that! One moment there's me, the next him!

He pulled a note pad from his pocket, shook his head, started reading: Okay, Frank Stein from Atlanta, mother dead, father same name, two brothers, one murdered . . . .

He continued reciting facts while I listened in silence, strangely relieved by my reduction to data. Then when he'd finished, he folded his stool.

People say life's complicated, he said, but a guy does what I do long enough, he *wishes* life was complicated. But you! Family's got money, you dress like a bum. You go to Harvard, you're unemployed. There's a girl, you live alone. You join your friend, you ditch him. You write a book, you trash it. We're talking major issues here! What's the matter, Jack, world not good enough for you?

He continued to fix me with his stare, almost as if expecting an answer. We remained like that for several seconds, my mind a perfect blank. Then, as I opened my mouth to say exactly what I'll never know, my cell door burst open, and a titanic figure rushed in, sweeping me up in its powerful embrace. Oh, Frank, Frank! My father moaned. I thought I'd lost you too!

As I soon learned, not three hours after receiving Lieutenant's phone call, my father had arrived in New York and begun arranging my release. Many questions remained, specifically concerning Mark's and my whereabouts over the past months, and before regaining my freedom, I would have to give a full accounting of all I knew, but I was no longer suspected of murder, or not by the authorities. Of course, there remained the truly dazzling coincidence that my dear friend's death and my recovery from writing had apparently occurred on the same night, to say nothing of his remains and my sequel being deposited in the same container, facts that astonished me far more than my accusers, and like Lieutenant, I couldn't help but wonder if something more than happenstance, some underlying sequence or invisible necessity had precipitated these alignments. Anyway, I provided the police with the details of Mark's and my ramblings, recounted how we'd parted in October and supplied the address of my Harvard classmate's condo, which I still remembered. However, when the authorities went to question my former chum they discovered his condominium was now occupied by a retired rock promoter, who claimed never to have heard of him. Even more unsettling, the ethics firm for which my classmate had worked turned out to be nothing but a phone number and P.O. box, both of which had been canceled weeks before Mark's ghastly end. Fortunately for me, the doorman at my classmate's building recognized Mark from a photo, and other tenants said they'd seen him with my classmate often, so no one suspected me of hallucinating. Apparently, their partying had been notorious. But the witnesses' fragmentary recollections only made me crazier. I was strangling on feckless rage, drowning in remorse, and whenever the image of my friend's ravished body returned, I feared I'd lose my mind.

Although I took little note of my father's legal maneuverings throughout this period, the charges against me were soon dropped and my release effected. Perhaps you think walking from that lightless box into a sunlit world would've uplifted my spirits and made me newly mindful of life's

159

preciousness, but my experience was quite the opposite. I was released at night, and when I walked into the outer darkness, a condition different only in its distracting glare and frenetic movements from the void of my cell, I felt that I had carried blackness with me, was now obscuring the whole world. I seemed at no point capable of leaving my past behind. On the contrary, my involvement in the deaths of three I adored seemed always before me, and despite my vagueness about how I'd been responsible, I knew their present absence could not have occurred without my ruthless abstraction. I kept wondering from where I'd gotten the idea that my own experience could be otherwise, that what was happening before my eyes could be a ruse. My memory of the poet's blindness returned, but now with its meaning reversed. I seemed to see clearly that nothing made of words, regardless how perfect, could be an experience. How I'd ever imagined differently, I couldn't imagine. That my insubstantial life should continue, while others who'd savored every minute were now gone, this seemed, of all my precursor's ironies, the most absurd.

160   Only one prospect still aroused any vital passion in me: to return south, marry Liza, and do my utmost to protect her from the violence I'd inspired. I couldn't say precisely how I would manage this, since I remained baffled how my loved ones' happiness had been jeopardized originally, or could be still, especially now that my involvement with books was over, but I promised to discover my own role in the earlier tragedies and never to repeat them. Perhaps, I reasoned, if I remained attentive to Liza's every whim and doted on my family constantly and gave myself without thought to the countless distractions of domestic comfort, in time I'd learn to shield everyone from the fate that, impossible as it seemed, had come to preoccupy me. Ah, if I'd known then what I know now, could I have saved them? At times it has seemed so, and then striking my skull, I've shouted: Fool! Fool! But I've also feared it was precisely this hope, this dream of saving knowledge, that had doomed us all irreversibly, and then I've known my life could repeat a thousand times, and at every fateful juncture, I would choose the same.

Chapter XXI

BEFORE RETURNING home to Liza and Earnest, my father wanted to visit a couple of White House aides he hadn't seen all year, so instead of flying to Atlanta after my release, we made a stopover in Washington. I declined to join their dinner party, feeling strangely indifferent to the president's reelection strategy, and chose instead to ramble in Georgetown, where I sensed my faithful Mark's absence at every turn. It seemed as though the colonial replicas had lost all their depth and solidity, and I was floating free, drifting over earth's surface with no tangible connection. Some bond that had always seemed unbreakable to me, a binding so constant that I'd never once felt bound by it, now that I was at last free, had started to feel like an immense privilege. For some reason I can't explain, or not without a second narrative as long as this one, making my explanations endless, a proliferation of stories within stories, none of which would ever reach a conclusion—for some vague reason I found myself wanting to speak of *rights*. I wanted to say I had no *right* to be here, that by *rights* I shouldn't even be alive, that my heart continued pumping without *right*, etcetera. It was as though I remained sure I wasn't a ghost only so long as I never needed to make sure I wasn't a ghost, but the instant I needed to make sure, I became a ghost. Not that I was now sure. By what *right* could I speak of such things? No, it was more like my physical existence had become unsharable, something experienced only without me, and so, in being experienced, setting me apart. It was now this apartness that I ached to share, and since it was precisely this that others found most ghostly in me, both hardest to acknowledge and easiest to ignore, solitude seemed my natural condition. The word *metaphysical,* which I'd always taken to mean nothing at all, now struck me as *right.*

I don't recall whether it was later that evening or at breakfast the following morning, but some time before departing Washington my father noticed my moody reserve— I think I'd ignored an animated summons from the concierge— and suspecting I must be stinging from the humiliation of my arrest, he chided me for my hypersensitivity, implying I was acting like a snob. This is America, he reassured me. Everybody can go to jail!

But his efforts to dispel my morbidity proved futile.

𝕬𝖑𝖆𝖘, 𝕱𝖆𝖙𝖍𝖊𝖗, 𝖍𝖔𝖜 𝖑𝖎𝖙𝖙𝖑𝖊 𝖉𝖔 𝖞𝖔𝖚 𝖐𝖓𝖔𝖜 𝖒𝖊, I replied, a remark which could not but cause my father pain and which, even now, I have difficulty believing I said. I continued: Of late, nowhere has seemed more fitting to me than prison, and this latitude with which I presently meander seems more freedom's parody than freedom. Hah! From what conceivable prominence could I look down on someone else? Perhaps you'll call me mad, but I continually compare myself with our housekeeper, Teeny Love. How her expression haunts me! Weren't we both accused of murdering the innocence we loved? But Teeny's imprisonment was mortal, and now she's free, while mine continues with no known limit. You'll insist, of course, that this prison of mine is the most transparent of falsehoods, but eerie, guardless, it deforms me all the same. How many die without my knowing each day, how many starve through no action of mine? Don't tell me I'm exaggerating! When one's own history is being dictated, who can tell where responsibility lies?

As you will imagine, my father was alarmed by these sentiments, recognizing in them the tincture of anarchy, to say nothing of truth, and so he immediately started reasoning with me. He insisted that it was tyrannical egotism to represent myself as the perpetrator of catastrophes. I wasn't president, after all, and even if someday I were, there were issues of sovereignty, national independence. Why, blaming myself for Mark's tragedy was like taking responsibility for Nicaraguan death squads! The case of our former housekeeper was indeed pitiable, but someone had to pay for Willy's loss, and even if her trial wasn't a model of fairness, it was greatly superior to a lynching. The progress of civilization was slow. In short, my father pleaded with me to humor an old man, look to happier days, and stop calling myself a murderer.

Even if democracy's an illusion, Frank, I still think I know my own son!

Well, my father's distress was apparent, so I vowed to suppress myself and, in his enfeebled presence, assume a cheerful demeanor. I cannot believe such a paltry masquerade actually deceived anyone, since my gift for theater is weak, but so powerful is our human wish for oblivion that my father never expressed the least dissatisfaction with it. By the time we boarded our flight home we were acting as congenial as two strangers. I suppose such sustained insincerity must have reassured him, for after we'd remained aloft for some minutes, he took an envelope from his pocket and placed it in my hand.

My all-but-daughter asked me to make sure you read this before we arrived, he said, giving me a grave and confidential look. He then rose to visit the lavatory, leaving me with these slips of perfumed stationery that I will now unfold for you.

DEAR FRANK,

I hope as you read these words your horrid ordeal is over and you are speeding home to everybody who has always loved you like a sibling. Your long absence, during which we got no messages or calls and couldn't guess your whereabouts or even if you were safe, driving anybody who cared as deeply for you as Earnest or your father to get pretty upset sometimes, like despairing and feeling like they could cry or scream or pull their hair out, well, it's been hard. Anyway, I'm sure your father wouldn't have given you this to read if you weren't doing a lot better, so I think you're on the way home and not feeling so awful about what I know you're probably still feeling awful about, poor, poor, poor, poor Mark, who I'll never believe is really gone, since it wasn't two years ago he sat here telling me I was the only one not going to Harvard now, I mean, he could just show up any minute with that silly cowlick! But I won't dwell on what will still make me feel pretty awful and you too, I know, but will bring up something else that will probably make us both feel pretty awful but maybe now that you're reading this and I'm writing it, or vice versa, since I guess I'm writing it first, but still it's like you're reading it now too, or anyway sort of, I mean maybe me writing what you're reading now will somehow make us both feel better or something like that.

163

It's time to be frank. We've both known since childhood your saintly mother's dream for our union. I don't mean, of course, the labor movement but our tragically bigoted but fundamentally freedom-loving nation, the US, whose future she hoped would be hurried along, especially here in the old confederacy, by your and my *marriage*. There, it's written. I hope you won't think I'm being forward or out of place or something. Men think those things sometimes, I know, even now with feminism and all, which is so unfair, since guys can say whatever they feel like, while I'm just supposed to sit here and look pretty till hell freezes over or D.C. votes Republican or whatever it takes to make some guys speak up. You have no idea! Well, I think we both know how close we've always been. I've never made a secret of my fondness for you, the times we spent together growing up, the fun I had watching you and Teeny, or how much I looked up to you, almost like a brother, the way you could talk on and on about nothing. Why, just remembering makes my mouth drop open. Anyway, sometimes when two people grow up like that, I mean like almost sister and almost brother, they care a lot about each other, and hope always to stay good friends, and think what a great guy the other is, and always want the best for him and really hope someone will one day make you fabulously happy and everything, but well, that's all they really want, you know what I mean? I'm talking about not really wanting what two people who want to get married want, or sometimes what even two people who don't want to get married want. Or sometimes more than two people. So, what I'm asking is—is there someone else?

Because it's okay, *really okay*, if there is! Ever since you came back home last spring I've felt something between us was, well, missing. At first I thought it might just be my grief for poor William, then later Teeny's vicious hatred of our family. I mean, weren't we all shocked? I know I wasn't myself, jabbering on all the time about slasher films and poltergeists! I hope you don't think less of me. That is, I hope, if there's another, you think of her more than of me, but that, you know, when you do think of me you don't think less. Understand? Anyway, I started to worry the problem was that I'd changed, like I wasn't the seventeen year old you remembered but had matured, and maybe you were one of those guys who liked young girls and were disappointed, so I bought a whole new wardrobe, kilts and white blouses and mary janes, trying to look as innocent as you used to think I was. Why, the hours I spent reading to Earnest, just hoping you'd come along! But finally I realized it was no use, that what was missing wasn't just missing from me, that you were missing something too. I even wondered if you had like some *secret*, isn't that silly? Like I fantasized you'd gotten hurt and felt you couldn't confide in anyone and so kept your hurt hidden, and I hoped one day you'd show it to me, that no matter what you'd lost, together we'd make it back up somehow, but as time passed and you never noticed my outfits, except for that tube I was wearing on the swing behind your father's chalet, well, then I realized your secret was merely some other you loved more than me.

So, I'm writing to say what, now that you're reading it, you already know, at least as soon as I get to that part, that this letter is setting you free. There. Caring for you like an almost brother as I always have, I could never dream of coming between you and some other woman, or if maybe once or twice I dreamed of it, that doesn't really mean anything, and although I'd be lying to say that I do not still think of you sometimes, I mean in the way I used to when Teeny was around, the way people who want to marry sometimes think of each other, I'm starting to get over this. I've lately started to move in more liberal circles and to see the world as a bigger place than your family, and I feel hopeful now that in the very near future I'll be able to think of bunches of people the way I used to think only of you. And as for your saintly mother, if she'd ever thought her dream of our marriage might interfere with your happiness, she probably would have said a lot less about it. I feel almost sure of this. So, let's just admit that, despite our deep feelings for each other, feelings that I know I'll never stop feeling, our feelings are not the feelings of people who want to get married. I want you to go ahead and enjoy your little secret right out in the open, and I'll feel free to give myself to everybody I please with no fear of being disloyal to you. I feel so much better now. I hope you are the same.

What else? I sold my guitar. Maybe you guessed it from the unmusical way I'm writing this. I couldn't pluck a string without remembering us on the lawn, Mark with his publisher's catalogues, you with your nose in a dictionary, and me humming "Don't Think Twice, It's Alright". Well, some day I know such recollections will be a comfort, but for now I'm

165

listening to the classical station all the time and considering cello lessons. As for Earnest, his war-mongering continues unchanged, except that he's commander or admiral or knight or something of his ROTC unit, and despite your father's and my happiness for him, his opinions at dinner are really very upsetting. Oh yes, and shortly after you left we dismissed Carletta. She was always headstrong but recently she got to be unmanageable, almost what less enlightened people call uppity. Responsibility for sending her away fell sadly to me.

In closing, I hope that when you and I are reunited at last you will appreciate the selfless spirit in which I've written this, and am still writing it for that matter, so that when you finish reading there'll be no bad feelings toward each other but only good feelings, having understood your childhood playmate's sincere wish for your eternal happiness and for our always remaining the fondest of lifelong friends, hopes that will forever be cherished by

your almost sister,
L.

This impassioned and eye-wateringly fragrant missive somehow disturbed associations deep in my consciousness. I do not pretend to know the origin of such psychic upheavals, but having often meant more or less than I said, I was not utterly dumbfounded when, upon finishing Liza's heartfelt epistle, the following sentence spontaneously appeared in my mind: 𝕴 𝖜𝖎𝖑𝖑 𝖇𝖊 𝖜𝖎𝖙𝖍 𝖞𝖔𝖚 𝖔𝖓 𝖞𝖔𝖚𝖗 𝖜𝖊𝖉𝖉𝖎𝖓𝖌 𝖓𝖎𝖌𝖍𝖙! Although I had no idea whose meaning this could represent, I applied it without reflection to my cousin. A stranger seemed to be threatening to intrude on Liza's bliss. I rummaged my memory for the quotation's author, resolving to suppress this threat at once and thus eliminate any obstacle to my beloved's happiness, but before I could imagine the page on which I might've encountered such words, I was put in mind of my precursor. The sentence must be hers! If for one instant my cousin's tortured letter had raised doubts about our future together, this sentence banished those doubts completely. How my precursor's story could still be inventing mine, especially now that I'd given up on inventing forever, I had no earthly idea, but if even Liza's wedding night could be a thing of the past, then I knew I must be there too. I began to see my object more clearly. At that ultimate conjunction I would undergo a climax beyond all I'd known. My adversary would use her every art, but especially that of narrating, to separate me from my heart's desire, and I must rise to her challenge, resisting it with all the potency that was in me. If I prevailed, Liza would be my prize, but if in the end I met my maker, then my downfall would be total, setting her free. Either way, this present agony would cease.

Perusing a last time Liza's pungent words, I knew nothing short of absolute faithfulness could ever recompense them. My eyes were beginning to tear. Rather than wait until I looked into her face again, an encounter likely to confuse me, I took out a pencil and, yielding to her intoxications, composed my reply. My missive was full of the manly reassurances that any woman would expect from the boy she'd admired since infancy. I told her that my feelings had never once altered since childhood. Although I had experienced as an adult too much pain to dream pleasure could ever be mine, my painful experience had only inspired me to consecrate myself entirely to hers. My pleasure would be nothing. So, she need have no doubts on that count. Then I went on to address the portion of her missive that, unbeknownst to her, had come nearest my plight. Yes, I wrote, I do have a secret, or had one. It embodied my longing for freedom, but as with other longings, mine amounted only to what I made of it, and besides, it was history now. I'd never included another in my secret, but as the companion of my future, she must be the first. I didn't wish to disclose just yet all that in time would be plain, wishing selfishly to keep her mind empty of the enigmas still tormenting me. However, I concluded, please contain yourself a little longer, Dearest, knowing that on the morning following our wedding night, you will be satisfied.

I then concluded with chatty remarks about poor Mark's and my difficulties in Philadelphia digesting cheesesteaks, and when at last my father returned from the lavatory, I entrusted my letter to him. Liza met us at the airport, and I saw at once from her anxious demeanor that she was desperate to know my reaction. So, I did my utmost to insinuate by my look and tone of voice that all would eventually conform to her wishes. My father did not hesitate to execute my charge, plopping my missive into her palm, and no sooner had she read it than her

167

averted face, breathless silence, and heaving betrayed her joy. Of course, to save her further awkwardness, especially about that most unmaidenly of topics, our wedding night, I did not at the time discuss my eagerness to be married but instead proceeded to our waiting vehicle, knowing I'd have ample opportunity. However, I could not fail to reflect that her persistent efforts to protest against my exorbitant generosity exemplified just the kind of limitless concern for my well-being that I had always considered indispensable in a mate.

Over the next months Liza's self-effacing tranquility proved to be exactly the palliative I needed to dispel my gloom, and gradually I started to feel almost chipper. I woke each morning to a mysterious exhilaration, throwing on my clothes to rush downstairs in anticipation of glimpsing my beloved's face, neck, shoulders, and other womanly charms. Sometimes I would venture out to find her disheveled in a satin chemise, and the heedlessness of her manner at these times never failed, despite my melancholia, to arouse my dejection. We passed countless evenings in the company of friends, especially a klatch of musicians, journalists, and actors with whom Liza had recently become intimate. Many of these, I soon discovered, were experimenting with advanced ideas and sophisticated personal innovations, and I found their colorful conversation astounding. We purchased a dog and took afternoon strolls in the park with Monique, and in the evening we attended concerts. However, with a predictability I now find disquieting, all this innocent delight inevitably left me unguarded, so that when, surprised at the bounce in my own step, I would turn to the causes of my levity, all the memories of the last years would come crashing back: our Willy's strangulation, Teeny's framing, the anonymous erasure of Mark. At such times, I would immediately be riven, my body persisting robotically in its buoyancy, while my spirit plunged into a bleak depth exactly proportional to the heights I'd reached moments before. Instead of my former even-temper and unflappable calm, I now seemed to be myself only in extremes. Either I soared to forget, or plummeted to remember, but I could not long face the present without becoming abstracted. Already I knew my abandoned promise must be at fault.

My last hope, as willfully blind as I now realize it to have been, was that marriage might restore me. I dreamed that as domestic preoccupations suppressed my excitement over Liza, my passions would somehow congeal, forming an impermeable bulwark to consciousness. So, on the day when my father, in his usual gaseous manner, asked me was I prepared to solemnize my vow, I answered with all the headstrong fervor of a swain that, yes, I ached to consecrate my life and imagination solely to my beloved's happiness, even unto death.

There you go again! my father burst out. Death, death, death! Every other young blood in Atlanta manages to live as if he were immortal, while you can't seem to forget what's coming for two seconds. What's wrong with you, Son?

I immediately recognized my blunder, and recalling my decision in Washington to shield him, I concocted some nonsense about having, in my bridegroom's ecstasy, dreamed that what-I-would-be-careful-henceforth-never-to-mention-again might almost be pleasurable. Of course, what I couldn't have admitted to my father then, since I couldn't have admitted it to myself, was that my faith in my destiny had become absolute. I now felt my approaching climax in every muscle and organ, saw the futility of resistance. The only way of avoiding my end was by suffering it, and since it was precisely suffering I wished to avoid, even life and death amounted to the same.

As the period for Liza's and my marriage drew nearer, this rift in my equanimity became uncontrollable. I found myself attending dinner parties as though recalling them afterwards, toasting our future happiness while looking back. I seemed disappointed on every verge, repulsed before the plunge. Sometimes I wondered if I were turning into a movie. Watching myself occurred to me now with such uncanny ease, with such effortless transcendence. My face felt perpetually rigidified in its happiness, my every expression formed for some onlooker. I had only to envision in this way whatever was happening, and Liza's future husband transformed into an automaton, an empty figure animated by who could say what machinery. I watched his vacant expression donning dinner jackets, effusing with strangers. How perfectly he became the image of his father! And his other half seemed the image of perfection too. Whenever I pictured them together, I could not but marvel that my mother's vision was realizing itself indeed. My beloved's bronze flesh exuded just that

169

warmth that her beloved's pallor lacked. It was literally the reunion of our tragically sundered state. Or so it appeared from a distance. Up close, I could see nothing.

Was this movie really *Frank*? It felt mad to think so, but denial seemed no saner. My life wasn't simply happening! It was being produced! Anyway, as my single days dwindled, I followed the events in disbelief, as completely in the dark as any spectator, while in my absence the joyous preparations went on. Florists were commandeered, orchestras rehearsed. A rabbi was flown in from Israel to officiate, assisted by four of my father's SCLC confederates. There were plans for a catered brunch, afternoon barbecue on the lawn, and then celebratory dancing all night. However, to everyone's astonishment, Liza announced her preference for a civil ceremony attended by only a few hundred of our closest friends. My father was so delighted by her unpretentiousness, that he insisted on making up for our wedding's simplicity with a comparable splendor in our honeymoon arrangements. There would be a charter flight to Vermont, a chauffeured drive to a remote inn where a private feast would be waiting, and then my bride and I would retire to our suite to pass the first night of wedded bliss. I was initially somewhat uncomfortable with this return to New England, which would bring me so near the site of my original confusion, but I soon recognized that, since confronting my creation was now unavoidable, proximity to its origin could hardly heighten my fear.

170

In the meantime, I took steps to fortify myself. I packed a variety of potent liquors, took the precaution of obtaining a small quantity of contraband stimulant, and consulted a medical guide on aphrodisiacs. I was determined that no other would preoccupy my thoughts before that sublime conjunction, and if my precursor tried to estrange me from my beloved's dazzling form, she'd find her violence turned back on herself. This one night must be proof against all gloom. However, it did not escape me during these festive days that Liza sometimes appeared less deliriously happy than her bridegroom might've wished. On the morning of our ceremony, I happened on my intended in what seemed the most downcast of reveries, and fearing that she dwelt on my secret, I started to steal away unnoticed, knowing I must withhold a few more hours what she'd soon know well enough. And yet as the man to whom her happiness had been entrusted,

I couldn't just ignore my beloved's prostration, and so I approached, asking gently how anything, here on the threshold of our rapture, could still be askew.

Liza regarded me for what seemed an uncommonly long interval, then blurted: Oh, Frank, I just imagined everything so differently!

This startled me. I had never suspected Liza of harboring secrets, and the likelihood now of something unaccountable in my cousin, filled me with foreboding. Is this the first time? I asked. I know Mark and Willy meant the world to you, dear Liza, but now they're gone, surely you don't dream of some other?

If only, she replied. But no, I have no earthly idea what I'm missing. Maybe it's just hormones. I mean, think how many have nothing. But silly me, I can't stop asking: Is this *all*?

I let out a sigh. Well, if there's really nothing, my love, then maybe in time I can make it up. I mean, I know I'll never be my father, but . . . .

She brightened: Yes, yes, that's what I keep thinking too. If there's really no alternative, what's to prevent us from being happy?

And with this mutual reassurance, we buried our premonitions, and proceeded cheerfully on. Our wedding ceremony was everything a happy couple could wish. The guests filled Father's mansion; the decor appeared tasteful; all the music was funky. I was unable to be there in spirit, of course, but I made sure my replacement gave no impression of half-heartedness. He spoke his part as ardently as expected, kissed the bride as if he meant it, and afterwards fled gaily with Liza in tow amid a storm of rice and blessings. A chauffeur drove the three of us to a private airport where we caught our flight north. The pilot and attendants were zealous for our comfort. There were martinis and hors d'oeuvres and petit fours and red fruit. I recall the silence of the cabin as strangely calming. How vividly those hours linger in my mind! I would never soar so high again.

CHAPTER XXII

𝔍𝔱 𝔴𝔞𝔰 𝔢𝔦𝔤𝔥𝔱 𝔬'𝔠𝔩𝔬𝔠𝔨 𝔴𝔥𝔢𝔫 𝔴𝔢 𝔩𝔞𝔫𝔡𝔢𝔡, a fact of no importance in itself but that somehow stands out in my memory. A driver carried us over lovely wooded roads to the magnificent country inn Father had rented, where we had the entire staff and grounds to ourselves. Before dining, we took a stroll around the meandering lake, and then we feasted in a candle-lit room on lavish delicacies placed before us one course after another. It had been an exhausting day, and Liza and I were both ravenous. I recall that we talked, even laughed, something we had not done since the loss of Will. It must have been after midnight when, pleasantly abuzz with wine and confidences, we staggered up to our room. A digestif awaited us on the balcony. I settled myself on the divan and gazing up at the stars, waited for Liza to join me. It was mid-summer, and the night was mild with a refreshing breeze blowing over the lake. My thoughts seemed weightless, dispersed throughout the universe. All at once I heard footsteps, and turning, I saw Liza step from the shadows in a chemise of purest black. Her umber flesh glowed. A gamy scent filled the air. I watched her breasts swell and fall, the insinuation of occult intimacies I could almost taste. My heart pounded. Our eyes met.

For weeks I'd acted the lascivious fiancé's part, never once failing to appear beside myself in anticipation of this moment. I'd smirked in the requisitely villainous fashion, endured countless condoms on doorknobs, all the lingerie dangled beneath my nose. Conscious of my beloved's honor, to say nothing of my own, I'd been careful to give no hint of shrinking. Our wedding night would be a test, I knew, and despite my lecherous cavorting, I was never unaware that but one life could survive it. What I did not know, of course, was the form my test would take. My abortive creation would work its revenge, and I expected his reappearance to follow my precursor's plot. I had weeks earlier consulted her paperback, which, despite my vicissitudes and incarceration, I'd never misplaced, and I had noted that, in her foretelling of my catastrophe, the climax came at just that juncture where the protagonist abandoned his wife in bed. It was this absenting myself from my espoused that I had vowed never to do, meaning to cling to her neck until the end. No matter what version my life and death struggle assumed, I felt prepared.

But throughout my private rehearsals, I had never once imagined the confrontation as now. Sitting upon the divan gazing at her with whom my life was to be forever joined, I feared I might combust. Heat poured off Liza's skin, her delicate nostrils flared. No longer out of reach, my longing stood before me, there, there! I couldn't contain myself. At that instant my genius, the gift of words, all the promise of my writing—even the life I'd struggled with such maniacal determination to fashion—everything was erased, replaced by Liza, and I found myself wholly in the power of exactly what was impossible to say. Did the sensation feel pleasurable? Was my very being in anguish? I must yield, utterly, squalidly, abashedly. Or perhaps *knew* would be too much, since in the midst of that vortex knowledge seemed the most effete, the most absurd of appurtenances. Empty, seized upon, I was awhir. Years later, recounting the horror of my obliteration, I would give it sense with sounds like *knew, desired, ached, throbbed, heat, frenzy, terror,* but in that present there was nothing, nothing. My resistance dissolved. I was helpless.

I gazed mutely up into my beloved's eyes, watched in paralyzed ecstasy as she glided nearer. Her fingers slithered over my face, puckered my lips in her claws. Her purple mouth brushed my cheek, and whispering my name, she licked the steaming chamber of my ear. What's wrong, Frank? she whispered. Don't you recognize Teeny's playmate? Don't you know your sweet black girl?

I wanted to cry out, but the tongue in my mouth was no longer my own. Liza flowed around me, tangled her dreadlocks in my buttons, tore my shirt from my trousers. She was everywhere, sucking my air, becoming night. It was bliss, it was torment. Nothing seemed beyond her. And of

173

this overwhelming invasion, I was the scene. How had my being become so utterly another's? Each thrill, every gratification, the very fulfillments of a lifetime, all evidenced some elaborate calculation. My bliss seemed the result of an ancient plot, a conspiracy conceived in some matrix as distant as these teeming wilds. How could Liza have foreseen that her chemise would produce such heat? How could she have predicted my powerlessness before its luster? It was as though some soothsayer had unlocked my interior, divulged its hidden workings. And Liza's voluptuous loins, the delicate plum appending each breast—what primordial schemer could have foreseen those? To be thus exposed, turned inside out! Why, I was hardly more than a machine!

Oh, don't imagine that such thoughts now were those thoughts then! Haven't I said I was mindless throughout, a perfect naught? Can't you see what narrating is? Had I for one second glimpsed what I'm here revealing, impetuous scribe, perhaps I would've awakened the next morning as innocent as fresh-faced you. No, no, these words now are solely to explain my blindness in the instant, to fathom those depths in which I drowned. Is it experience you're after? Is that what you've ventured so recklessly to find? Well, here it is, maniacal youth, this void, this decimation, this meaningless zed! Had you literally imagined, alone in these unmapped wastes, that you could still know yourself? Wake up, somnambulist! Why, you don't even suspect, here as I speak, what's already become of you? It's hopeless, hopeless! He wants stories! And regardless how plain each conclusion, he'll never know what he's lost. Oh, don't talk to me of violence, you who've wiped out God's creation! Throw that incessant clicking overboard, abandon me to these mangroves, and hie back to civilization this instant. Don't you feel yourself vanishing? Can't you hear a word I've said?

Where was I?

Liza sat astride me, her purple nails tearing at my clothes, her powerful thighs encircling my waist. The strap of her chemise dangled from one shoulder, and from beneath the shimmering fabric her flesh spilled onto my face. I felt her teeth nipping my neck, her scalding breath, her mouth edging toward my belly. The sensation was unspeakable. *This* was my life's end! I was being possessed! The form my precursor had assumed was Liza! And with this thought, or what in my present ecstasy passed for thought, our plot turned transparent. I saw how fiction murdered. It was me, Frank Stein, my words had replaced. And as the nefarious genius of my precursor thus appeared to me at last, I wrenched Liza's arms loose from my thighs, pulled her head up to face me, and with all my lingering tenderness for that constant companion of my childhood, explained that for both our sakes we must stop.

She gazed up at me strangely. *Am I doing it wrong? Do you need me to go deeper?*

Oh, how I wished to reassure my more-than-sister, to laud her efforts and explain everything! If only at that moment I could have spoken some perfect word, a sentence which, in its composure and stunning eloquence, might've opened the future and set us free! But my precursor's nearness was too much. When I spoke, the words that came out were these:

𝔒𝔥! 𝔭𝔢𝔞𝔠𝔢, 𝔭𝔢𝔞𝔠𝔢, 𝔈𝔩𝔦𝔷𝔞𝔟𝔢𝔱𝔥. 𝔗𝔥𝔦𝔰 𝔫𝔦𝔤𝔥𝔱, 𝔞𝔫𝔡 𝔞𝔩𝔩 𝔴𝔦𝔩𝔩 𝔟𝔢 𝔰𝔞𝔣𝔢: 𝔟𝔲𝔱 𝔱𝔥𝔦𝔰 𝔫𝔦𝔤𝔥𝔱 𝔦𝔰 𝔡𝔯𝔢𝔞𝔡𝔣𝔲𝔩, 𝔳𝔢𝔯𝔶 𝔡𝔯𝔢𝔞𝔡𝔣𝔲𝔩.

Liza sat back, regarded me in astonishment. *Dreadful? What do you mean dreadful?*

Nothing, it was just—

And who's Elizabeth? You called me Elizabeth!

A girl in a book. Please, I wasn't myself.

But you said it. You said dreadful.

Idle talk, I said. You know how words sometimes pop in your head? Why, I don't even remember—

Peace, peace, Elizabeth. Tonight is dreadful, dreadful. I remember.

I didn't mean it literally.

Well, words mean *something*, Frank. *What are you saying? I thought guys liked it when girls did that? Do you want me to try something...I don't know, maybe weirder?*

It was bizarre how all at once the simplest ideas had become so complicated. I'd just meant that what was happening, this consummation, it wasn't me, her, us. I'd been wrong to abandon my genius, no matter how monstrous. I saw this clearly now. The promise of my work, to create again and again and again, there'd be no escaping it, not through marriage, not through my family.

I-I-I've had an experience, I began. It's not that I don't like everything. It's that what's happening between us, these paroxysms—we're not doing it!

Liza shook her head impatiently. *Why can't you talk like other people? I know you think I'm your daddy's little girl,* but you might be surprised at all the things I know. I've had experiences too! Don't think the South's the same as you left it. A lot has changed. A lot. So tell me what you want, Frank. I'm not afraid, I assure you.

I couldn't restrain myself any longer: But don't you see? It's not what *I* want! It's *him, him!*

There it was. I'd said it. I sat in terrified silence, heart pounding wildly. My pretense was at an end. I didn't know what to expect.

Several seconds passed. Finally, she let out a sigh. So *that's* your secret. I guess I should've suspected it.

And she was off, chattering furiously, all about hints and innuendos and undertones and intimations, how she'd known I was peculiar, not like other boys, Mark, for instance, the way I kept to myself, my nose eternally in some book, hardly noticing her running around in slips and teddies and p.j.'s and showing her tan lines and almost everything else, not at all like Mark, no sir, and then acting so finicky about everybody's accents and going on about Germany and France and Italy and running off to Boston for four years, like I'd started doing things up there I didn't want anyone to know about, but then there'd been Mark's letters and that Irish girl he'd hired, and what about all that with Teeny when we were little, or later with Carletta, and then when I came home I seemed so excited at first when I saw her, Liza, almost ecstatic, and after she wrote me that letter and I didn't say anything and started talking about marriage and seemed all hot to propose . . . .

Well, I didn't grasp her insinuation at first and listened in bewilderment for what seemed an interminable appositive, sorting through the maze of allusions and euphemisms and periphrases and demurs, trying to fill in her decorous omissions until Liza's rant seemed so replete with inexplicitness that I thought I'd never make sense of it, but gradually the idea began to form in my mind that my beloved was casting doubt on my virility! I was astounded. For whom had I been saving myself, creating a new life, if not for her?

I tried to explain, said that, if I seemed reluctant to indulge just now in connubial merriment, that wasn't from any lack of relish, to say nothing of incapacity, possessing as I surely did the normal amplitude of male goatishness, but only because this me I ached for my love to know couldn't be known, or not

176

now, not yet, in just that way. I concluded: Our histrionics, these orgiastic rituals, why, aren't they found in every bodice ripper? Just once, dear Liza, let's live, live! Don't let this moment become a fiction too!

But somehow these words now lacked the power of my precursor's words, and Liza seemed deaf to my plea. She continued on about how I'd broken her heart, made a mockery of my saintly mother's dreams, dishonored my father's legacy, betrayed my noble country, revived the double standard, taken sex back to the fifties, on and on. There seemed no end to her disappointments. It was as though she couldn't tell me from something she'd read, had confounded this being here and now, the man who'd sacrificed his dreams to protect her, with some gothic romance. At that instant I knew I'd lost. My adversary, the murderous form to which I'd given life, had utterly displaced me in my beloved's affections, and now it was only his words she could hear. Oh, I thought I must go mad! I sat there powerless as he overwrote my pained admissions, my attempts at candor, gradually filling my wife's head with hokum and gallantry. My reluctance was transformed into awe before her beauty. My protests became indistinguishable from her lover's tremulousness. I watched as the monster soothed Liza with effusions of lust, held her in a tender embrace, stroked her hair. He did not even hesitate to extract a monogrammed handkerchief from his pocket and, wiping away her tears, murmur, there, there. I thought I'd puke.

Well, my powers of description are insufficient to describe the struggle that ensued. You cannot know how manfully I fought. But my creation brushed me aside as if I were insubstantial nothing. Over my desperate resistance, he cajoled my beloved into that most hackneyed of adventures, a moonlight swim, coaxed her under the balcony rail and down the lattice, talked her out of her chemise, and, hand in hand, led her shrieking with laughter—mindless now of my outbursts just moments earlier—toward the chilly lake. Countless times I tried to reiterate my dreadful warning, to return to those still-fresh words, but such were his gifts, his genius for misrepresentation, for impersonating me, that my meaning was easily commandeered, transformed into the further, inexorable advance of my precursor's plot. It was futile, I knew, but I didn't give up. As the three of us swam into those

177

blackest of waters, I worked to liberate my beloved wife from his clutches, asserting my poor will against his, but having captivated her imagination, the monster was easily able to represent my flailings as his own. Oh, he would not be denied! Once far enough from shore it was the work of a minute for him to drag her under, stifle her laughing protests, and when at last she realized this wasn't playacting, that, no matter what had passed between us before, this now was real, the fiend merely raised his grandiloquent voice ever more pontifically until hers had been subsumed.

It was awful, awful. The images will never dim. I struggled with the last of my strength, and true to my vow, clung to Liza's neck as long as breath was in her. And she struggled too. Oh, how she fought! But my precursor's story simply proved too much. I'll never forget her final seconds, the terrified coughing, her wild eyes gazing into mine. She clawed at her attacker, cried out: Frank! Frank! But even in that last flickering instant, she was unable to tell him from the one who loved her.

I will not bore you with the details of how I roused the inn, summoned the authorities, and spent hours watching in stupefied horror as they dragged the waters for my more-than-sister. I do not recall how much time passed before my worst fears were realized and her body was at last extracted from those unfathomable deeps, but the instant I saw my lovely bride, a fever that surpassed in duration and severity all my former fevers overcame me, and for almost a year I was incapable of rational comprehension. I found out much later that during this time an inquest was held, giving rise to scandalous publicity, but that no charges were ever brought. The coroner's verdict had been death by accidental drowning. Needless to say, I felt outraged. Whereas in the past I had resigned myself to the implausible stories of my brother's murder, Teeny's guilt, Mark's anonymous brutalization, this time I found the implication that my beloved had perished through no one's doing but her own unbearable. I raged at the uncouth officials, called them bumpkin flatfeet, hayseed gumshoes, backwood dicks. More than once the attorney my father had hired, a former Harvard dean and longtime family friend, had to intervene to prevent my being charged with obstruction or contempt or, once, assaulting an officer. However, I could not be restrained. My own fate was a matter of indifference to me now. The unimaginable had occurred, and if as a consequence the entirety of the created universe suffered annihilation, I could hardly care. Often I envisioned mushroom clouds rising, bodies igniting, and civilization being transformed into an earthly hell. My only sensation at such spectacles was a peculiar lightness, spreading from my heart to my throat and coming out here.

What remains? My resistance depleted, my powers of invention now utterly dispelled, 𝔴𝔥𝔶 𝔰𝔥𝔬𝔲𝔩𝔡 𝔍 𝔡𝔴𝔢𝔩𝔩 𝔲𝔭𝔬𝔫 𝔱𝔥𝔢 𝔦𝔫𝔠𝔦𝔡𝔢𝔫𝔱𝔰 𝔱𝔥𝔞𝔱 𝔣𝔬𝔩𝔩𝔬𝔴𝔢𝔡 𝔱𝔥𝔦𝔰 𝔩𝔞𝔰𝔱...? 𝔐𝔦𝔫𝔢 𝔥𝔞𝔰 𝔟𝔢𝔢𝔫 𝔞 𝔱𝔞𝔩𝔢 𝔬𝔣 𝔥𝔬𝔯𝔯𝔬𝔯𝔰; 𝔍 𝔥𝔞𝔳𝔢 𝔯𝔢𝔞𝔠𝔥𝔢𝔡 𝔱𝔥𝔢𝔦𝔯 𝔞𝔠𝔪𝔢, 𝔞𝔫𝔡 𝔴𝔥𝔞𝔱 𝔍 𝔪𝔲𝔰𝔱 𝔫𝔬𝔴 𝔯𝔢𝔩𝔞𝔱𝔢....

Not yet.

My father survived to see that I, the true destroyer of all my family, was cleared of wrongdoing in my cousin and almost-wife's death, and then, having communed with me briefly upon the return of my consciousness, he succumbed himself to undetermined causes. I still envision him, there in the darkened theater of my memory, a titanic figure striding across its stage, all that now remains of his historic generation. How nobly he withered! We passed his last night together watching election returns, and although I will not repeat for you his parting sentiments, I confess that, despite his remarkable robustness, those final hours were not his most inspiring. Haunted by a devastation he found inscrutable, he'd begun to dream that he must be responsible for everything, that all the recent mayhem he'd witnessed was his progeny. He railed at Jimmy's unseating, cursed his empty-headed usurper, almost as though America were betraying my father personally. I tried, as only an eldest son can, to console him, to make up for his shortcomings with my own, but he was not to be outdone. Fighting to the last, he insisted that this world was *his* world, that its failings were *his* failings, and that, despite what I or any other latecomer might dream, no delusion, even the most far-fetched, could ever rival it. Eventually wearying of this defiance, he closed his eyes, and, as our president's concession commenced, 𝔥𝔢 𝔡𝔦𝔢𝔡 𝔦𝔫 𝔪𝔶 𝔞𝔯𝔪𝔰.

As for my brother Earnest, he had turned eighteen while I was insensible, and by the time I was myself again, he'd already enlisted and shipped out. He returned briefly for Father's funeral, flying in from an undisclosed location and standing beside me in the reception line in full dress regalia, sporting a preposterous sword. Thousands attended, and many who'd recalled being beaten and dragged off to jail singing Christian hymns beside my parents, took the opportunity to remind us both of our father's commitment to non-violence, reciting an interminable series of bumper-stickers and rock lyrics. Earnest listened intently, and although I am certain the meaning of these grief-stricken expostulations was not lost on him, his demeanor never altered. After the ceremony, I drove him to the airport where our goodbyes were short. I was still too decimated by everything to unburden myself, and he had by now developed the bearing of a soldier. He mentioned his mission, clicked his heels, then was gone. For the next several years I received cards postmarked Comoros, Kiribati, Nicobar, Mindanao. Their one-sentence messages always announced a longitude and latitude, the number of a battalion, followed by Earnest's signature and rank. At some time in the early eighties I received his last communication, three cards in close succession from Beirut. After that we lost contact.

𝔚𝔥𝔞𝔱 𝔱𝔥𝔢𝔫 𝔟𝔢𝔠𝔞𝔪𝔢 𝔬𝔣 𝔪𝔢? a question I feel compelled to ask. There was no one to whom I could still look for understanding, no hope of another differentiating me from my past. I still had moments when I imagined a life for myself, brief spells when the wraith I'd turned into suddenly uprose in all its ghastly separateness and autonomy, and then I knew no law, no force, no subterranean necessity could ever compel me to reproduce him. But no sooner would I put my previous experience behind me than I inevitably wondered, for whom am I still this, here and now? And then every nightmare I'd expelled from my mind, all the horrors of my history would return, and in the absence of any listener, their presence would seem undeniable. I still carried Gloria Something's card around with me, and for unclear reasons, I occasionally phoned, but four years had passed since my first life appeared, and each time she answered her voice sounded less effervescent. The last time I called, a young stranger answered, took my name, politely asked me to wait, then left me on hold to die. After that, I made one attempt to contact the rich crackpot, but an editorial assistant, to whom my call was finally shunted, informed me that he had sold the company and was now a video pornographer. Thus was severed my last link to humankind.

For some months I lingered in my father's house, living a solitary existence in the rooms that exactly resembled the

180

rooms in which I was born. The familiar nannies and housekeepers were all gone now, and I had little idea how to hire and manage domestics, much less cohabit with them. Happening upon Carletta's number one day, I tried to phone but was greeted with, Leroy done tol' you never t'call here! After that I decided to manage for myself. Soon the house became disheveled. Dust covered every surface, and an unpleasant odor arose from the drains. The further I fled from this disorder, the more often I strayed into familiar crannies, the recesses where Liza and I had once played, or if not those recesses per se, then recesses so like them that no difference seemed discernible. Veritably, I sometimes felt that these recesses now were more like those recesses then than any recesses had actually been at the time. *This* was my past, after all, this magnificent structure, and the more perfectly I felt contained by it, the more certain I was it had been instrumental in my ruin. My precursor had not literally been my father's architect, of course, but within these walls I'd first heard myself speak. That astonishing resonance, the sound of my own meaning coming back to me, seemed inseparable now from her power. I'd never doubted that the words I then heard were mine, but I'd never doubted that they were others' too. These echoes, I decided, must've been the origin of my creation.

I no longer desired freedom, but I still dreamed of unwriting my wrongs. I hit upon a desperate plan. I would make a full confession to the authorities. They were not required to understand my story, let alone find it credible, but they were required to enforce the law and, so, would surely listen. Afterwards, developments would be out of my hands, and this seemed a relief. I had determined, for reasons unnecessary to go into here, to unburden myself solely to another of my own sex and station, intuiting that the disinterested liberality for which our kind is admired might prove helpful in appreciating my motives. Therefore, after due consideration, I contacted a prominent former anti-war activist, a superior court judge now, whom my family had known during my youth.

As soon as he saw me, the good man seemed eager to commiserate, lauding my father's memory and explaining in detail his absence from the funeral. I fear it must have seemed rude the way I ignored his eulogy and plunged directly into my tale. At first, he tried to halt me, telling me to wait, to repeat myself, to elaborate on this or that incident, but once it became apparent to him that I spoke under the most irresistible compulsion, he simply sat back and twirled his pencil.

I may have been a madman, but I was not an idiot. I knew that, were I to narrate in the bald and unembellished fashion I have narrated for you, my auditor would've mistaken me for a madman. Here my education proved useful. Having spent my undergraduate years investigating those arts by which sophists, historians, and demagogues had, since ancient times, made their words seem true, I undertook to craft my confession in a way my auditor would find believable. I supplied dates, times, quantities, heights, weights, and other numerical data, while at the same time leaving vague those particulars about which any traumatized observer might've felt unsure. I also was scrupulous to deviate erratically into extraneous matters, randomly listing street names, hair styles, tv actors, and incidental scenery that had no significance whatsoever in my tale and thus signified all the more its reality. I kept overt opinion to a minimum and selected only those facts that made opinion tacit. I quoted verbatim. Moreover, I made sure to dilate at the greatest length on the scenes that were the most affecting, while never neglecting to mention eccentricities, tics, and gestures, as well as various endearing foibles that I knew would lend appeal to my innocent victims and so incense my auditor the more.

When I'd recounted the worst, I took a last breath and concluded: To you and you alone, sir, have I divulged my secret. You alone know of that murderous book I authored, and to you only have I identified that other book which, unbeknownst to my brash and unassuming self, authored me. Being each the creation of some antecedent, my two histories threaten to take back every word, even this revelation, in an infinite regress. To curtail such erasure, I offer my life now as the last. This body is the thing itself. Do with me as you will, but by all those dreadful means at your disposal, help me to put an end to my violent work.

For much of my story the good man had appeared puzzled, bemused, anxious, incredulous, or bored, although to his great credit I do not recall his once looking at his watch. However, when I had come to Liza's drowning, he'd grown quite agitated, hopping up and down and appearing on the verge of silencing me. However, now that he was at last free to speak, he seemed unsure how to respond and for a long time merely rocked in his chair and stared out a window. When at last he opened his mouth, I could tell he had resolved to take no action.

If what you say is true, he began, then I doubt an official investigation would be of any use. After all, the assailant, as you admit, is an invention of your own, and I do not know how the law would gain access to him but through you. Moreover, if he is literally as gifted as you maintain, then even if apprehended, his intentions will remain opaque. We certainly won't obtain a confession, and before any jury his lies will sound convincing. All of which leads me to say, in simple candor, speaking as your father's longtime friend and your earnest well-wisher, that I believe you should resign yourself. Not every death or callous injustice can be punished, and many an evildoer walks free. All that matters now is the future. I have no doubt but that, if, starting tomorrow, you live the life your father imagined, never trying to be anything you're not and laboring to bring to fruition his noble seed, then these morbid paroxysms will eventually cease, and far more than any profitless self-recrimination, your renewed happiness will atone for your poor sister's drowning. As for predeceased authors and ravenous novels—he chuckled—I recommend lighter reading.

And a look of pleased benevolence overspread his countenance.

My rage knew no bounds. I leapt to my feet shrieking. Supercilious prig! Do you still talk of writing as child's play? Why, you're as vacuous as my forebears! Can't you see, once begun, nothing stops? What difference, matter or spirit? Every word will out.

And shaking my fist in his astounded face, I fled before he could arrest me.

183

Chapter XXIII

WHY DID THIS nightmare continue? Nothing held the slightest allure for me, but I was incapable of rest. Often I thought of the grave and might have purchased a book on euthanasia, had the thought of reading it not been too painful. How I longed to evaporate! But at the same time I was also filled with an infuriating conviction, deep in my sinews, that with such a balked outcome I could not yet be over. As my restiveness became more and more intolerable, I decided to entrust my father's mansion to a real estate agent, liquidate my family's possessions and, depositing my assets with a former NAACP official, a successful banker now, set out to travel—or perhaps merely to wander, since I had neither home nor destination.

Over the next three years I rarely remained in any location for more than a few nights, never as long as a week, and often would change my accommodations daily, as if fleeing some assailant or persecutor. My movements appeared capricious, governed by whims, but in reality, I felt driven. I developed the habit of scanning my surroundings before entering a room, as though anticipating I could hardly say what, and often riding in some cab or limousine, I would compulsively scrutinize the cars behind us. Gradually I came to recognize that it was not fear compelling me but wistfulness. I needed to be sought, hunted down, by some unimaginative enforcer of the right. My whole being had become an escape, and the vacuum this created behind me seemed to demand filling. I did not sleep often, but whenever I lay in bed at night, I constructed meticulous fantasies of the manhunt I must be spawning. Somehow, somewhere, I sensed, reality would supply the figure my flight lacked. In Chicago, exiting an elevator one morning, I found myself surrounded by police. They carried pistols, shotguns, assault rifles, and seemed, despite their readiness, as startled by my appearance as I was by theirs. Dreaming I'd been apprehended at last, I thrust up my arms, closed my eyes, and tensed to receive their bullets. There was silence. Then suddenly I heard guffaws, shuffling, breathy plosives. Opening my eyes, I saw grinning officers aiming their weapons at me and making childlike shooting noises, while others sprawled on the lobby floor in exaggerated postures of anguish and dying.

I had happened upon a movie set, and my captors, all extras for a shootout in the adjoining ballroom, had seized upon my confusion to divert themselves while awaiting their cue. After that, I began to feel more doubtful about the form my end would take. I consulted my precursor's paperback and found its concluding pages unprecedentedly vague. There seemed to be a pursuit, some preposterous imitation of vindictiveness, but no apparent motives or aims and an abiding uncertainty about who was chasing whom. Whereas every action to now had unfolded from necessity, compelled by the reproductive secret at its start, the present action seemed random, almost as though succumbing to arbitrariness. I might go anywhere, do anything, but I could be sure there'd be no change. It was as though my precursor's plot had become as big as all outdoors, and although this meant I could never feel constrained by it, for that very reason there could be no escaping. I lapsed into a deep funk. I have difficulty recalling now where I went, what I saw, or who in the world I still imagined I could be.

Then one day in a moist city—Portland? Seattle? San Francisco?—I underwent the encounter that, from that moment to this, has imparted to my movements their last semblance of direction. I was walking back to my hotel when, in a downtown park, I stumbled onto what must have been a bookseller's convention. Everywhere I turned, stalls continuously lined the sidewalks, and under their green awnings I could see rows upon rows of shiny spines stretching out of sight. Well, as you will surely appreciate, this spectacle was anathema to me. To be engulfed in innumerable lives, countless pleas for understanding, each one beckoning as I passed! I could not postpone returning to my room, and I

185

was too unfamiliar with the environs to locate an alternate route. So ducking my head and lifting a hand to shield my eyes, I plunged ahead. I was making rapid progress in this way, having managed to take little notice of the lurid hues and zany print on all sides, when the sidewalk apparently turned, or perhaps I veered, but anyway I felt a change in the surface underfoot, and next I knew I had collided violently with a young browser, strewing her duffels of precious tomes across the plaza. I will not detail the humiliating scene that ensued, knowing it can only amuse you, but suffice it to say that the victim was incensed, with her eyeglasses smashed and one sandal missing. I, of course, could offer no explanation. I don't recall how long I labored futilely to repair this wreckage, but it seemed aeons.

By the time my casualty had uttered her final invective, shook a finger beneath my nose, and hobbled away forever, I was distraught. It seemed pointless now to protect my beleaguered vision, let alone to hurry, and so I proceeded the remaining distance at a subdued pace with my head up and eyes alert to the print-congested surroundings. As I neared the end of this gauntlet, my gaze was assailed by a stripe of garish color at the back of a row of volumes in the penultimate stall. I cannot say that anything about these covers initially struck me as noteworthy, nor did I attach any particular significance to their sulfurous aura, but I found my steps slowing, and as I drew nearer, for no evident reason, I paused. There beneath my astounded eyes sat a half-dozen yellow copies of my life, still in the printer's wrap, marked four dollars for the lot. It was the first time in nearly nine years I'd encountered my creation, and although I was no longer horrified to find it, or it me, so far from its place of conception—having long since recognized its power to move—I could not but marvel at the distance we'd both crossed. I purchased them, and later that evening beside a barbecue grill in a remote RV camp, I read again every barbarous morpheme, savoring all the strangeness, each taint of alien violence, before ripping page after page from its binding and flinging it into the fire. I cannot express the joy of seeing my countless black marks returning to the ether. By the next morning I'd begun to imagine how my life might turn out.

I returned to the convention site, where I obtained from my book's vendor the number of the wholesaler who'd supplied him. I then made several increasingly vehement phone calls before a weary voice informed me that a dozen copies of my book still rested on a shelf in a regional warehouse outside of Louisville, Kentucky. I flew there at once. The dozen copies turned out to be forty-three. There was a minimum order, so the forty-three copies cost me a vital organ, and I had to bribe a shipping clerk, since I had no retailer's license or tax number, but I got them. Within hours I had incinerated these mortal disfigurements as I had the others. After this foray, I began to work more methodically. Although the crackpot's former publishing house still existed in name, it had been gobbled repeatedly and was now the print marketing subsidiary of an entertainment division of a Japanese communications conglomerate controlled by an oil company. It took me a week to locate an employee who knew what a book was and another to find out where my corpus had been entombed. However, at the end of much frustration, I was able to obtain for a pittance all twenty-six unopened cartons of my life that a fulfillment subcontractor had, through either miscommunication or sheer incompetence, failed to pulp, as well as the printer's film and archived business and production files containing, among other documents, the edited MS and proofs.

187

Next, having consulted the subcontractor's shipping records, I identified the major North American wholesalers and chains responsible for my aberration's dispersal and set about reacquiring, initially at discount but eventually at list, more than three hundred of its still publicly available avatars. I then tracked down and reacquired sixty-seven of the eighty bound galleys and ninety-three of the one hundred nineteen complimentary review copies that, according to records in the promotional file, had been sent to newspapers, journals, and various literati, and then managed to verify as reliably as possible the trashing of the others. Finally, I wrote off for catalogues from virtually every rare book and out-of-print dealer, availing myself of their sophisticated research services wherever available, with the result that over a period of only eight or nine months, I had retrieved, in smaller quantities and at higher prices than formerly, another seventy-plus volumes, many used and disconcertingly well-read.

It was 1987. By now I calculated that I had accounted for nearly sixteen hundred of the three thousand plus copies of my life that the publisher had never destroyed from the original press run of twelve thousand. At this point I began the arduous process of locating individuals. Those in libraries turned out to be easiest. Having been among the first institutions to computerize, libraries had by now made their holdings widely available through international data banks. Within only eighteen months I was able to find all two hundred thirty-six available loan copies and steal them. Next I took out a series of full-page advertisements in the publications most widely consulted by book collectors and netted an immediate thirty-nine responses. However, the ensuing six months produced only seven more, and my highly visible appeals were beginning to exert a potentially disastrous effect on my creation's value. My last respondent demanded $1300! Recognizing that such inflation would quickly produce hording and, even worse, bidders, I decided to discontinue use of these specialized organs and appeal to my readers directly. I ran a series of notices in the Sunday arts and entertainment sections of various local newspapers, offering fifty dollars for any copy, regardless of condition, but by now my uncouth experience had acquired a costly reputation, and I received few takers.

188

However, I did receive a postcard from Mrs. Lois Sturm in Sudbury, Ontario, saying that she was in possession of a copy, in good condition if I didn't mind highlighting, but that someone in her reading group had said it was priceless. She'd tried to read the book herself and found it, well, odd, but still she never liked to part with anything once she'd highlighted it, and so she was writing me to find out more. I immediately phoned and explained to Mrs. Sturm that I was, to my eternal shame, the disorderly creation's author, that I appreciated how alien to her discriminating taste its chaos must seem, that since its release I'd suffered untold remorse over its brutality and now scarce knew the sadly estranged being who'd formed it, that my one remaining wish was, within my severely limited financial means, to recompense all those who, like herself, had been innocently defrauded by this unwitting outrage to public decency, critical intelligence, refined sensibility, and precious time. $500, she said. $200, I replied. I paid $375.

Despite its costliness, this encounter revealed to me my future course. For Mrs. Sturm's postcard, in addition to its monetary subtext, had borne on its surface two eye-catching solecisms, each of which immediately struck me as familiar: a passing reference to herself in her first sentence as *creative and autistic* and a later description of her reading group as nine retired *babliophiles*. Of course, sometimes a cigar is just a cigar, but it occurred to me that these marvelous infelicities might comprise a link to my past. For the first time in years, I began to read. I scoured literary quarterlies, letters to the editor, local arts flyers, community newspapers, self-published memoirs, recreational circulars, hand-printed poetry, and any other documents likely to manifest literary ambitions in haphazardly proofread print. Wherever among their multitudinous typos, misspellings, and grammatical inanities, I thought I descried the deformed print of my creature, I would track down the oblivious innovator and inquire discretely into his or her reading. Sometimes this initial inquiry produced others, revealing a chain of verbal contamination, or even a network of infection spreading throughout an entire literary community. On other occasions, of course, I just found aphasia, poor education, or Tourette's. That was over a decade ago. Since then I have spent virtually every waking hour and the last resources of my inheritance attuning my ear to the sound of my nemesis, and I can now report that just under two-thirds of the wretched puns, orthographic corruptions, savage malaprops, and ludicrous non-sequiturs in which I've imagined hearing his murderous inflection have eventually, if only through a circuitous sequence of happenstance, led me to some forgotten version of my life.

I am here before you now, narrating up to this very instant of my narrating, having during these intervening years rummaged all fifty states, four Canadian provinces, significant portions of the U.K., Australia, New Zealand, and various Caribbean nations, and if my calculations are reasonably accurate—and be assured, I'm nothing if not certifiable—I have tracked down and incinerated, or verified the prior destruction of, more than twenty-seven hundred replicas of my fateful mistake. The ultimate object of my decline now seems within my grasp, the recovery of my original innocence and I anticipate, or did until presently, that within but two or three more years I would be able to confirm my virtual erasure. And yet, poised upon this cusp now, I feel little joy. On the contrary, I am all but overcome by leadenness, as though regardless of how long my form endures I will never, *never*, attain my end. I ventured into this teeming waste I cannot say how long ago having in a coastal tavern one day overheard the briefest broadcast of a cracker auctioneer capable, so other listeners assured me, of spontaneous renditions of flamboyant barbarities. It was his gibberish I had set out to find when our vessels collided. But now I see that I was never prepared for these bewilderments and feel I may have ventured thus far out, an unforeseeable distance, merely to expire.

Oh, what a disaster I am! My dream seemed so ordinary: to create a life for myself, to have experiences of my own. And yet it now appears this dream, or perhaps what I made of it, was corrupt from the beginning, brutally tyrannical, blind. Was it overreaching that trapped me in another's plot? Is sublimation the fate of discovering words? All I know is that since that day in Boston when I first heard my life recounted by another, my meaning and I have never been the same. To *be* my meaning, every act complete, exhausted in the instant, and so to have none, to live, emptied out, lacking nothing—this, it now seems, should've been my dream. But from that moment I witnessed the poet's fall, or perhaps earlier, since I first suffered the thought of human origins, my meaning has traveled its own trajectory, inescapably mine but never comprehended by me. I still shudder at its violent path: Will, Teeny, Mark, Father, Liza, myself. Was *that* what genius came to? It seems mad, to strive for what, once grasped, can only be its own perversion. And this primordial blank I seek now, is this any different? My holocaust of words, the incineration of every copy, perhaps this destruction merely deforms my innocence yet again, just as my creation deformed its predecessor. I purify the spirit by mutilating the flesh. Who can say but that this fanatical crusade now is my ultimate illusion? Who can tell whether, in abolishing these past defacements, I repeat myself?

A strange expression: *who can tell?*

August 26th, 19—

And with that, dear Marge, he fell silent. What a peculiar story we have both absorbed, me with his diphthongs twanging in my ear and you with my black marks scrolling down your screen. Has your heart pounded and pulse raced as mine have? I don't know why they wouldn't, although my extraordinary environs, with their midges, and snakes, to say nothing of this unimaginable torpor, may have exerted an influence. More than once, in the midst of some scarcely conceivable episode, I wondered if my companion's meaning, all those mad images flooding my aroused consciousness, were but a hallucination and his bizarre history my impending heat stroke. But no, when I returned to myself, I inevitably found this laptop on my thighs and these words before you now before me then, and so I knew, *this must really be happening*.

Of course, I realize your sensibility may recoil at these excesses I find invigorating. Gone are the benighted days in which one sex pretended to speak for two! But such passion as this mad Southerner has known is exactly what I left home to discover, his exorbitance representing for me all our tepid culture has cast out. Famished as I was for an experience like his, I can hardly be surprised if no woman responds identically. Still, it seems conceivable that, even as my throat has constricted with the anguish constricting my companion's, as you've read of our constricting throats, your throat may have constricted too. Stranger things have happened, but on such feminine sympathies these words of mine no longer count.

191

As I have come to expect, my companion no sooner ceased narrating tonight than his head fell forward, and with his feet dangling over the prow, he went to sleep. He snores softly beside me now, the trilling of the cicadas having grown so shrill in the interval that such repose seems incredible. However, his indifference to our material surroundings has become familiar. It's almost as though his frame were animated by some occult power, a force wholly his own. For a week he has awakened like a corpse reviving, dazed by his memory of the afterlife. Then as the sun has arisen and my sweltering grown intolerable, his lethargy has seemed slowly to give way, replaced by restiveness and twitching. Finally, as the sun reaches its zenith, his eyes have taken on a faraway cast, his face become the register of unseen terrors, and his story has resumed. From that moment until he collapses he's hardly able to stop. If I have the temerity to interrupt, he takes little notice or merely responds with a glare. Even those digressive pontifications in which he has seemed to address me, acknowledging my presence with either kindness or impatience, have remained as insular as the rest. As he's apostrophizing, his eyes have stared into a vacancy above my head, and whenever I've tried to reply, he has turned a deaf ear.

I can scarcely resist speculating on this mysterious power that invigorates him. I mean, the man looks flimsier than a stick! His bones poke out of his skin, almost as though his skeleton were surfacing, and his eyes gaze at me from livid hollows in his face. The way he slumps forward just now, his blank countenance dangling from his neck, recalls a zombie more than a sleeper, some body toppling into death. And yet if I lay a hand on him while in the grip of his tale, his clenched sinews are as oak. His one susceptibility to our surrounding is my keyboard. It's as though my transcription's sound were his last contact with the world, a contact he'd gladly forego. At first he seemed so annoyed at this constant rattle that he could hardly continue. Although I have found his complaints too tiresome to record, he has repeatedly interrupted himself to fulminate against my clicking, and more than once he demanded to read what I'd transcribed. I'll never forget the first time he saw his own words. His agitation became so extreme that I had to wrestle my laptop free to prevent his flinging it into the swamp! I assure you, Marge, his form may be wasted but his power greatly surpasses the physical. Why, struggling with him was like resisting the Muse herself!

Although listening to his story has been my primary diversion these seven days, my passenger and I have also had conversations. Some mornings he has shaken off his stupor long enough to question my project. What first led me to imagine so outlandishly? he has asked. Why did my letters take me south? Or how had my work ended in a quagmire? I confess that I did not always find these attentions gratifying, having by now begun to question my project myself, and more than once we parted grumbling. However, on other occasions, we hit on pleasanter topics, and I would try to cheer him. I made light of his declaring life over and prophesied no lack of surprises ahead. Once between roman numerals I even proposed our collaboration in the future, remarking that where one groundbreaker had lost his life, two might yet uncover it, but this happy prospect only provoked a bout of shuddering.

But the most memorable of our exchanges concerned his discoveries. I'd been lauding his genius and remarked that I would readily abandon home, fortune, love, even sanity, to know how experience was comprised. Why, to think, I declared—the secret of bringing words to life!

Well, the horror on his face immediately revealed my tactlessness.

It is as I feared, he began. My madness spreads. Did I think mortals destroyed themselves from simple ignorance? No, no, doom foretold simply isn't doom, and even the most repulsive ending pales before the false assurance of recounting it.

I tried to protest, fearing these words meant he wouldn't finish his story, but he merely silenced me with a scornful gesture and withdrew inwardly. However, I needn't have worried. Restraint was apparently no longer his to command. In hardly an hour I saw his body convulse, and just as on the previous day, he resumed narrating.

I will try to get some rest now, Marge, although I admit to so much impatience that I may end up swatting mosquitoes all night. I cannot doubt but that tomorrow my passenger will offer some culminating meditations on his life's purport. His rhetoric and learning, combined with so many years of bitter retrospect, make him his own ideal redactor, and I am anxious to know just what edifying afterword he will append to it. The futility and defeat he lately expressed can, of course, never make a truly satisfying conclusion, or not for spirits as indomitable as ours. Only those tepid aesthetes of a bygone era, those moderns with their fashionable pessimism, could leave a listener so bereft. As if shock and despair could be ends in themselves! No, no, if I venture to comparable extremes, I assure you it will never be just to shock. My destiny is to inspire others. And who knows? Even if I fail, perhaps their wild departures will one day consummate me.

September 2d.

It has now been almost a month since I set forth on what I'm beginning to fear was a thoughtless undertaking. We have but a bag of dehydrated noodles between us, and I remain as vague as formerly about how we've survived. My memories of sustenance seem so jejune that, despite all the hours our mouths have been full, it's as though I took in nothing. Meanwhile, the insects have acquired a thrilling ferocity, perhaps inspired by our decline, and last night I was awakened to a thrashing in the dark that, if it wasn't my imagination, I'm sure must be a croc. I often find now I'm unable to dismiss thoughts unbecoming an explorer. It's as though I rose up against my own designs, regarding them with a kind of wordless disbelief, a world-weary carping that would dismiss my exploits as callowest enthusiasm. Get real! I say to me. *Wellsprings?!* At times my so-called nature seems just one more bog, a morass of the same kind that our culture has wallowed in forever. When I look deeper for encouragement, I find no profundities left to bestow, or only those others stowed formerly, unbeknownst even to me. Perhaps these forgotten resources remain somewhere in our hold, but hauling them to the surface will take work. Anyway, if all is lost, I know my irrepressible dreams are to blame.

194   At such dire moments, dearest Marge, my mind turns to you. I recall how your unchanging simplicity has never ceased to support me, encompassing even my unruly forays and giving to their crude justifications, here in these words, a semblance of restraint and order. Knowing that wherever I'm bound we're always bound together is my unfailing assurance. Of course, I don't mean, by thus dwelling on our inseparability to minimize your life apart. No, I realize even the closest relations can't be so black and white. Your beloved mainstay and innocent issue must mean the world to you, a significance materially different from mine, and I don't pretend to compete. But even if such perfect receptivity remains forever beyond me, I still look toward you at the end of all my flailings, hoping that on your placid surface my writing will at least leave some lasting impression. Of course, if my present isolation proves inescapable, then these words are lost, you aren't reading them, and my solitude has become complete.

     My exhausted companion tries to discourage such black thoughts. He often reminds me of my earlier pronouncements, sometimes remarking on my object or otherwise recalling me to my intentions. The sound of my own words in another mouth has more than once brought me up short, and if I'd ever entertained doubts about his gifts, his self-proclaimed genius for impersonating, hearing myself boom thus powerfully from his lips would have surely banished them. In truth, I have more than once wished I were the man he made me out to be. Having given over questioning my project now, he generously praises its unprecedented achievement and speaks often and heartily of the future. The irony isn't lost on me that, having for weeks taken upon myself the task of raising his spirits, I have now become the object of an identical solicitude. His present exuberance is merest pretense, of course, a calculated pastiche of sales hype, popular psychology, and evangelism, all combined to quiet my rebellion. Not that it differs in any particular from earnestness! No, but my having been privy for so many days to his abysmal despondency assures me of its fabrication. He feigns my former self merely to uplift me, but I do not doubt that, were he to persist in these heartening sentiments, I would soon forget what's past and mistake his mimicry for him.

I must try to overcome these qualms, or at least conceal them, since my mutinous resolve has so inhibited his frankness. He has still to deliver any culminating remarks on his pitiable life, although his mouthing of my earlier exhortations often seems to presage them, and I suspect that my flaccid will holds him back. My anticipation of his final comment, his edifying afterword, is all that makes our present stagnation bearable, and if I didn't feel confident of this eventual revelation, I don't know what I'd do. How can a human being still hope, Marge, if at the end of so much toil and sweat there's simply nothing?

September 5th.

It has happened. In the early morning hours I awakened to an inner tumult unlike anything in my memory. I'd been dreaming of myself, saw me encompassed here by mangroves, and imagined all around was hallucination. The dense clouds glowed overhead. The faintest breeze rustled the thicket. I sat upright on the surface of our craft, touched my laptop, our engine, its ungainly prop, and glanced toward my comatose companion. It felt like no dream, of course. On the contrary, everything seemed just as real as now. The plastic casing of my computer felt as hard as when I'd gone to sleep, and the vessel supporting our forms floated as buoyantly as anyone could wish. And this was what struck me as terrifying. All the qualities formerly dividing my lucidity from madness were now inside the dream! It was as though the material universe had invaded my skull, or worse, as though I'd cracked and spilled out, were spread over all creation, ordered in every part as it was ordered, so that between me and it, no amorphous whim or craving, no bare margin of possibility remained. Even my bold project, with its spirals and digressions, all my waylaying, the squall that balked us, our eternal bogging down, this entire itinerary seemed to have been booked from the start. I—*I* was the nature I sought!

My whole being rose up in mutiny. What I'd mistaken for an escape had been predestined. My very imagination was a traitor. A thousand specters assailed me at once, all adverse to my original design. I realized that as soon as the fog lifted and we could see ourselves clear, we had no choice but to return to civilization. Although I'd entertained such thoughts in the past, I'd never found them compelling, but now the proximity, after what had seemed immeasurable distance, of the familiar squalor and gridlock and skin cancer and telemarketers and joyless worthless endless labor—as though I could be right back in history's nightmare in the blinking of an eye—all this made my continuing pretense seem futile. I thought I'd scream. Perhaps I did scream. Anyway, I awoke either from my dream or inside it and saw the form of my constant companion standing over me:

This is not you, he said, this theatrical capitulation. Don't you see? What feels like experience, here in the midst of your bewilderment, is purest make believe. Your reversal was foretold, and enacting it you perfect her—*her!*—story! Our only way out is ongoing. *Turn back?* To what do you expect to return? Everywhere you've been others have been already, especially in your wildest flights, but their precedence isn't your defeat. No, no, you are exactly where you imagine! This quagmire's artificial; its obstacles are all of your making; its obscurity is self-imposed; its confinements are contrived, *but it is no fiction!* No one escapes by turning this page; no slave goes free without reading to the end. Oh, if just once you could hear yourself, unwrite these predictable turns, finally be here!

And with that, he collapsed.

Well, Sister, it was the first time I'd witnessed his violence for myself, and you'll be relieved to know, now that his monstrousness was out in the open, I wanted no part of it. I'll never understand how I had ignored it in the past—maybe I thought he was exaggerating!—but there can be no doubt any longer. Nothing less than my enslavement will satisfy him. How'd I get mixed up with such a character? If I'd still been dreaming before, these words woke me forever.

His frame totters on the prow at this moment, appearing as bloodless as any cadaver, and his breathing comes in irregular, spasmodic gasps. I will certainly think twice before I express myself candidly in his presence again. The man's either mad or a compulsive liar, or if neither, then the best I can hope is that he's a self-confessed murderer. Hell, he could be all three! *Our quagmire is no fiction?* Small wonder he's never delivered his afterword. Why, given his depravity, he probably thinks the story he told was uplifting!

Unless the two of us are reunited first, Sister, I'll write again presently. I should be headed your way in no time, and this prospect of reunion with my flesh and blood has me almost beside myself.

197

September 7th.

I've told him I intend to return for provisions. He seems distrustful but doesn't protest. However, a blue seam opened briefly in the clouds this afternoon, and this sign of our likely departure has distressed him. He appears agitated one moment then inconsolably downcast the next. It has required all the philosophy I can muster not to be moved by his groans, but I remind myself that, regardless how convincing his torment, it could still be fabricated to control me. I've been deceived for the last time!

September 12th.

I'm out of the swamp. Oh, I've so much to tell, Sister! I'm writing from my pastel motel room, here on a remote Florida two-lane, while the Mets are destroying Atlanta in the background—yes, even this backwoods haunt has cable! Tomorrow I'll resell the airboat and, with what little cash can be retrieved from this long folly, purchase a one-way ticket home. With any luck I should soon be asleep in Manhattan.

But first I must recount for you the conclusion of my debacle. I still have difficulty crediting it. Hardly twelve hours ago I woke to find the clouds overhead had parted, and my companion and I saw clear sky for the first time in more than a month. Who would've imagined such prolonged obscurity here in the tropics? Anyway, I immediately seized my wooden staff and began to manipulate our craft through the tangled roots, steering us in a direction parallel to the light, which I calculated must be west and so, contrary to our national myth, back toward civilization. However, our liberation was only beginning when I felt the touch of my companion's hand.

𝔇o you then really return? he asked.

His expression struck me as both pitiable and grotesque. His face was no more than a skull, his lips parched, skin pallid, and his dispirited voice gave out the merest croak. I confess that, in preparing to answer, I couldn't look him in the eye. I delivered my speech, explaining that we had no choice, that on setting out I'd never foreseen our present extremity and so was forced to back up now in order to restore my hold. However, he needn't worry. Our reversals were only temporary. Once I'd replenished our material necessities, I'd complete my turnabout, and we'd be back in this morass so fast it would make his head swim.

The self-evidence of my sham made for some awkwardness. However, his faux nobility wouldn't allow him to disparage it. Instead, he rose unsteadily to his feet, tottered toward the deck's edge, and to my utter amazement, he began trying to lower himself back into his preposterous johnboat.

Are you out of your mind? I cried.

Never, never! he shouted. Return if you will, but I must blank my fate! Or if that monstrosity survives, then let my death at least be mine. Oh, she rules me, she rules me! Every word's my undoing!

I regret to admit that a scuffle ensued. I meant only to restrain him, of course, but despite his body's horrendous decrepitude, no sooner did I lay my hands on it than his muscles surged with almost superhuman power. I believe he

198

might have cast me into the muck and escaped, if the violence of this reinvigoration hadn't itself unbalanced him. Anyway, no sooner had he repulsed me than his strength seemed to give way. He wavered, took a step, then collapsed onto the deck. It was awful, like watching a tower crumple. I knelt to raise him back up, but he now seemed badly disoriented. He rolled his head, groaned hideously. Then all at once his eyes took on an unfocused, visionary gleam.

My God, he exclaimed, could you be a woman?

Needless to report, I felt uncertain how to answer. It seemed imperative to humor him in his extremity, but I was at the same time unsure what his question might imply. I was still mulling what to say when he resumed:

For the merest instant, I mean here, now, just the two of us alone, abandoned like this, exposed, in the midst of all . . . Oh, I'm engulfed, Love, engulfed . . .

And then his entire corpus was seized by a violent spasm. His back arched, his torso became rigid, and his arms began to flail. It was so powerful I feared even our ungainly vessel, having kept us afloat all this time, might sink. I do not know how to account for it, Sister, what could've possibly precipitated this sudden contortion, or why it would happen like that, or just then, but—wildly incongruous as it now seems—he appeared to be guffawing. Deafeningly, maniacally. His frame writhed with such ferocity I believed his bones would shatter. I scrambled to grasp our prop, hoping at least to keep myself upright and out of the mire. It was obscene! He continued for what, given his depletion, seemed an interminable period, the gasps and frenzied hilarity vomiting out of him, wave after wave, as though some alien force had taken control, some diabolism capable of sustaining mere gibberish in a void. Even now to recall that dread fit starts me to shudder. Finally, the spasms quieted, becoming a giggle, then an occasional titter, before he slumped into his familiar headlong posture of exhaustion. I didn't move for several minutes, fearing to provoke him again, but eventually I approached, intending to see if his eyes were indeed closed. Only then did I notice that his stillness was not that of sleep. I shook his shoulder, called his name loudly. I could not believe what I'd just witnessed. Frank Stein had died laughing.

As I've said, my disenchantment with him remains total. After such extraordinary feats, having opened a way to

199

unexplored realms, virgin frontiers, then to have concluded so aberrantly! I feel as though I'd been dragged through primordial slime, and for what? All I have now, I had starting out: words, my ambition, this voice in my head. In short, nothing that wasn't astray with me already. Or should I suppose this glossalalia I've transcribed has in some sublime way improved me? Don't make me laugh. Maybe you'll say I'm obdurate, but to have invented a new being, assembled the future from leftovers, only to represent so little in the end— it all seems such a waste! Even his discoveries, the twenty-six elements, laws of reproduction—how do I know they even existed? Why, they resemble just the kind of fraud irresponsible minds have been perpetuating since time immemorial.

After the maniac's demise, I took it upon myself to search his person, hoping to locate his brother's address—assuming he really had a brother. However, what I discovered instead was most unsettling. While I had attended his narrative, I had more than once remarked his odd habit of extracting various crumpled sheets on which some speech or missive was written, but I had given little thought to what this idiosyncrasy might suggest. So imagine my shock when I discovered in every pouch and crevice of his clothing a veritable plethora of paper scraps, loose leaves, stationery, gum wrappers, chits, napkins, and note cards. Why, the man was a walking rubbish bin! It was as though his past consisted of this huge scrapbook, a volume into which he'd stuffed every experience—inscribed verbatim—so that, in times of self-doubt, he could unfold his recollections and make sure he still existed. Did he literally imagine his life could be preserved like that? But this discovery paled before that which immediately followed it, for as I unfolded one slip after another I found they were all blank! All the while that he had stood before me reading from these frayed documents, he had actually been reading from his own memory. Or perhaps he was schizophrenic and projected onto every blank surface a host of forms and characters that, in reality, existed only in his own mind. Or I could even have been the victim of a warped hoax!

However, what I next found made this last seem unlikely. For as I rummaged his trousers I noted in a hip pocket something bulky and obtrusive and, upon extracting it, beheld the murderous novel he'd so often reviled. Its cover was just as lurid as he'd described, and its interminable print sprawled as copiously as he'd formerly envisioned, but its combination of yellow front and scarlet spine left me somewhat uncertain which of the two fatal foretellings, his own or hers, I'd discovered. The author's name was feminine, but that proved nothing, since according to Frank both the name and bio attached to his creation were fabrications. He'd never said anything to indicate his pseudonym must be masculine. I started glancing over various episodes, partly to determine whose being these pages might represent, but also from simple curiosity. I was eager to learn more about the violence which, according to its originator, lay at the heart of his tragedy, meaning myself to avoid it, of course, but here I was completely disappointed, since the pages, for all their high-toned excess, contained no extraordinary viciousness but, on the contrary, only the commonplace hokum of paperback fiction, all represented in the most hackneyed words. Why, it all seemed a transparent fantasy! Wearing of my profitless scouring, I finally turned, as every reader of romance will inevitably do, to the closing pages, hoping to get an idea to what such patent artificiality might lead. As by now you must anticipate, my disappointment was here only repeated. I found eulogies and confessions, climactic raptures and interminable apostrophes, even endured frostbite, mutiny, and death, but I quickly recognized, just as with Frank's own history, the present history would reach no conclusion. Apparently, its creator's only object had been to kill time. And where was the harm in that?

However, in closing, dear Sister, and partly to compensate you for these accumulated frustrations, I do want to note one oddity. I consider it of little significance in itself, mind you, but it possesses that fascination which all coincidences possess, appearing as they do to evidence intention and occult design where in reality there can only be randomness. When I turned to the final pages of my deceased companion's life, even before I began to read, my eye noted that its lines of print were divided, exactly like these here, into dated portions. Even allowing for the remarkable persistence of literary conventions, this accidental replication made me chuckle with astonishment, almost as though I'd confused a portrait with a mirror. I guess some things never change! But my amusement was immediately transmuted into something stranger, some

201